Jaci Burton is a *New York Times* bests  Oklahoma with her husband and d children, who are all scattered aroun of their own. A lover of sports, Jaci ca is by what sport is being played. She v television, including an unhealthy amount of reality TV. When she isn't on deadline, Jaci can be found at her local casino, trying to become a millionaire (so far, no luck). She's a total romantic and loves a story with a happily ever after, which you'll find in all her books.

Find the latest news on Jaci's books at www.jaciburton.com, and connect with her online at www.facebook.com/AuthorJaciBurton or via Twitter @jaciburton.

Praise for Jaci Burton:

'A wild ride' Lora Leigh, No. 1 *New York Times* bestselling author

'It's the perfect combination of heat and romance that makes this series a must-read' *Heroes and Heartbreakers*

'Plenty of emotion and conflict in a memorable relationship-driven story' *USA Today*

'Strong characters, an exhilarating plot, and scorching sex ... You'll be drawn so fully into her characters' world that you won't want to return to your own' *Romantic Times*

'A beautiful romance that is smooth as silk ... leaves us begging for more' *Joyfully Reviewed*

'A strong plot, complex characters, sexy athletes, and non-stop passion make this book a must-read' *Fresh Fiction*

'Hot, hot, hot! ... Romance at its best! Highly recommended!' *Coffee Table Reviews*

'Ms Burton has a way of writing intense scenes that are both sensual and raw ... Plenty of romance, sexy men, hot steamy loving and humor' *Smexy Books*

'A wonderful d!' *The Romance*

'Spy the name Jaci Burton on the spine of a novel, and you're guaranteed not just a sexy, get-the-body-humming read, but also one that melds the sensual with the all-important building of intimacy and relational dynamics between partners' *Romance: B(u)y the Book*

'The characters are incredible. They are human and complex and real and perfect' *Night Owl Reviews*

'One of the strongest sports romance series available' *Dear Author*

'As usual, Jaci Burton delivers flawed but endearing characters, a strong romance and an engaging plot all wrapped up in one sexy package' *Romance Novel News*

By Jaci Burton

Play-by-Play Series
The Perfect Play
Changing The Game
Taking A Shot
Playing To Win
Thrown By A Curve
One Sweet Ride
Holiday Games (e-novella)
Melting The Ice
Straddling The Line
Holiday On Ice (e-novella)
Quarterback Draw
All Wound Up
Unexpected Rush
Rules Of Contact
The Final Score
Shot On Gold

Hope Series
Hope Smoulders (e-novella)
Hope Flames
Hope Ignites
Hope Burns
Love After All
Make Me Stay
Don't Let Go
Love Me Again

Shot on Gold

Jaci **BURTON**

HEADLINE
ETERNAL

Published by arrangement with Berkley,
a member of Penguin Group (USA) LLC.
A Penguin Random House Company.

First published in Great Britain in 2018
by HEADLINE ETERNAL
An imprint of HEADLINE PUBLISHING GROUP

1

Cataloguing in Publication Data is available from the British Library

ISBN 978 1 4722 4803 9

Typeset in 10.5/15 pt Janson Text LT Std by Jouve (UK), Milton Keynes

Printed and bound in Great Britain by CPI Group (UK) Ltd, Croydon, CR0 4YY

HEADLINE PUBLISHING GROUP
An Hachette UK Company
Carmelite House
50 Victoria Embankment
London EC4Y 0DZ

www.headlineeternal.com
www.headline.co.uk
www.hachette.co.uk

This one is for my readers.
Your dedication to this series has rocked my socks off.
A mere thank-you will never be enough, but thank you.

ACKNOWLEDGMENTS

To Erin, Jessica and Ryanne, and to Derek for being so great at the cover shoot. Thanks for making this cover happen.

To Claudio Marinesco and Rita Frangie, for creating the most beautiful covers for all the books in the Play-by-Play series. You have wowed me with every single one and I thank you.

And to my editor, Kate Seaver, who thought this book was a great idea—thank you for always encouraging me. What would I do without you?

Dear Reader,

At the time this book was written, it hadn't yet been decided whether US professional hockey players would join in the 2018 Olympics. When it was determined that the National Hockey League would not allow its players to participate in the Olympics, this book was already in production and couldn't be altered. So for the purposes of this book, pro hockey players are participating in the games.

Since this is a work of fiction, locations and names and some events have been changed and do not reflect what actually occurs during the international games.

I hope you enjoy reading *Shot on Gold*.

Jaci Burton

Shot on Gold

ONE

WILL "MAD DOG" MADIGAN STOOD ON THE CARPET leading to the ice in the hockey arena.

He wasn't supposed to be here—not today, anyway. But he'd gotten up early this morning, needing a run after his long flight yesterday. He'd needed to clear his head, and when he'd ended up at one of the two arenas that would serve as home for several of the ice events here at the international games, he couldn't help himself. He had to see if he could get inside. Fortunately, the team's coach had been arriving and spotted him, and he had access, so he let Will inside.

But only for a few minutes, coach had said.

A few minutes was all he needed.

The arena was huge, and there'd be attendees from all over the world watching the games. On the ice, there'd be hockey, as well as figure skating, curling and speed skating. He took in the sheer size of the arena, then dragged in a deep breath of chilled air. There was something about the smell of a rink, that crisp scent of icy air that clung to his lungs and gave him life. It replenished him, gave him a sense of purpose and affirmed he was right where he was supposed to be.

Like now, looking over the ice rink for what would soon be the international games in Vancouver. He felt damned fortunate to be here and he couldn't wait for the games to start. He was itching to put on his skates and get out there, test the ice and get some speed going under his skates. Then all he'd need was his stick and a puck to chase after.

He loved playing hockey. It fulfilled him in ways he would have never thought possible when he had been a kid fighting it out with his friends at the local rink back in Chicago. Back then it had been all fun and games, shoving and laughing and playing all day.

Even then, it had been in his blood. Now, it was his job playing forward for the St. Louis Ice hockey team.

And to be selected to play for these games, not just once, but twice? It was a damn dream come true. He planned to soak in every minute of this experience, so he could remember it forever.

Four years ago he'd been twenty-three, an excited young guy who'd partied his ass off the entire time. If he'd been honest with himself, he couldn't remember much about the experience. On the ice, of course, he'd put everything into his game play. Off the ice had been a constant party. This time he wanted to soak in the experience, really live it. This time would be different.

He could already imagine playing in the upcoming games, even against some of his own teammates, who'd be playing for their home countries. They'd talked about it before the games began. On their pro team, they fought for the Ice. Here, they'd play for their country and they'd respect each other for that.

When it was over, they'd all be teammates again.

"That's it, Mad Dog," Coach Stein said as he came up to him. "Time to clear out."

Will nodded. "Thanks for getting me in."

"We'll see you back here tomorrow after the rest of your teammates arrive."

"You got it."

"Try to stay out of trouble until then."

Will laughed. "You know I will."

Coach Stein gave him a head tilt and a disbelieving look. "Do I?"

Will gave him a grin. Okay, so he had a rep. Even Coach Stein, who was the coach of the New York team, knew his reputation. He went out the way he came in, through the front doors that were locked and guarded by a security guy, who nodded and let him out.

He stretched, started off with a walk, then eased into a run as he made his way back to the village he'd call his home for the next three weeks. His roommate hadn't arrived yet, so he had no idea who he'd be bunking with. Hopefully someone fun.

They weren't allowed to bunk with teammates. He was certain it was the committee's way of getting them to branch out and make friends with people from other disciplines, and often other countries. Last time he'd bunked with a bobsledder from Latvia.

They'd partied their asses off the entire time. He'd had a blast. He was looking forward to reconnecting with several of the friends he'd made during the games four years ago.

When he got back to his apartment in the village, he stripped and climbed into the shower. A hot shower was one of his favorite things. Maybe even top-ten favorite things, especially after a grueling hockey game.

Thanks to his run he was hungry, so he got dressed and headed out to the other building where the dining hall was located.

It was fully stocked—and huge. It was like a hangout here, and the size of a couple of football fields.

You could get anything you wanted, with food from almost every country participating. Last time he was here he'd made sure to eat something from every country. It seemed only respectful to sample the various cuisines.

And, hey, he liked to eat.

He planned to do it again.

Many athletes had already arrived, though the dining hall wouldn't be fully packed until the end of the week. Several of his teammates were flying in today, so he'd catch up with them later. For now, and since he wasn't shy, he sat with some of the snowboarders, figure skaters and downhill skiers.

The great thing about the games was that everyone was friendly. You could take a seat and strike up a conversation with anyone.

"How was your flight?" a guy named Hans asked him.

"Long. Yours?"

Hans smiled. "Same. Slept in a bit this morning. Looking forward to getting my skis on those mountains, though."

Will dug his fork into the egg-white omelet and nodded. "I got a glimpse at the hockey arena earlier, but they wouldn't let me skate on it yet."

Telisa, one of the figure skaters, looked shocked. "They let you in already?"

"My coach was there so he snuck me in. But I couldn't get on the ice."

"Oh. You're lucky." Robbie was Telisa's husband and the other half of their pairs team. "We're nearly drooling over the figure skating arena. We can't wait to get in there."

"They said they'd open it up to us this afternoon," said Rory, one of the individual figure skaters. "We have to practice and stay limber."

"Huh," Will said. "Maybe I'll mention that to my coach. Can't get stiff."

"Unless it's your dick," Zeb, one of the skiers, said. "You want that to be stiff at all times."

Will laughed, then noticed he'd gotten a suggestive look from one of the women across the table. He thought her name might be Monie or Monica or something. No idea. The names had flown fast and furious when he'd sat down.

He wasn't interested in sex. Okay, that was a lie. He was always interested in sex. But there was plenty of time for that, and for the next few weeks there'd be a hell of a lot of it going around.

The only thing on his mind right now was getting on the ice. After that he could think about sex.

AMBER SLOANE SET HER BAGS DOWN AT THE FRONT counter, taking in the multitudes of athletes surrounding her.

She was here. In Vancouver. Her third—and final—international games.

This was her last shot at gold. At twenty-four, she'd be considered old for a figure skater. Her biggest competition was here. She spied Tia Chang in line about four people ahead of her, her posture near perfect even standing in line, her dark hair shining like a fall of midnight down her back as she absent-mindedly checked her phone. It was like she had no cares at all.

Seventeen. God, that had been a lifetime ago for Amber. At seventeen she'd been a nervous wreck at the Worlds. But she'd come in first.

It was only the international games where she'd failed to grab the gold. She'd won both bronze and silver, but the gold eluded her.

This was her last chance. Her mother told her it was her time to shine.

Amber thought her chance escaped her four years ago, when Elena Bulosova of Russia had just inched her out for that gold medal.

Amber's long program had been better. The judges had to have been blind not to see it.

But this was her year. She'd revamped her entire program and worked her ass off the past four years. And now, she was ready to put it all out there and win.

Or she'd be done. Because there'd be no more games for her after this year.

"Amber!"

She heard the shout of her name and turned, then smiled when she saw her friend, Lisa Peterson.

Lisa threw her arms around Amber.

"I've missed you," Lisa said.

"I've missed you, too, Lisa. How excited are you to have the games in your home city?"

"Excited beyond belief." Lisa pulled back, then looked around and whispered, "So, guess what?"

"What?"

"I pulled some strings, and don't ask me how I pulled those strings, but you and I are going to be roommates again."

Amber raised a brow. "Seriously?"

"Yes." Lisa grinned.

Amber couldn't be more excited to have Lisa as her roommate again. Lisa was outgoing and talkative and incredibly sweet. "That is fabulous. I'm so excited. Though you aren't going to boot me out of the room at two in the morning again because you've brought some hot guy in to bone, are you?"

Lisa crossed her fingers over her heart. "I promise I won't do that. We'll boot as-yet-unselected-hottie's roommate out."

Amber laughed. "Perfect."

They waited in line together and discussed their careers.

"How's snowboarding?"

"Kicking it," Lisa said. "And if you'd come to Vancouver like I keep asking you, I'd teach you how to snowboard."

Amber felt very guilty about that. For the past four years, Lisa had invited her several times to many events, and to her home for a visit.

"I know. I'm sorry. After winning the silver four years ago, I've done nothing but work on a new routine."

They made their way to the front desk and checked in, got their credentials and packets, then grabbed their luggage.

"There's more to life than just your work as a figure skater, Amber," Lisa said, taking out the map that would lead them to their building. "You have to find time for fun. For a life."

"I know. After this year, I'm going to travel and have nothing but fun."

"That's what you said four years ago."

They walked outside and Amber pulled her sunglasses off her head and slid them over her eyes.

"This year is different. I'm confident about my routine, and I know this is my last time at the games, win or lose, so I intend to enjoy it."

Lisa stopped and turned to her. "Which means you plan to have some fun?"

Amber offered up a tenuous smile. Did she even know how to have fun? "Sure."

"Excellent. We'll start tonight after we unpack."

She felt a giant lump of trepidation. What was she thinking telling Lisa she was out for a good time? Her mother's voice rang in her head.

The work is everything, Amber. Focus, keep your head down and skate. No distractions.

No distractions. Fun was a distraction. That had been drilled into her head from the time she was six years old and had first strapped on a pair of ice skates. Since then it had been all work.

And the reward would come when she won the gold. She knew that.

But still, her mother wasn't allowed in the village, and what she didn't know, she didn't know.

They opened the door to their apartment. It was spacious and lovely, with cream-colored décor, a living room, kitchen and two queen beds in the large bedroom.

"This is awesome," Lisa said. "And the living room has a fold-out sofa. You can even stay here if I have a guy over."

Amber laughed. "Good to know."

"Seriously. And who knows? You might even be busy with some stud of your own and I'll be bunking on the couch."

Highly unlikely, but she wasn't going to spoil Lisa's grand plans.

"Come on, let's unpack and go check out who's here."

"Okay." She carried her luggage into the bedroom and set it down.

This time would be different. She was determined. And she was so happy Lisa was her roommate again. If anyone knew how to have a good time, it was Lisa.

Amber had worked her ass off the past four years. She intended to show that on the ice. She was disciplined and ready.

But when she wasn't performing, she intended to party. Or, at least, learn how to party.

She had to start somewhere. She was twenty-four years old and it was time to start living.

TWO

THE ACTION WAS ON AT THE CLUB TONIGHT. WILL walked in with a bunch of his teammates, along with his new roommate, a Swedish snowboarder named Elias, who was totally up for having a good time.

It was great to have a club at the village. The committee always did a great job of making sure the athletes had entertainment without having to go far. There were restaurants and music venues open every night, along with the club where everyone could meet up, enjoy music—but without alcohol, which wasn't allowed in the village. Not that you couldn't get it or bring it in if you knew the right people or knew how to do it, but it wouldn't be served in the club or at the dining hall. Which didn't bother Will in the least. He didn't plan to drink much. Boozing it up before competition started would only leave him hungover and sluggish and that would affect his game play.

He knew some athletes could party from the start of the games until well after the finish, and still perform at ace capacity. And Will could party as well as the rest of them, but he took it easy during the season and he intended to pace himself here.

"Let's get drinks first," Elias said.

Will nodded and they all made their way to the bar. It looked like a lot of athletes had arrived today, because the club was full.

"Shots?"

Will arched a brow at Ivan Petrov, a fellow hockey player. "What did you do, Ivan? Smuggle in vodka?"

"You know it."

He wasn't at all surprised. "A little early for shots, don't you think?"

"Never too early for shots. Warm you up."

Will laughed. "I think I'll just have a soda."

"I'm in for shots," Elias said.

Elias and Ivan did shots, while Will and the rest of them opted for sodas, juice or water. Then they made their way around the club, stopping to talk to people they knew. The advantage of having been to the games before was that Will knew a lot of people, so he'd lost sight of his group by the time he'd finished catching up with several guys from the bobsled team he'd friended four years ago.

Which was fine. He knew he could easily find his friends again. He wandered around, checking out the tables to see if he could spot the guys.

Instead, he spotted Lisa Peterson, a snowboarder he'd met during the last international games. Lisa waved him over.

She got up and hugged him. "Hey, Will. So glad to see you again."

"You, too. I'm happy you're here. How's the knee?"

"All healed up and ready to kick some ass."

"Glad to hear it. You as hyped up and ready to go as I am?"

"You know it, buddy. Oh, Will, this is my friend, Amber Sloane. Figure skater. Have you met her before?"

He hadn't, but damn if she wasn't fine looking, with long wavy blond hair and amazing blue eyes. "I haven't. Will Madigan."

Amber stood and they shook hands. "Nice to meet you, Will."

"He goes by Mad Dog when he's on the ice," Lisa said with a wide smile.

"I see."

She didn't even ask why. Everyone asked why. She was so formal. So incredibly shy, too. Wasn't she just the sweetest thing he'd ever seen?

"Where are you from, Amber?"

"Long Island."

"I'm from Chicago."

"I know. And you play for the St. Louis Ice."

Maybe that's why she hadn't asked about the Mad Dog thing.

He arched a brow. "Are you a hockey fan?"

"Yes."

Still wasn't much of a talker. He was used to overconfident women, not ones who barely said a word. But there was something about Amber that intrigued him.

"Oh, I see someone I have to say hello to," Lisa said. "I'll be right back. Good to see you, Will."

"You too, Lisa."

Amber looked like she wanted to sink under the table, so he motioned to the chair. "Mind if I sit with you?"

"Oh. Sure."

"Are these your first games, Amber?" he asked.

She looked down at her water glass, the one that looked as if she hadn't even taken a drink out of it. "No, actually. It's my third."

"Your third? Really? Wow. So you're a veteran."

"A veteran. Old, by game standards." Her lips curved and oh

man, did that ever transform her face. She was beautiful, but with a smile? Damn stunning.

"You're hardly old. What are you? Twenty-three or so?"

"Twenty-four." She swept her finger around the condensation of her glass. "In the figure skating world, twenty-four is ancient. My biggest competition this year is seventeen. Trust me, I feel every bit of that seven-year difference."

"Damn. That must weigh on you. There's so much pressure to perform in so many of these sports, to be at your best every minute of every day. It's no wonder there's so much burnout. At least it's that way in hockey. I always feel that grind to be the best. It has to be the same for you, right? Those young kids coming up all the time, trying to shove you out of the way, so they can be the next big star."

Amber was shocked that Will was so perceptive, that he'd picked up right away on the high pressure of her sport. "It can be brutal."

"So why push yourself and come back for more? Did you medal previously?"

She nodded. "Bronze the first time, silver the second."

"Ah. I get it. You want the gold."

"Yes."

"The one advantage you have over them is you've done this before. You've felt that pressure in venues like this where they haven't. So go kick your competition's ass and get it."

"I intend to."

The one thing a person who wasn't a competitive athlete never understood was that need to win. Will understood. Everyone here understood. That's what she'd always loved about these games, about staying in this village. She was surrounded by people who got it, that burning desire for gold. That and she was away from her parents—from her mother—who had put unrelenting pressure on her every day of her life.

She had always been motivated to win. She could push herself to do better every time she was on the ice.

But, to her mother, she had never been sharp enough. Whatever jump she'd done hadn't been high enough or angled correctly.

She had never been good enough for that gold, according to her mother.

She loved her mother and she knew her mother loved her. But being here, away from her, was the best vacation ever. Her coach pushed her, of course, but it was different. He wanted what was best for her. And when she skated well, she knew it and so did her coach.

With her mother, nothing she ever did on the ice was right. Her mother constantly berated her for what she did wrong. Years of that had worn her down, had made her feel that she'd never be good enough for the gold.

Which was partly the reason she had come back again this time, why she had worked so damn hard to qualify. Part of it was because she wanted that gold medal. The other part was to prove her mother wrong.

She *was* good enough. This was her year and everything was going to go right.

"I can't believe we didn't run into each other four years ago," Will said.

"Yeah, funny that." Except she'd seen plenty of Will four years ago. How could she not? Good looks, oozing charm and women flocked to him as if he held the secrets of the sexual universe.

And he'd never once noticed her or even realized she existed. It had been like she was invisible. Which wasn't a surprise. All she'd done was practice and perform, then hide in her room. She'd never hung out in groups. Lisa had dragged her out to eat, but when it came time to party, she'd begged off, claiming it wasn't her thing. In reality, she'd so wanted it to be her thing.

But she was older now and this time she was trying to be braver. Which was why she had ventured into the club with Lisa and now found herself trying oh so hard to make conversation with Will Madigan, who likely thought she was the most boring person he'd ever met.

Come on, Amber. You can do this.

"So . . . what about you, Will? I know the US hockey team won the silver last time. You back for the gold, too?"

He smiled and everything inside of her quivered. "Hell, yes. I was lucky to be selected. We're all really damn lucky to be on the US team."

"Awesome. But no break for you."

"Trust me, I'd rather be here than taking the two weeks off while the games are going on. I skate all the time. It's my job. This is like a fringe benefit."

She took a sip of her water. So far so good. She'd made conversation, which was hard for an introvert like herself. And he hadn't made an excuse and fled the table yet, which happened to her a lot.

She took the time to study Will, now that he was up close. He was incredibly good-looking, with dark hair that was a little longer than average. His eyes were a striking steely gray that she found utterly mesmerizing. And of course, his body was incredible. He wore jeans and a tight dark brown Henley that hugged some incredible muscle. She wouldn't mind getting her hands on all that muscle. Though she wouldn't really know what to do with it if she did.

Lisa was an expert on sex. Amber? Not so much.

Sex was a given at the games. They plied all the athletes with plenty of condoms. Amber had a nightstand drawer filled with them. The last two times she'd come to the games they'd gone unused. This time she was determined to use them. She just had to find a guy willing to take her on, which she knew wasn't going to be easy.

"It must be amazing to be chosen to play hockey at the games."

He took a swallow of his drink and nodded. "Like the best damn dream come true. And it's here in Vancouver, which is one of my favorite places."

"Is that how you know Lisa?"

He nodded. "We met at the games last time, and I've taken some vacation time up here. Gotta love the mountains, plus the snowboarding is amazing."

She arched a brow. "So you snowboard, too?"

"A little. How about you?"

"I tend to spend all my time working."

"Oh, one of those workaholics, huh?"

"Yes." At least he didn't make fun of her. Points for Will.

"We need to change that, Amber. It's time for you to let go and have some fun."

She took a long swallow of her water, thankful she had something to occupy her hands—and her mouth. "I intend to do just that."

"Well you're here, and you're prepared for your competition, right?"

"I am."

"Then it's time to party. Come on."

She had no idea what he had in mind, but she was more than ready for . . . whatever. When he stood, he grabbed her hand. She felt the instant jolt of attraction and hoped that what he had in mind was dragging her up to his apartment for hours and hours of hot, steamy sex.

An hour later, she found out his version of "whatever" meant games of beer pong with Lisa and several other people. Though she had no idea where the beer had come from. But they were in someone's apartment, so she assumed someone had brought it in. She'd been introduced to hockey players, skiers, snowboarders, speed skaters, bobsledders, curlers and so many athletes she'd never met before. A few of her figure skating friends were there, too.

Lisa had been joined at the hip with Blake, a hot Canadian downhill skier with a thick mane of platinum blond hair and amazing green eyes.

She could only hope Lisa made good on her promise and they'd be hitting the sheets in Blake's room tonight.

Unfortunately, based on Will paying zero attention to her, it looked like Amber was going to be in her room alone tonight.

Just like always. She pushed her disappointment deep down inside, so used to being let down it was second nature to her. She'd made attempts to join in, but she just wasn't as outgoing as the rest of the group, so eventually she found a seat and watched.

It was what she was good at—observing, not participating.

At least she'd met Will Madigan tonight and now he knew who she was. So that was something.

Baby steps, Amber. She'd get there eventually.

So Will Madigan was out of her league. She was certain she'd meet up with some guy who'd want to have sex with her while she was here. And then she could unload her stupid virginity and live like the wild woman she was certain lurked somewhere deep inside of her.

THREE

AS THE NIGHT WORE ON, WILL MET UP WITH SOME OLD friends and met a few new ones. He was having a blast. There was nothing he loved more than hanging out with a large group of fun people. And you could never have enough friends.

He slung his arm around Lisa, trying to distract her as they played pool. She shrugged him off.

"Not a chance, Madigan," Lisa said. "I'm not missing this shot."

He laughed, then coughed as she shot the ball.

Lisa was right. She was cool as the ice in his water glass as she expertly landed that ball in the center pocket.

"Sorry, buddy," Will said to Drew Hogan, a fellow hockey player. Drew was currently Lisa's opponent.

He grinned. "Not a problem. I'll get her on the next shot." Except Drew's phone rang. He pulled it out of his pocket. "It's my wife, Carolina. Someone take this shot for me."

"I'll do it," Mikhail, one of the skiers said.

Will walked away and headed over to the bar to refill his drink.

As he went to the bar he noticed Amber sitting at a table by herself flipping through her phone. So after he grabbed his glass, he wandered over to her table.

"Making a hot date for later?"

Her head shot up and she gave him a wide-eyed look. She dropped the phone to the table as if it were on fire. "Oh, uh, no. Just checking e-mail."

He pulled up a chair and sat. "So, you've got a boyfriend back home, huh?"

She let out a laugh. "No."

He got that she was shy. She'd hung around the group earlier, and then he hadn't seen her after that. He thought she'd left, so it surprised him she was still there.

For some reason he wanted to draw her out. "Do you play pool?"

She looked over at the pool table. "No."

"I could tell earlier you weren't into beer pong, either."

"Uh, not really."

He moved his chair so he now sat closer to her. "What do *you* like to do, Amber?"

She shrugged. "Skate?"

"Oh, come on. There's more to life than skating. Surely that's not all you do."

"Of course not. I like movies and reading."

"Okay, what kinds of movies?"

"Horror and adventure and comedies and animated and mysteries and . . . okay, all kinds. Like the books I read. I don't settle into one genre. I read everything."

She probably used books and movies as an escape. But an escape from what?

"Okay. If you had your ideal night out—that didn't include movies or reading—what would you do?"

"Um, let me think about that for a second." She chewed her lower lip and he found himself staring at her mouth. She had generous lips and a beautiful face. Her skin was creamy with a sprinkling of freckles across the bridge of her nose. And the icy blue of her eyes mesmerized him. Her body was curved in all the right places, the kind of body a guy would want to get his hands on.

Tonight she wore jeans and a blue silk top that hugged her breasts in ways that made his own jeans tighten. She had small breasts that went with her small waist, but her hips flared out into exceptionally long legs. Since he was a pretty tall guy, he liked women who could match him, stature-wise.

Plus, he had a thing for long legs on women. And he'd wager she looked amazing when she skated. Which suddenly got him to thinking about her skating naked.

Now that *would* be amazing.

"Ice cream."

He pulled himself from one hell of a sexual fantasy. "Huh?"

"I'd want to go out for ice cream."

He laughed. "That's your idea of a big night out?"

She shrugged. "I like ice cream."

He stood and held out his hand. "Fine, then. Let's go."

"Where?"

"There's an ice cream place in the village."

She frowned. "There is?"

"Yup. Come on, ice princess, let's go get you some ice cream."

WILL HAD CALLED HER AN ICE PRINCESS. AMBER couldn't decide if that had been a compliment or an insult. But considering he had left his friends and was walking outside with her in the village—alone—she supposed she should take it as a compliment.

"Cold out," Will said.

She smiled as she looked over at the shops lined up side by side, making her feel as if she was wandering the streets of a quaint small town instead of a manufactured village that had been created just for this event. She hoped they kept this together after, because it was lovely. "Isn't it great?"

He looked over at her. "You like the cold?"

"I feel like I was born in the cold. I spend so much of my life on an ice rink, this is my preferred temperature. It's where I've spent most of my summers on Long Island, so it's not like I'm used to the heat."

"Ah. Always practicing, right?"

"Yes. My mother didn't want me wasting my summers hanging out with my friends. Not that I had any of those."

He stopped. "No friends?"

She realized she'd offered up way too much information. "Oh, it wasn't bad. I had coaches and teammates and it was always fun."

He gave her a dubious look. "Still, wouldn't it have been nice to go to the beach in the summer, or on vacation?"

"Competitions were my vacations. I got to travel a lot—all over the world. I was very fortunate."

He held the door open to the ice cream shop. "And you never resented what you might have missed out on?"

She turned to face him after they'd walked inside. "If I never had it, how could I resent it?"

"Oh, come on, Amber. You know what I'm talking about. Parties with friends, and prom. Did you go to your prom?"

"I was skating in an exhibition in Russia during my senior prom. So, no. Besides, who would I have gone with? I didn't really know anyone at my school, and I was traveling so often that most of the time I had to be homeschooled to catch up."

There was a line with a few people ahead of them, so they got in it. "That sucks."

"It was my life. And it was a good one. I met so many people from many different countries. It's been an experience many people will never have. I don't resent it at all."

She'd had a unique life, for sure.

"Hey, as long as you're happy with your life, that's all that matters."

She smiled at him, then leaned down to stare at the ice cream flavors in the case. "I am. I have been."

She was definitely happy right now. She was in an ice cream store with Will Madigan. It didn't get much better than this.

Though it could get a lot better than this. She just had to take things slowly, and figure out how to become bolder, to figure out how to ask for what she wanted.

"So what do you want?"

She straightened and met his gaze. "Excuse me?"

"Ice cream. What flavor do you want?"

"Oh." She realized they were at the front of the line now and the proprietor of the shop was waiting for her to make a decision. "I'll have raspberry chocolate in a cup, please."

"And I'll have mint chocolate chip, two scoops in a cone," Will said.

They took their ice cream and sat at a booth near the window. Amber slid her spoon into the ice cream and tasted it. It melted over her tongue and she closed her eyes, falling in love with the delicious flavor. She couldn't help the moan that escaped her lips.

When she opened her eyes, Will was staring at her.

"What?"

His lips curved. "That good?"

"Oh, it was that good. I'm not supposed to have anything sweet."

He frowned. "Why not?"

"Because my personal trainer and my mother watch my calorie intake. So when I can get away from both of them, like an event here, where neither of them are allowed, I indulge."

"Good for you. And I'll bet you work off all those calories when you skate."

"I work off plenty of them. But I understand they're looking out for me. Carrying around extra weight on the ice hurts my performance. Plus, I have to look good in my outfits."

"I'll bet you look damn good in your outfits."

She took another spoonful of ice cream, trying to avoid moaning this time as the sweet flavored cream slid down her throat. "I wouldn't if I ate anything I wanted to."

"Yeah? What are your cravings?"

"Hmm, let's see. Thick crust pizza with sausage and extra cheese. Lasagna. Chocolate chip cookies. Brownies. Oh, and cheeseburgers. I really love cheeseburgers. With onion rings."

He laughed. "That's a damn fine menu, Amber. Surely you can have some of those things at least once a week, right?"

"I get healthy proteins, like lean chicken and fish. Only when I finish a competition am I allowed to indulge."

"Allowed? Come on, honey, you're a grown-ass woman. You can make your own decisions."

She looked down at her ice cream, suddenly losing her appetite for its creamy sinfulness. She pushed it aside. "I do make my own decisions. Like now. I'm full."

Will looked over at her cup. "You barely ate two bites."

"It doesn't take much to fill me up." Which was her mother's mantra.

Eat half of what's on your plate, Amber. You're thin anyway, so you don't need a lot of food.

Except she was always hungry, and drinking more water never filled her up.

"Yeah? Well I'm eating this entire cone and two scoops, which I know I'll burn up on the ice. You should do the same."

Will didn't understand how hard it was for her to maintain the balance between strength and figure. But she did. She'd worked so hard, and nothing was going to derail her.

Not even the tempting raspberry chocolate ice cream that sat in front of her.

This had been a mistake. She should have never come here with Will. But since she had, she'd politely wait until he finished his ice cream and then she'd make her way back to her apartment.

"Would you like to taste mine?" he asked.

She shook her head. "No, I'm good."

"So's this mint chocolate chip. And I promise I don't have germs."

Oh, she'd love to put her mouth where he'd had his mouth. That wasn't the issue at all. Just the thought of swirling her tongue where his tongue had been caused flames to lick along her nerve endings, making her wish they were outside where it was cooler.

"Do you like mint, Amber?" he asked.

"I do."

He leaned forward, offering the cone. "Take a lick."

She was going to self-combust if he kept talking to her that way.

"Okay." She started to take the cone from him, but instead, he wrapped his hand around hers and held the cone steady. She leaned forward and flicked her tongue over the top of the cone, watching the way his gaze was glued to her mouth, which only made her previous heated state grow more incendiary.

She sat back and pulled her hand from his. "It's really good."

"Yeah, it is really good," he said, and Amber was certain he hadn't been talking about the ice cream.

She'd been hit on by a lot of guys over the years, mainly at skating competitions, and especially at the international games. She'd ignored them all to focus only on her goal of winning. Never before had she been affected by flirting or guys coming on to her. She knew she'd be nothing more than a one-night stand, and she wasn't much interested in being some guy's forgettable bang.

But there was something about Will Madigan that intrigued her. He was hot, and had a magnificent body. She liked that they were compatible from a skating point of view, but she'd had attractive male figure skaters hit on her before and they had certainly been more compatible than Will, so what was the deal with this guy? Why him, other than she'd madly crushed on him four years ago when he'd never once even looked in her direction.

That was probably it. He'd noticed her tonight, and she felt vindicated. Plus, she was determined to live it up during these games.

Though she was going to do it on her terms. She was going to be the one doing the choosing, and it was going to be on her timeline. When she was ready.

She wasn't going to jump in the sack with the first guy on the first night.

Even if said guy was hot and sexy and had eyes that made her melt.

"Are you sure you're not going to finish that?" he asked, motioning to her cup of ice cream.

"Yes, I'm sure."

"Somewhere out in the world some little girl is crying about that raspberry chocolate."

She laughed. "I'm sure."

They got up and threw away their trash. Amber zipped up her parka and slid on her gloves, then they headed outside.

The chill bit into her skin. The wind had picked up as well. She reached into her pocket and put on her beanie so her ears would be covered.

Will shoved his hands in his coat pockets. "Looks like it might snow tonight."

"That'll be great for the mountains."

He nodded. "I can't wait to watch snowboarding. And slalom skiing."

"And bobsledding and luge and hockey." She turned to him as they walked briskly back to the apartments. "I really do love hockey."

"Thanks. Me, too. I'm going to admit I've never watched figure skating. Sorry."

She laughed. "It's okay. Not everyone loves skating."

"Hey, I didn't say I didn't love it, I just said I've never watched it. With you gliding around on the ice, I bet watching you skate will become my new favorite thing."

She laughed. "Sure it will. Come watch all of us. There are some amazing skaters."

The first flakes of snow started to fall. Amber stopped and looked up at the sky, then held out her hands. "It's snowing now."

Big fat flakes followed—their descent slow but steady. It was a beautiful sight and made her jittery and excited. There was something about snow that signaled the beginning of the games to her.

"You can feel it, can't you?" Will asked.

She looked at him, saw that same excited grin on his face. "Yes. You feel it, too?" She balled her fingers into a fist and pressed it against her stomach. "Deep inside. Nervousness coupled with excitement, like I can't wait to get started."

"Yup. I feel the same way. If I could be on the ice right now skating with a stick in my hand and a puck to chase after, I'd be a happy man."

She laughed and hooked her arm in his. "See, we're a lot alike.

We may have different disciplines, but it's all about the competition. I even get that little flitting butterfly in my stomach watching the other skaters compete. I want so much for them to win. I want it as much for them as I want it for myself." She looked up at Will. The snow was coming down hard now, his hair covered in the white flakes. "Is that silly?"

He took his hand out of his pocket and grasped hers. "Not a damn thing about you is silly, Amber."

His words warmed her chilled body. She smiled up at him. "Thank you."

"Now let's go inside and sit by the fire. I'm freezing my balls off out here."

She laughed and let him tug her by the hand toward the door. When they got inside, he shook the snow off his hair, sprinkling her with snowflakes. She swiped at him.

"Hey, leave the snow outside."

"I can't. It's attached to me. I'm just sharing with you."

"Thanks a lot."

There was a great room off the lobby of the main building that housed the dining hall and several TV and game rooms. She'd loved this room as soon as she'd seen it. It had a huge rock fireplace and several seating areas with tables. And of course, there was a drink station at the back of the room, which was a definite plus.

They found a table near the fire. She shed her coat, already feeling the heat.

"Want something to drink?" Will asked.

"I'll have hot tea."

He took off his coat and slung it on the back of his chair. "I'll be right back."

Her phone pinged, so she pulled it out of her coat pocket to see who had messaged her. It was Lisa.

You disappeared. Where R U?

She typed a response. Went for ice cream with Will.

Her fingers hovered on the keypad. She thought about telling Lisa where they were now, but she honestly wanted more alone time with Will and she wasn't sure whether or not Lisa would drag the entourage of friends into the great room.

She pressed "send," then chewed her bottom lip in indecision. What kind of friend was she to lie to Lisa like that?

Lisa sent a response. Will is hot. Have some fun! We're off to sneak in some ice bowling.

She smiled, shook her head and also sighed in relief, realizing she shouldn't have worried. Lisa would never pass judgement on her, and she should have been honest and told her she wanted some time alone with Will. She'd be sure to talk to her about it when she got back to the room.

"Here's your tea." Will set the cup down in front of her, then slid into the chair next to hers. He had a glass of ice water.

"Aren't you cold?" she asked.

He shook his head. "Not now that I'm in front of the fire."

She sipped her tea. "Oh, Lisa texted wondering where I'd disappeared to."

"Did she think I kidnapped you?"

"No. Also, she said they're going to sneak in some ice bowling."

He laughed. "She's always up for adventure."

"This is true." She took another swallow of the tea, letting the warmth of it ease the last of her tension away.

"So . . . you wanna go ice bowling?" he asked.

"Not really, but you can feel free to join them if you'd like."

He cocked his head to the side and studied her. "Trying to get rid of me?"

"Trust me, I'd tell you outright if I wanted you to go away."

"Good to know you have no problem getting rid of men who annoy you."

"None at all."

He sipped his water and she found herself watching his mouth. Probably smooth and hard at the same time. She might not be all that experienced, but she had a very rich fantasy life. And now that she was by the fire and fantasizing about kissing Will, she suddenly felt very hot. She had to stop staring at his mouth and wondering what he'd taste like.

So she foolishly took another sip of tea, because fueling her internal fire was such a brilliant idea.

"Do you kick a lot of guys to the curb, Amber?"

She blinked. "What?"

"From what you told me, it sounds like you have a lot of guys chasing after you and you have to fight them off."

She let out a short laugh. "Oh. That's not what I meant at all. But at competitions sometimes they'll hit on me as if I'm a sure thing. And I'm not."

"So you're not a fuck-and-go kind of woman like a lot of people are here at the games?"

"No. Sorry."

He frowned. "Why are you sorry?"

"Because if that's what you're looking for from me, I probably wasted an hour of your time just now when you could be getting next to someone else."

"So you think I'm that kind of guy?"

She shrugged. "Most of the guys I've met are that kind of guy."

"I'm not. Okay, I have been, but trust me, any woman I've been with has been on board and just as eager to get down as I was."

She enjoyed watching him squirm and try to explain himself. "Oh, I believe you. Otherwise we wouldn't have gone for ice cream. You wouldn't have wanted to waste your time doing something so innocuous when you could have been coaxing me into your bed instead."

He frowned. "I never coax. Women go willingly."

"Of course they do."

He sighed, then downed the rest of his ice water in one swallow. "I'm not helping my case here, am I?"

"I wasn't aware you were trying to make one."

"You are tough, Miss Sloane."

Her lips curved. "That might be the best compliment any guy has ever paid me."

"Is it?"

"Yes. Usually they only mention one of my body parts."

"Well, most guys are assholes."

She laughed, then set her empty cup of tea on the table.

"Did you want another?" he asked.

"I'm good with just one, thanks. But if you're getting another for yourself, I'll take a tall ice water."

"Okay."

She watched him walk away. Halfway to the bar he was stopped by a woman, a petite brunette Amber didn't recognize. The woman hugged Will and they chatted for a few minutes before she walked away and Will continued to the bar.

She could imagine Will knew plenty of women who'd like to be sharing his bed right now. He stood at the bar talking to some guy. He was extremely outgoing and friendly, so it didn't surprise her that he knew a lot of people.

She wished she'd had more opportunities to meet people growing up. Of course, there'd been competitions, but her mother had always discouraged her from getting too friendly with her competitors. Mom had been afraid friendship could be used against her, so Amber had typically kept to herself. She'd been polite, but not outgoing enough to form close friendships.

She'd always been so lonely at events. Just like now. Until four years ago when she'd met Lisa, who'd forced her to leave her room on occasion and socialize. Not a lot and no partying. But still she'd been introduced to others, eaten meals with them. That had melted the ice somewhat and she'd felt a little better about herself once she'd actually made a few friends. Not that she'd continued those friendships beyond the games, which she'd felt awful about.

Will made his way back to the table and laid the water in front of her.

"Thanks."

She saw he also had another water for himself.

"I noticed you didn't drink a lot tonight, even at beer pong."

"Nah. I'm trying to hold back on the alcohol. Last games I partied a little too hard. Not that it affected my game play, of course."

"Of course." She gave him a knowing smile.

"But it's easier on me if I stay clearheaded."

"I totally understand."

She saw the dark-haired woman approaching their table.

"Hey, Will, I just wanted to give you my number." She handed Will a piece of paper. "And thanks."

"Sure, Helene."

The brunette nodded and smiled at Amber, then walked away. Okay, that was interesting.

"One of your former conquests?" she asked, feeling like an idiotic jealous girlfriend as soon as the words left her mouth.

"No, that's Helene. She hooked up with one of my teammates last time we were here. He didn't come this time and she was asking me about him. I think she's got it bad for him."

"Oh. And how does he feel about her?"

Will shrugged. "I have no idea. But I'll pass her number along to him."

She took a sip of her water.

"Were you jealous?" he asked.

She knew she should have kept her mouth shut. "I figured it was someone you knew. Maybe dated or slept with or something."

She was just making it worse. She should shut up now before she embarrassed herself further.

"I'm not the man whore you might think I am, Amber. Get to know me and you might find I like making a lot of friends, but I'm pretty selective about who I fuck."

She'd asked for that. "I'm sorry. You're right, I was assuming and I lumped you in with all the other guys who've hit on me. And you haven't even hit on me."

He shot her a devastatingly sexy smile. "Yet."

She laughed, relieved that he didn't take her for some jealous stalker type. "Okay. Yet."

"So what's on tap for you tomorrow?" he asked.

"They're opening the ice arena. I can't wait to get a feel for it."

"Same here. Which means we should probably get in bed."

When she arched a brow, he laughed.

"Separate beds," he said. "I still have some jet lag to sleep off."

"And I have to get up early tomorrow morning to hit the gym before I get on the ice."

"Isn't skating enough of a workout for you?"

"It warms up my muscles, so I'm not trying to do jumps cold."

"What time are you working out?"

"I have my time on the ice at nine-thirty, so I'll probably go to the gym about six for a run, then have breakfast after that."

"Damn, woman. You're an early riser."

She smiled. "I get a lot more done that way."

"I guess you do. I'm impressed."

He was just full of compliments, wasn't he? And wasn't she just so enamored of him complimenting her? "What time do you get to skate tomorrow?"

"Noon."

"Oh, so you get to sleep in."

"I could, but some of the guys want to meet before that to go over strategy, and we'll get in a weight-lifting workout, too. How about we meet in the gym at six?"

She was surprised he'd make that offer. "You really want to run with me?"

"I really want to run with you. Unless you're one of those people who get in the zone when running and want to do it alone. I can sleep another hour."

If she was smart, she'd tell him to get that extra hour's sleep. "I'd love to have you run with me."

"Great."

Obviously, she wasn't smart.

They got up and Amber grabbed her coat. Will took it from her and held it out for her to slide her arms in.

"Thank you."

He pulled it around her. "Can't have you getting cold. Not around me."

"Trust me, Will, that's not going to happen."

Just being near him rocketed her temp up, especially when he looked at her the way he was now, his eyes going dark with sensual promise.

"Button your coat," he said.

She did and they headed outside toward their buildings. She thought they'd part here, but he walked with her to hers.

She turned when they got to the front door. "Thanks for walking me."

"You're welcome." He moved in closer. "Got your key?"

She fished it out of her pocket and held it out. "I do."

"I'll see you in the gym tomorrow morning," he said.

She thought the way he stood so close that he was going to kiss her. She wasn't sure she was ready for that, but if he did, she wouldn't pull away.

Instead, he stepped back and she had to tamp down the disappointment.

"See you tomorrow, Amber."

"Good night, Will."

He was obviously waiting for her to go inside before he left, so she turned and used her key card in the door, slipped inside, then waved at him before heading to the elevator that would take her to her floor.

She smiled all the way up in the elevator.

FOUR

SIX A.M. RUNS SUCKED, ESPECIALLY WHEN YOU DIDN'T have to get up that early, and especially when you were only doing it to impress a woman.

Sometimes Will was a moron.

But he had to admit that running the indoor track with a gorgeous, sweaty Amber was worth getting up early for. She had on some tight purple cropped sports top along with yellow and purple pants that went just past her knees and looked like they were part of her skin. They outlined her incredible figure. She had an amazing body—toned and fit, and damn the woman had some serious stamina, because as they rounded the start of the track in the middle of mile three, she didn't look ready to quit anytime soon. And if she could keep going, he could, too.

"How are you doing?" she asked.

"I'm doing great," he said through panting breaths. "But if you need to stop . . ."

"No, I'm good. Water break at the end of the next mile, though."

"Sure."

The next mile? How many miles did she intend to run? Sure they were maintaining a fairly slow pace, but still, as they made their way around and finished mile three, Will was feeling it. He hadn't eaten yet and he was starting to get hungry.

"Are you hungry?" he asked as they stopped for water.

"Not yet. I plan to do five miles. If you need to go eat, though, feel free."

"I'm fine." No way in hell was he going to admit defeat. But if he ever ran with her again, he'd need to put down a little protein first. Water wouldn't propel him through five miles.

He pushed through it, though, and afterward, they headed to the cafeteria where he ordered three eggs, bacon, toast, potatoes, fruit and salmon.

Amber had an egg-white omelet and fruit, along with black coffee.

"No wonder you're so slender, he said as he balanced two plates on top of each other. He laid those down and went back for coffee and a large juice.

"And I'd like to know how you're going to eat all of that," she said as she tenderly speared her fork into a grape.

"Easy. I'll burn it all off on the ice later. Not to mention the five miles I already ran."

He dove into his food without saying another word, his stomach demanding retribution for those five punishing miles. Everything tasted amazing, and if Amber hadn't been watching every bite go into his mouth, he might have gone back for seconds. But he could always eat again after he skated.

Meanwhile, Amber delicately tasted every forkful, chewing slowly and thoughtfully with each bite.

"It doesn't bite back, ya know," he said.

She took a small sip of her coffee. "What?"

"Your food. You approach it with caution, like it's going to attack you at any minute."

"Oh." She laughed. "If you eat slowly you get full faster."

"Uh-huh. Sure." He was full now, finally, and he felt great. "Or you can shovel it all in and make your stomach happy."

She laid her fork down. "A full fat stomach doesn't look so awesome in a figure skater's outfit."

"So you're saying I'm fat."

Her gaze roamed over him. He didn't mind that.

"I wouldn't know. I haven't seen your abs."

He leaned back in his chair. "Just say the word and I can make that happen."

"I'll be sure to let you know as soon as I'm interested in getting you naked from the waist up."

"Or the waist down." He gave her a grin, absolutely enthralled by the blush that stained her cheeks.

"Yes, that, too."

Surely she wasn't that innocent, was she? And if she was, he was going to have to watch out for her, because sharks circled the waters here, and he felt protective of Amber.

He liked her. Though since this was her third go-round at the games, she could obviously take care of herself just fine without his help.

Which didn't mean he wouldn't stick close.

"Do your parents come to the games?" he asked.

She nodded. "My mother will be here. She's never missed one of my performances."

"That's pretty awesome."

"Yes it is. My dad will probably come for the finals. He's very busy."

"What does he do?"

"He owns an investment firm. He travels a lot so he can't always watch me skate."

"I'm sure he's very proud of you. It's not every skater who can make the team for the games."

She nodded. "Thanks. What about your parents, Will? Will they be here?"

He shook his head. "My parents own a bar in south Chicago. They can't close it up to come over here, because there's no one else to take over. They'd lose too much money. But you can bet they'll be watching every game on TV."

"There are no other family members to mind the bar?"

"I've got a younger brother still in high school. My parents are both only children. They have great employees, but no one they'd trust enough to leave the bar in their hands. I've offered to pay for them to come, to pay their losses for having the bar closed. But they said no. They're proud people, always wanting to make it on their own."

"That's a shame. But I understand where they're coming from. Still, it's too bad they can't see you play."

"It's okay. They bring in a lot of revenue when the games are on TV there. All our friends come in and watch there. They serve food and tons of drinks. It's great for business."

"I guess that's a good thing, then?"

"For them it's awesome. And it's really okay that they're not here. I get enough cheering from the fans."

She reached out and touched his hand. "But you miss your family being here."

He'd reconciled himself to his mom and dad not being there the first time. It was enough that they wanted to come. He knew the realities of their lives. He'd lived his childhood through the rough times, all the times only one parent—or sometimes neither—had showed up at his hockey games. It had become a part of his life.

And they'd always supported him, encouraged him and made sure he could do what he loved. He would never make them feel guilty for the choices they made. "It is what it is. They're making what they feel are the right choices for themselves."

"I suppose that's true. Sometimes I wish my mother hadn't been at some of my events."

"A little overbearing?"

She laughed. "She can be at times. Which is why I love being here at the village."

"So you can hide out from her?"

She offered up a serene smile. "It's magical here. I'm on my own. I can make my own decisions without being told what to eat, what to wear, what time to go to bed and who I can or can't see."

"Come on. Surely she's not that bad."

"She's that bad. I know it comes from a place of love. She's a former dancer. She understands discipline and what it takes to be a winner. But sometimes . . ."

She didn't finish the sentence.

"Sometimes you'd just like her to back off and be your mom instead of your coach?"

"Something like that. Aren't your parents the same way?"

He laughed. "Honestly, not at all. My parents taught me a work ethic. You get up in the morning and you show up when you're needed. No one's going to make a success of yourself but you. If you want to win, you push hard. That kind of thing. Hockey is in our blood. My dad played in high school, and my little brother and I were on skates as soon as we could walk. But if I'd wanted to be an accountant or a doctor or anything in between, my parents would have been fine with that, too, as long as we worked hard at whatever we chose, and as long as we loved what we were doing."

Amber dragged in a breath, then let it out. "That's really sweet.

To have that kind of support, to know they're always going to have your back, is everything."

He leaned back in his chair. "So what if you decided to give up figure skating like tomorrow, Amber? What would your mother think about that?"

She gave him a straight stare. "I . . . well, I wouldn't give it up. It's just not possible."

"Why? Because you love it, because it's in your blood, or because it's what your mother wants?"

She continued to look at him and he could see her mind working, could feel the emotional knot of tension balling up inside of her.

Finally, she picked up her phone. "Oh, I need to go get ready. It's almost time for me to get on the ice." She stood.

He got up, too. "Sure."

She grabbed her coat. "The run was great. Thanks for coming with me."

"Anytime."

"So, I'll . . . see you later?"

"Yeah. See you later."

She gave him a sweet smile and walked away. He watched her, more curious about her now than ever. He wished she'd opened up more about how she really felt. But she didn't know him well enough to trust him with her feelings yet. He understood that. To her, he was just some guy she'd had breakfast with, that she'd run with. She likely thought he was some random dude—probably one of hundreds she'd met—that was trying to get into her pants.

But he wasn't that guy. He liked her and he could tell she was a ball of tension and nervousness. If she could just let go and be who she wanted to be, she'd be a lot happier.

Then again, who the hell was he to tell her how to live her life?

It wasn't like he was some goddamn expert. He really knew nothing about her.

Why did he even care? He'd never cared before about any of the women he met here. Hell, they'd been mostly hookups. Satisfying ones on both sides, but it wasn't like they'd ever delved deeply into their backgrounds. The games were for winning at your sport, and when you weren't competing, you were out having some fun.

So why was he so into Amber? Okay, the why was obvious. She was beautiful. But there was a haunted quality about her that intrigued the hell out of him, too. Admittedly, he was interested in the physical side, for sure. But there was an emotional side to her that he wanted to tap into and get to know. And for Will, that was a damn first.

He should probably bag it and concentrate on the hockey and leave women with baggage alone.

He made a mental note to do just that and grabbed his coat, determined to focus on competing and fun. Nothing more.

FIVE

AMBER STRETCHED, MAKING SURE TO GET HER FULL extensions while she was on the carpet and before she ever put on her skates.

"Did you run this morning?" Valeria asked.

"Of course I did." Her trainer was always on top of her physical routine.

"When was the last time you skated?" Yegor, her coach, asked.

"In Colorado, with you, right before I flew over here. So . . . three days ago?"

Yegor waved his hand in disgust. "Bah. You'll be rusty."

She rolled her eyes. What was she supposed to do? Ice up the aisle on the plane? She loved her coach, but sometimes the man was ridiculous.

"I won't be rusty. I'm never rusty."

"Get on ice," Yegor said. "We'll see."

Now it was her turn to wave her hand. "As soon as I'm done stretching."

"Yes," Valeria said. "Go away, Yegor. We're not finished here."

Yegor glared at Valeria. "And who is in charge?"

Valeria glared back. "Right now? That would be me."

Amber fought back her grin at the two of them arguing. Yegor and Valeria had been married for twenty-five years. They'd been her trainer and coach since she was ten. She loved them both and they were like her second set of parents. In fact, she'd spent more time with Yegor and Valeria than she had with her own parents, so she was used to the two of them bickering with each other, typically over training versus skating. She'd also seen them cry and embrace each other when she won an event.

She adored them, even if on occasion they did get on her last nerve.

She lifted her head and thought about that. Yeah, they really were like her parents.

"Lie down," Valeria said. "We need to stretch your hamstrings."

She lay on her back on the carpet and lifted her left leg, letting Valeria give her a full stretch. "Was it like this for the two of you in Ukraine?"

"Like what?" Valeria asked.

"Always arguing?"

Valeria laughed. "When we skated together, it was even worse. Always the arguing. And you know Yegor, he has the loud voice."

She looked up at Valeria. "Did he make you cry?"

Valeria smirked. "No, he made me yell louder."

Amber laughed. She could see that. Valeria was no shrinking violet. Though she was petite, she possessed both an inner and an outer strength, and Amber had never once seen her back down to Yegor when she thought she was right, especially where Amber was concerned. Valeria watched Amber like a hawk, and when she thought Amber was injured or tired, she'd pull her off the ice for a break or a rub down.

She couldn't have gotten this far, especially the past four years, without either of them. When she'd told them both she wanted to compete again, neither of them hesitated. They had both been completely supportive of her decision. She trusted them implicitly. She knew they had her back, and if either of them felt she wasn't up to the task, either body-wise or talent-wise, they would have told her. That had given her the confidence to take another shot at winning the gold. And both had helped her get ready for the grueling competition.

After Valeria finished, Amber felt limber and ready for the ice. She put on her skates, her adrenaline pumping despite this being nothing more than a practice skate. But it was on the competition ice, and to her, that meant step one in readying herself for this race for the win.

As she laced up her skates, she looked around, sizing up her competitors. Tia was already there, listening to her coach talk to her. There was also Olena Brutka from Ukraine, who had come in second in the Worlds last year. She was damn good and Amber had been keeping an eye on her.

Besides, Tia, though, Amber's fiercest competition would be Sasha Petrova of Russia. She had seen Sasha's routine. It was nearly perfect. Sasha was an ice queen who rarely, if ever, made mistakes. She was eighteen, in her skating prime, and everyone was talking as if this was her year.

Amber intended to prove everyone wrong. All she had to do was skate her best, because her routine was without flaws. It was also tough as hell. But if she could pull it off, she stood a solid chance at winning the gold.

The announcers told them to take the ice and her heart skipped a beat.

It's just practice, Amber. Relax.

"Go on," Yegor said, making flapping motions with his hands. "Skate."

She nodded and stepped out onto the ice, gliding along with the other skaters. There was no music, there would be no routines performed today. Instead, she'd limber up and get the feel for the arena, for the way the ice was set up. She started off skating the entire circumference, measuring it in her head so she'd know how much room she had when she performed her routine. Measurement-wise it was the same as any other ice arena she'd performed in, but until she familiarized herself with this one, it was foreign to her. So she went around and around several times until she acclimated, until she could do it with her eyes closed, mentally counting every step.

Once she'd done that, she started to twirl, to skate backward, to ease into her comfort zone. She ignored the other skaters around her as she went into her first jump, a double toe loop, getting a feel for the landing, how the ice felt under her skates.

She felt comfortable. Solid. Secure. That initial jump had felt good, so she tried a double axel and eased out of it with no problem. She didn't perform any of her routine, just glided along the ice and occasionally worked into a jump at various parts of the ice to gain some familiarity.

When it was her turn to get off, she did so reluctantly. She could have spent hours on the ice and she so wanted to work her routine, to see how it felt. But they could only allow six skaters on the ice at a time, so she skated to the base of the gate and stepped off easily.

"How did it feel?" Yegor asked.

She gave Yegor a confident smile. "Like I was at home."

Yegor nodded. "Good. Good. Tomorrow you'll go through routine. Then we'll see."

"How do you feel?" Valeria asked.

"I feel awesome. Limber. No aches or pains."

"Perfect. You want a massage?"

Amber shook her head. "No, I'm good for now. I'll probably need one tomorrow after I go through the routine a few times."

"Okay."

"Go," Yegor said. "Get out in the village and make friends. We meet tomorrow and practice routine."

"All right." She hugged them both, then took off her skates and started to head out. At the last minute, she changed her mind though, and decided to hang out and watch the next group of skaters. Tia would be out on the ice in this group.

She took up a spot in the front row, so she could get a clear view of the skaters. Not that she'd see much since, like her, they were just warming up. But maybe she could get a feel for their readiness and their form.

Tia, as always, skated lines of grace and beauty, even when she was just warming up. The young girl had a bright future in figure skating. Amber noticed at competitions that the crowds were enthralled with her routines. Who wouldn't be? Her routines were flawless, and her music always spoke to people's hearts.

Amber wished she could hate her for being so good, but how could you hate on someone who felt her routines so passionately at such a young age? It was obvious she loved what she did. Amber had felt the same way when she was Tia's age. She could still remember the awe and wonder of her first games.

And also how lost she'd felt being isolated at the village by herself, without her mother by her side. She'd had her coaches, of course, but even they hadn't been by her side twenty-four hours a day. Amber wondered if Tia felt the same way.

Typically, Amber didn't socialize with her competitors. Making friends with the people you competed with was never a good idea. Her mother had taught her that a long time ago.

But maybe it was time to change that. When Tia came off the ice, Amber smiled and nodded at her. Tia gave her a tenuous smile in return, then headed off with her coaches.

Sasha was in the next group, and it was evident even in warm-ups how much power she possessed. It was her biggest strength and it served her well when she did her jumps. Sasha always had the highest jumps. Amber tried not to compare her own jumps to hers, but it was hard not to. She wanted to be the best, and being the best meant being better than Sasha.

Amber had been so focused watching Sasha that she hadn't noticed Tia standing just off to her left next to the seats. She was also watching the skaters. When Tia looked her way, Amber motioned for her to come over. Tia hesitated at first, then looked around, as if she couldn't believe Amber meant her.

Not surprising, considering Amber's typical unfriendly stance. Heaven only knew what the other skaters thought of her. Or said about her. She tried not to think about that, and instead motioned to Tia again.

Tia walked over.

"Come sit with me, Tia," Amber said.

"You sure?"

"Yes. We'll watch everyone skate."

Tia shrugged. "I guess that'd be okay."

Amber knew exactly what it was like to put up a front as if you didn't care, but deep down inside you wanted friends more than anything. She'd been lonely her entire life. If it wasn't for Lisa forcing her to be her friend, she wouldn't have any, and she'd likely have hightailed it for her room as soon as practice was over today. She had Lisa to thank for dragging her out of her introverted shell.

Amber decided to give Tia time to acclimate. So they watched the skaters in silence for a few minutes. Then Amber asked, "What do you think of our competition this year?"

Tia looked over at her. "I think Sasha is the one to beat. I hope that doesn't hurt your feelings."

Amber laughed. "It doesn't, because I feel the same way. She doesn't make mistakes. Though I think you're pretty formidable, too."

Tia looked surprised. "Me? Really? I'm too new."

"And your lines are beauty in motion. I could watch you all day, Tia."

Tia shifted her gaze away and back onto the ice. "That's . . . really nice. Thanks."

"Just the truth."

Tia went silent for a few minutes and Amber figured she was shy.

"I'm super jealous of you," Tia said.

Amber blinked, then shifted in her seat toward Tia. "Me? Why?"

"Because you have such a confidence on the ice. Even when you're just stepping out onto the ice, your head is held high, you have a smile on your face, and it's like you own every inch of it."

Amber laughed. "Thank you for saying that. I love to skate."

"It shows. You skate beautifully, as if you're a part of the music, as if no one else is even around. I don't know how you do it with all the crowds and the noise and the clapping."

She nodded. "It can be a distraction. You have to tune into the music and forget that all the people are out there during a competition. It takes some practice, but you just have to be one with your music. Actually, while I was watching you I was thinking about how you look when you perform, how your movements are an extension of your music. So if you're nervous, Tia, it doesn't show."

For the first time, Tia smiled. "Really? Thanks. That's good to know. I always think people will be able to see my legs or my hands shaking."

"I've never seen it. And it helps to take a couple really deep breaths right before you go on."

"That's what my coach says."

"He's right."

"So how do you handle being off by yourself?" Tia asked, obviously becoming more at ease. "There are so many people here."

"My advice? Make friends and make a lot of them. Get out of your room and socialize."

"I'm underage so I can't go to the club."

"I was, too, my first time out, but there are activities for you. And groups for everyone who's underage."

She nodded. "Yeah, I haven't done any of that yet. My roommate is seventeen and from Finland. She's trying to coax me out."

"Go with her and do everything you can. Soak it all in. And when some of the other events start, go to them. They're fun to watch and they give you a chance to meet people."

"I'll do that."

"But always go in groups. And don't let the boys hit on you. They just want in your pants."

She laughed. "That's what my mom said."

"She's right. Have fun—but not too much fun, because you don't want to lose focus on the competition."

Tia studied her. "I can't believe you're being so nice to me. We are competitors, you know."

"We're also teammates. I think you're supremely talented and I want you to do well."

"Thanks, Amber."

They ended up exchanging cell phone numbers, because Amber wanted to make sure Tia had a person she trusted to text or call in case she needed someone. They watched the last round of skaters, then Amber headed out.

The ice had felt good, and she'd made a friend among her competitors today.

So far, so good.

SIX

WILL SHOT THE PUCK TO HOGAN, WHO PASSED IT BACK to him. The skate was light and easy. They had no opponents, just their team out there. It was mainly to get a feel for the arena. They didn't even have nets up yet.

The ice felt damn good under his skates. He was itching for a hard skate, a chance to really use his stick and slam the puck hard, to have an opponent to skate against, someone to slam up against the boards.

That would come soon enough, and damn if he wasn't ready as hell for competition to start. But for now, an easy warm up and a skirmish against his own defense would have to do.

He should have known his defense would make him feel ready. As he and Drew Hogan worked their way down the ice, Hogan slid the puck his way. Parker was right there to stop his progress, their sticks colliding in a fight for the puck. Stravinsky joined in and they hustled the puck away from Parker and made their way down the ice. Stravinsky shot it over to Hogan while Will got into position near the nonexistent net, battling sticks with the defensive players. As soon as Hogan shot him the puck, he visualized where the net would be and shoved it in.

"That looks like a score to me," Coach Stein yelled. "Take a water break."

Drew bumped against him as they skated their way over to the bench. "Now that's what I call teamwork."

Will curved a smile. "We look pretty good. I'll be happier when they bring in the nets, so we can slap the puck in there."

"Nets will be out tomorrow. Then we'll get heavy into practice."

"Are you guys as ready for this as I am?" Adrian Parker asked.

Will nodded. "You know it."

"I'm already tired of beating up on our own offense, and this is our first skate. I'm ready to beat up on the other guys."

Will laughed. "Hey, some of those other guys are our own teammates."

Parker grinned. "I know. That's the fun part."

That was one of the interesting parts of these games. His team back home was made up of guys not only from the US, but from Canada and Russia and a few other countries. Here at the games, some of those guys would be playing for their home countries, which meant his own teammates would be competitors, and some of his typical competitors were now his teammates.

Fun stuff.

He would have been able to play with Tyler Anderson, his teammate on the St. Louis Ice, but Tyler's wife, Jenna, had recently given birth to their baby boy, so Tyler had opted out and Drew Hogan from the New York Travelers had been chosen to take Tyler's place.

Will liked Drew. He was a formidable forward, and he'd be a great asset on this team. Actually, the entire team rocked.

He was so ready to get this party started.

SEVEN

AMBER HAD WANDERED THE VILLAGE ALONE ALL AF-
ternoon, familiarizing herself with the shops and locations. There
was so much to see and do.

She was used to being by herself and found it relaxing to wander
where she wanted. It was doubly easy because they were in Vancouver where everyone spoke English. The shopkeepers were all welcoming and she liked chatting with them.

She'd stopped in one of the craft shops to buy yarn. She loved
knitting, because she couldn't read during waiting and down times.
She was always too distracted, but knitting was something she
could do. She bought some beautiful teal yarn that would make a
pretty cardigan.

When she got back to the apartment, Lisa was just coming out
of the shower.

"Oh, you're back," Lisa said. "I was just about to text you."

Amber laid her purse and her package on the kitchen counter. "How did your practice go today?"

Lisa grinned. "Stellar. How about yours?"

"It went well. I even talked to Tia, one of my competitors. We sat and watched some of the other skaters."

Lisa made her way into the kitchen and pulled a bottle of juice from the fridge. "That's outstanding, Amber. Look at you, being all extroverted."

Amber skirted around Lisa to grab a juice drink for herself, unscrewed the top and took a swallow. "I wouldn't go that far."

"Hey, it's miles above how you were four years ago."

"I'll give you that. I mean, I'll never be you."

"Ha. Well, no one can be me."

Amber rolled her eyes. "So true. But I am getting out there more. I did a walk around the village today. Ate lunch by myself. I haven't been back to the room since this morning."

"See? You *are* doing better. I'm proud of you."

Amber laughed. "Thanks. Oh, and I had breakfast with Will this morning. He also went for a run with me at the gym."

Lisa's eyes widened. "Do tell."

"Nothing happened between us. Just a run and breakfast. Then I had to leave to get ready to skate."

Lisa leaned back in her chair. "But you *want* something to happen between you."

"I don't know. Maybe. I don't want to be a one-night stand for any guy."

"I don't know why not. Sex can be fun, Amber. It doesn't have to end in a big commitment. And frankly, you don't want that from any guy you hook up with here."

She sighed. "I know."

"We talked about that, remember? Jump into the sex waters, have a little fun and don't get emotionally attached to anyone. If you want to limit yourself to one guy—or maybe two guys, great. But it's okay for you to be a sexual being, honey. Isn't that what your hormones have been telling you?"

For the longest time, she'd thought she was sexually dead inside. She'd been so focused on skating, she never gave guys a second look, especially the drunken frat boy, grabby type of guys. But then she realized there was a major part of life—the fun, sexual part— she was missing out on. The only thing was, she didn't just want to be some guy's lay and then quickly forgotten. There was something deep inside of her that strongly objected to that.

"Yes, you have been telling me that. And I want that. I want to have fun. I want to have sex. I just want to be selective about it rather than falling into the sack with the first guy who suggests it."

Lisa nodded, then took a sip of her drink, obviously pondering her next words before she said them. "And has Will suggested it?"

"Not directly. I mean we've sort of talked about it in a roundabout, flirtatious kind of way, but I think he understands that I want to take things slow."

"Okay. And he's still around, right?"

"I guess. I mean, we'll see. I haven't heard from him since breakfast."

Just then her phone buzzed, so she reached for it, read the message and looked up at Lisa. "It's from Will."

"And what does it say?"

"It says, 'Hungry. Wanna have dinner?'"

Lisa grinned. "Outstanding. So go have dinner with Will. Then see what happens after dinner."

Amber couldn't deny the small thrill of anticipation, or the delight at getting a text message from Will.

You're being ridiculous.

Of course she was. But she was also giddy. So she'd ride the wave of giddiness and, like Lisa said, she'd see what happened after dinner.

EIGHT

WILL WAITED AT THE DOOR TO AMBER'S HOUSING UNIT. When he saw her step out of the elevator, his heart rate kicked up a few beats faster. She had on her white parka, the dark fur from the hood teasing her cheeks. It was snowing again, so she stopped at the door, pulled her beanie from the pocket and slipped it over her head. She spotted him as she pushed through the door on her way outside and graced him with a genuine smile that rocked him back on his boots.

"Hi, Will."

"Hey. You look pretty." Her cheeks were already pink from the cold. It was snowing again, the flakes dropping onto her black beanie. She also wore dark skinny jeans that were tucked into tall boots.

"I do? Thank you. That's so sweet of you to say. Can I say you look hot?"

His lips curved. "You can say that."

She looped her arm in his. "Are we heading to the cafeteria?"

"Nope. We're heading offsite for dinner."

"Really?"

"Yeah."

They walked a ways out of the village, toward a parking lot. Will pulled out a set of keys.

"You got a car? How did you get a car?"

He walked her to an SUV. "Let's just say I know people."

He opened the door for her and she slid inside and buckled her seat belt, her internal excitement engine revving up.

She thought she'd be stuck at the village for the entirety of the games. She wouldn't care if they were going somewhere for fast food.

Will got in and buckled up, then started the engine and cranked up the heater. They headed out of the lot and down the road.

"So this is why you wanted to meet early."

"That, and other reasons."

She looked over at him. "Care to share?"

"Not at the moment. But you'll know once we get there."

"Okay." Mysterious, too. Will was getting more and more interesting every time she was with him.

She focused on the scenery as Will drove. Vancouver was breathtaking. The snow had stopped falling and the sun had come out, so she fished her sunglasses out of her bag and slid them on, taking in the view of all that white and green blanketing the mountains. The trees towered so tall she could barely see the tops of them as Will took them through some fairly treacherous turns. But he took his time and she enjoyed every moment of gawking as he drove them down the mountain.

When he pulled into a parking lot and she spied the restaurant perched precariously on top of a hill, she felt pure awe.

"The views here must be incredible."

Will put the SUV in park and nodded. "Yeah, I've heard good things about this place. Let's go check it out."

They went inside and were immediately greeted by windows that showcased not only Vancouver, but the Burrard Inlet. Obviously there wouldn't be a bad seat in the entire restaurant.

Will stepped up to the desk and gave his name. They were immediately seated near one of the windows. Amber took off her beanie and her coat and then looked over the restaurant. The cedar ceiling and gorgeous stone fireplace created a cozy atmosphere. The fire gave off a delicious warmth, despite all the windows. She looked out over downtown Vancouver and watched the sun go down over the water. The views were breathtaking, the sun an orange fireball as it sank slowly behind the mountains. Amber felt so fortunate to be able to see it.

"This view is spectacular," she said, pulling her gaze away from the breathtaking scenery and onto other steal-your-breath sights, namely Will, who sported a day's growth of stubble on his jaw, which only served to give him a sexier look. If that were even possible.

"I thought you might enjoy it."

"Thank you for bringing me here."

Their waiter came over with menus and asked what they wanted to drink. Amber chose water. Will did as well.

Amber looked over the menu. "I have no idea what to order. Everything looks amazing."

"We should have an appetizer," Will said. "I don't know about you, but I worked up an appetite during practice today."

She looked up from her menu. "Did you eat lunch?"

"Well, yeah. But that was hours ago."

She laughed. "Okay, then. Appetizers it is."

When the waiter came back with their waters, they ordered an appetizer and their dinner.

"How did your skate go today?" he asked.

"It felt good. How about yours?"

"Not long enough. Not tough enough. It's better when you have someone to skate against other than your own team."

"I imagine that's true. I did stay and watch some of the other skaters on the ice. And I talked to one of my US teammates."

"Don't you always talk to your teammates?"

"No."

"Like . . . ever?"

"Ever."

"Why not?"

She tapped her fingers on her water glass. "My mother said it wasn't in my best interests for me to get friendly with my competitors."

"Yeah, but shouldn't you be friendly with the ones on the US team when you're competing internationally?"

"No. We're all competing for one spot—first place. It doesn't matter what country we're from. At least that's what my mother thinks."

He studied her while he took a sip of his water, then asked, "You always do what your mother tells you?"

She arched a brow. "Is that an insult?"

"No, it was a legit question."

"It sounded like an insult. I'm not a child, you know."

"Obviously. So you agree with her assessment?"

She shrugged. "I don't know. Sometimes yes, sometimes no."

"What would happen if you disagreed with her?"

Amber had tried that before. It hadn't ended well. But she didn't want to have that discussion with Will. He would think she was a child. And maybe her mother treated her like one. But she also knew her mother wanted her to win, and winning sometimes meant you couldn't have what you wanted.

Like friends. Or a boyfriend.

Or fun.

That last one might have been an exaggeration.

She sipped her water and shrugged. "Sometimes sacrifices have to be made."

"Is that you talking, or your mother?"

She had been enjoying herself. Now she didn't like the direction this conversation was going. "You don't know her, so you're making judgements based on supposition instead of knowledge."

"That's true. I'm not trying to hurt your feelings, Amber. I'm just trying to understand how a grown woman doesn't act on her own best judgement."

"I—"

She was about to argue with him further, but their scallops arrived, so instead, she decided to table the argument for the time being. Which was probably a good idea, since they were miles from the village, and if she got angry with him, it wasn't like she could storm off. She was stuck with Will.

At least for now.

They dug into the scallops. Or rather, Will did. Amber slid one onto her plate and cut it in half, then tasted it. It was perfectly broiled and delicious.

"That's all you're having?" Will asked.

"I don't want to spoil my appetite for the main course."

"Fine with me. I'll eat the rest of them."

He did, too. Not that the appetizer portion was very large, but scallops were rich, and Amber knew her limits. She'd ordered salmon for dinner, and she intended to eat every bite of it, so the last thing she wanted was to stuff herself on appetizers.

Or the amazing-smelling bread the waiter had just laid on the table. Will, however, had no problem tearing into it.

"Would you like some?" he asked, offering the basket to her.

She'd like about ten slices of warm bread. With as much butter as it would hold. Instead, she shook her head.

Sometimes, staying in fighting shape for competition sucked. So instead, she watched Will eat bread and thought about how great it must taste.

As soon as she retired she was going to eat an entire loaf of French bread, with a whole stick of melty warm butter—and no guilt.

At fifty-one, her mother maintained her trim figure by dancing as much as she could and teaching dance. And by watching her calories.

Amber had no intention of doing that when she hung up her skates. She'd still skate, of course. She'd always skate. But as far as counting every calorie that went into her mouth? The hell with that.

"Hey."

She looked up at Will. "Yes?"

"You went quiet on me and that's my fault. I didn't bring you here to pick a fight with you and I'm sorry. You have a right to do whatever you damn well please, and that includes listening to your mother's advice. And I have no right to give you my opinion on anything, because what the hell do I know about you or your life?"

That was the exact speech she was going to give him when they returned to the village. But he beat her to it, and apologized. "I appreciate that. And it's okay. A lot of people don't understand the dynamic between my mother and me. She can be overbearing at times. I'm the first to admit that. But I'm no doormat, either. I understand what it takes to be a champion. So I mostly agree with her, even if she's often a pain in my ass."

He laughed. "So she's kind of like your coach?"

"No, I have a coach. And he's a pain in my ass sometimes, too. He pushes me hard on the ice. She pushes me hard off the ice."

"Jesus. That must be unbearable for you."

"It can be. But I have my escapes."

"Reading and movies?"

He'd remembered their conversation. "Yes. And music. I'll often plug in my earphones and just skate so I don't have to listen to either of them. What about you? Anything get on your nerves?"

"My coach. My teammates. My competitors." He popped the last scallop into his mouth, chewed, swallowed and took a sip of water. "Oh, and losing. That really pisses me off."

She laughed. "I agree."

Their dinner arrived. Her salmon looked and smelled amazing. She couldn't wait to dive into the risotto as well. She looked over at Will's plate. He'd ordered the salmon trio, with Chinook, sockeye and coho salmon. It looked incredible.

The first bite melted in her mouth. She closed her eyes and let the flavor consume her.

"Kind of like having an orgasm, huh?"

Her eyes flew open. "What?"

He motioned with his head toward her plate. "The salmon. It's that great."

"Oh. Right. Sure. Orgasmic." She'd given herself plenty of orgasms. But she wouldn't equate the flavor of this salmon to an orgasm.

Maybe she hadn't been doing it right.

Will studied her and she suddenly felt as if he knew everything about her. Including the fact that she'd never had sex. Which was utterly ridiculous. How could he know?

She decided to concentrate on the delicious food and not her own stupid thoughts.

"If you hadn't become a competitive skater, what would you have done with your life?"

She looked up from her plate. "I've never thought about it before."

"Really? I think about it all the time."

"You do? Why? Is it because you don't love playing hockey?"

He took a bite of his salmon, swallowed, then shook his head. "Nah. I love what I do. It's in my blood and has been from the time I was a kid."

"Then why ponder another career?"

He smiled at her. "Because it's fun to play 'what if.' What if I'd never played hockey. What would I have done? Become a plumber, maybe. I have friends who are plumbers."

"And you think being a plumber is exciting?"

"I like working with my hands. Plus, plumbers are always in demand. It's a good business."

"True."

"So, yeah, I could see myself going in that direction. Or maybe a firefighter."

She had been eating as she listened, but she paused. "Why a firefighter?"

"Because you save lives. Plus, it's hard work and dangerous. And exciting."

"In other words, you want to be a hero."

"I think if you go into that line of work wanting to be a hero, you're going into it for the wrong reasons."

"That's true."

"So what about you?"

She thought about it as she ate. "Maybe a teacher. I like kids."

"Little ones or big ones?"

Her lips curved. "It doesn't matter, but I always loved science. I could see myself teaching high school."

He arched a brow. "Think you could take on unruly high school kids?"

"Kids just need someone who understands them and respects them. And who won't take shit from them. It doesn't matter what age they are."

He looked at her. "You'd make a great teacher, Amber."

She laughed. "Yeah, in another life."

"You could do it now. Or, you know, after all this."

"Maybe."

"Have you given any thought to what you might do after the skating thing is over?"

"No. All I've thought about is winning gold. I don't think past that, because winning is my focus. It has to be my focus."

"Good point."

"What about you? Any thoughts on what you might do once your hockey career is over?"

"I'll take over my parents' bar, probably. They'll want to retire at some point and they want someone in the family to take over, which means my brother and me. But I don't intend for my hockey career to be over anytime soon. I'm too good at this."

She laughed. "Spoken like a guy who has a healthy ego."

"Hey, neither of us would be here if we didn't think we were the best at what we do."

"You're right about that. We are the best." Sometimes she forgot how good she was. It was why she'd gotten on the US team. Not that she needed an ego stroke, because she didn't. But if she didn't believe in herself and in her talents, who would? Certainly not the judges.

She needed the judges to believe she was the best. She'd worked hard the past four years to make sure that happened.

They finished their dinner and both declined dessert. When the check came, Amber reached for it, but Will snatched it up.

"You do realize that I'm perfectly capable of paying for a meal."

"I'm sure you are," he said. "But I'm the one who invited you out, so, if you don't mind, I'd like to pay."

When she gave him a look, he said, "Next time we go out, you can pay."

She wouldn't argue with that. "All right. And thank you for dinner."

"You're welcome. Thanks for coming with me."

They headed out to the SUV. Amber paused. It was dark now, but the lights of Vancouver were a beautiful backdrop. Since she didn't know when they'd be able to leave the village again, she took a moment to breathe in the scenery.

Will moved in next to her, draping his arm over her shoulders. "Nice out here, isn't it?"

"Yes." The snow had stopped. It was cold, but she loved the cold. It always made her feel at home. And with Will's arm around her, she felt a warmth seeping into her body. She could stay like this for hours.

"So I guess we should get back," she said.

"You don't have a curfew yet. We can hang out here for a while if you want."

She turned her head to look up at him. "In the parking lot?"

"Why not? The view is good. Unless you're cold."

She shook her head. "I'm never cold."

"No, I'd say you're pretty hot."

She laughed. "Is that a line?"

"It's the truth. You're beautiful, and you have a sassy mouth." He had turned to face her, and he rubbed his thumb over her bottom lip. Her skin prickled with chill bumps, but it wasn't the cold causing her to shiver. Will's touch incited desire in her that she'd never felt before.

And when he cupped her neck and brought his lips to hers, for a few seconds she forgot to breathe. But when he fit his mouth to hers, she sighed in complete abandon.

She'd been kissed before. Lots of times. Some of those times had even been good kisses. But this kiss was the heaven of all kisses. Hot and delicious and with passionate intent. It was the kind of kiss a woman dreamed about her entire life, the way you wanted to be kissed, as if the man kissing you really meant it.

She leaned in and clutched his arms, taking in the strength of him through his parka, absorbing the softness of his lips as he moved them over hers. And when he slid his tongue in her mouth and swept it against hers, she unashamedly moaned her appreciation.

He moved his arm around her back and brought her close to his body, and all she could feel was rock-hard muscle.

She wanted more. A lot more. Without the impediment of thick down jackets in their way. She wanted to run her hands over warm, naked skin while their bodies writhed against each other. She wanted his mouth on other places of her body. She wanted an orgasm that she didn't have to give herself. She wanted the feel of a hot, hard cock moving inside of her. She wanted legs tangled together and his body moving over hers.

She wanted sex. Sweaty, hot, orgasm-inducing sex.

And she wanted it right now, because every sexual part of her throbbed. She pulled away and looked up at Will, at the desire in his eyes.

"Let's have sex," she said.

He looked taken aback. "In the parking lot?"

She laughed. "No, of course not. Back at the village. Your room or mine. I don't care."

"Okay, then." He took her hand. "Let's go."

Finally. She was finally going to have sex.

NINE

WILL HAD A HARD-ON THE SIZE OF CHICAGO, AND IF
Amber kept rubbing her hand up and down his thigh like that, he
was going to careen off the road and down the mountain and kill
them both.

Not that he'd let her know that because damn if he didn't love
the way she kept touching him.

But eventually he was going to have to tell her to stop because
they were about to arrive at the village, and he wasn't going to walk
up to the apartments with a raging erection.

Amber must have been aware of it as well, because she removed
her hand when they were a few miles away, which gave him time to
get himself under control.

When he pulled into the parking lot, he glanced over at her.
"So . . . your place or mine?"

"Yours, if you don't mind. I gave Lisa a hard time four years ago about always kicking me out of the apartment whenever she had a guy in there. I'd hate to do the same to her."

"Not a problem. I'll just shoot a text to Elias and let him know he'll have to bunk somewhere else tonight."

"You sure he won't mind?"

"Nah. He'll be fine with it."

"Okay."

She waited until he parked the SUV.

"But before you text your roommate, I should tell you that I've never had sex before."

He blinked, then shifted in his seat to face her. "Really."

"Yes. I figured if that was going to be an issue for you, I should tell you ahead of time."

She was a virgin. Wow. That topic hadn't come up a lot with women he'd been with. Okay, or . . . ever. "That's kind of a big deal. Isn't it?"

"Not really. I mean, it's more terminology than reality. It's not like I haven't played down there before by myself. So I doubt I'm actually even a virgin anymore other than I haven't been with a guy before."

Oh, shit. Now his mind was filled with images of her masturbating, and his dick got hard again. "Amber."

"Yes?"

He inhaled, then blew it out, trying to think about anything other than Amber naked, her legs spread and her fingers working in and out of her pussy.

Fuck. That was not helping his hard-on go away.

"Okay, so this is a big deal. Your virginity is a big deal."

"It really isn't, Will. It's just a thing. It's a technical thing I'd like to dispense with. You know, get it over with. And you seem like a nice enough guy and I trust you."

He dragged his fingers through his hair. She trusted him? Why? Not that he wasn't trustworthy, because he sure as hell was. But shouldn't she want romance or something to coincide with the giving up of her virginity?

"Don't you want . . . more?"

She cocked her head to the side. "More what?"

"I dunno. Candlelit dinner and champagne and some romance."

She snorted out a laugh. "Uh, no. I'm not bartering my virginity for romance, Will. I don't need to be married to give it up, either. Or in a relationship. Or in love. I just want it out of the way, so I can stop thinking about it. It's a given I'm late to the sex game. I'm tired of it weighing on my mind. I need to be focused on winning gold, and there are a lot of hot men here."

He arched a brow. "Oh, so you want me to fuck you and take your virginity so you can get in the game?"

"It's not like that at all. We've already had this discussion. If I wanted to just fuck some random guy, I'd have done that years ago. That's not what I want at all."

He leaned back in the seat. "Look, I feel special that you chose me, but I'm not sure I want the responsibility."

She laughed. "What responsibility? It's not a marriage proposal. Nor is there any type of commitment involved. But if you don't want to do it with me, I totally understand."

He dragged his fingers through his hair. "It's not that I don't want you. I don't know if you noticed or not, but I've had a raging boner the entire trip back up the mountain. And that was just from kissing you. I can already imagine what it'll be like to get you naked, to suck on your pussy and make you come, to feel my cock moving in and out of you."

He watched as she sucked her bottom lip between her teeth, then licked her lips. His words had turned her on. Hell, she turned *him* on. He'd been a walking erection around her ever since they locked lips. He wanted her, there was no doubt about it.

So what the hell was he waiting for? She'd already told him he was off the hook as far as any responsibility. The problem was, he felt responsible. Maybe her virginity didn't mean anything to her, but it sure as hell meant something to him.

"I need to think about this."

She nodded. "Okay, I understand."

He picked up her hand. "In the meantime, don't hop into the sack with the first asshole that offers, okay?"

She laughed. "That's not going to happen."

"Good." He kissed the back of her hand. "Ready to go inside?"

She nodded. They got out of the car and he walked beside her. When she started toward the door to her apartment building, he tugged on her hand and brought her close. He wrapped an arm around her and kissed her, this time not light and easy like he had at the restaurant, but deeper.

And yeah, his cock went hard again, and he'd regret this all night long, but he needed to taste her again, needed her to know how much he wanted her.

When he released her, she made a low humming sound in the back of her throat. Then she lifted up on her toes and brushed her lips across his. "It's really hard to leave you," she said.

He took her hand and pressed it up against his raging-hard cock. "Tell me about how hard it is."

Her lips curved, that sexy smile of hers not at all curbing his need for her.

"You don't have to leave at all."

Why did he want to think about this? Whose stupid idea was it to wait, anyway?

But he took a step back, determined to think this through before jumping into bed with Amber.

"I'll see you tomorrow."

"Think about me when you're in bed tonight."

"I'll be jacking off tonight thinking about you, Amber."

She smiled. "That's very good to know. 'Night, Will."

She went inside, and he waited until she closed the door.

He pivoted on his heel and decided to take a long walk in the cold, determined to cool down his raging erection before he went inside for the night.

TEN

AMBER WAS NUMBER SIX IN HER GROUP, WHICH MEANT she would skate last. It also meant she did a lot of stretching, pacing and mental warm-ups. But it also gave her a chance to check out the short program of some of her competitors.

Gretchen Bader of Germany was fourth and skating now. She'd come in third at the World competition and Amber knew never to underestimate Gretchen. She was extremely strong in jumps and she could sneak up on you in a competition and kick your ass. From the looks of her short program, her jumps were just as strong as ever, which meant that Amber would need to be flawless.

Next up in the group was Hua Ping of China. Hua had a lovely grace to her skating. She wasn't as strong on the jumps, but even in the short program Amber was mesmerized by the beauty of her movements. The judges would be, too.

While she watched Hua, she put her skates on since she would be up next. There were no judges present. She wouldn't skate in the short program for a few days. But just practicing sent a thrill into her nerve endings. It meant they were nearing the reality of competition. And once competition started, she'd be on her game and ready to win.

But for now, Hua had finished her short program practice, so it was Amber's turn. She listened to Yegor's instructions, then took the ice.

There were already people in the audience. The place wasn't as full as it would be when competition started, but the arena was half-filled with people.

Her mother wasn't there yet, thankfully. Mom had the dance studio, and while Amber was her child, the studio was her other baby. She wouldn't leave it until she had to, which meant she'd fly up here just in time for Amber to compete.

Amber did a few warm-up laps around the ice, then took her starting position. When the music started up, she flowed through the routine, getting a feel for doing the short program on unfamiliar ice.

Everything felt good. Her skates slid across the ice just fine, her compulsory jumps went off without a hitch, and she sank into the music perfectly. She tuned out the cheers of the smaller crowd with no issue. Then again, she'd always been able to adjust to crowd noise. Her music was all she heard when she was out there.

She slid to a stop and paused for a few seconds after her routine ended, satisfied that everything had gone well. Then she skated off.

"You looked good out there," Yegor said. "Jumps looked fine."

"How do you feel?" Valeria asked. "Any muscle tightness?"

"No. But that was a short program. We'll see how I feel after I practice the long program tomorrow."

She never liked taking such long breaks in between working her programs. Typically, she skated every day, but between the flights and the delay in getting on the ice, it had been several days. Now that she'd be allowed daily practice, she'd get into the groove again.

She went into the workroom with Valeria, who stretched her quads and hamstrings and gave her a back massage. After, she took a shower and dressed in black leggings and a long gray top. She laced up her boots, then decided to go in search of some food. Between this morning's run followed by a gym workout, and warm-ups followed by the skate, she'd worked up an appetite.

She grabbed her parka, about to head outside when she spotted Will leaning against a wall in the main lobby. She walked over to him.

"What are you doing here?"

"I watched you skate."

Her heart skipped a beat. "You did?"

"Yeah. So where are you off to now?"

"Cafeteria. I'm hungry. How about you?"

"I could eat. Mind if I go with you?"

"I don't mind that at all. I'd love your company."

He pushed off the wall and moved in closer. "You're very sexy when you skate."

No one had ever said that to her before. "It was my short program. All compulsories. Nothing sexy."

He picked up a lock of her hair and sifted it through his fingers. "That's where you're wrong. Every move you make is sexy, Amber. The way you glide along on skates, those jumps, even the way you extend your arms. All sexy."

She slanted a disbelieving look at him. "I think you want to get in my pants and your view of my skating is biased."

"Possibly."

"Besides, you haven't even seen my long program yet. Now that's packed with some sizzle."

He leveled her with the wicked desire in his gaze. "Babe, you haven't seen *my* long program yet, either. Trust me, I'm packing some heat, too."

She laughed. "I'm looking forward to that. All you have to do is say the word."

"I'm still pondering that."

He helped her on with her parka and they headed out the door. The sun was out, so she slid on her sunglasses. "I've never known a guy to play hard to get."

"I'm not hard to get at all. It's more like I want to make sure that you're sure about this."

"I haven't changed my mind. You're still my guy—at least as far as sex is concerned."

"Good to know."

They walked across the yard to the main building. When they went inside, they headed into the cafeteria. There were a lot more people here than there had been the past couple of days. With the opening ceremonies tonight, everyone who was competing was here now.

"I see Lisa over at that table," Amber said. "And isn't she with some of your hockey guys?"

"Yeah."

They made their way to the table where Lisa and a few other snowboarders had commandeered a large table. She also saw Drew Hogan, Ivan Petrov and Jimmie Oster, along with several of the other US hockey players she'd met the other night.

Lisa got up and put her arms around Amber. "Hey, sweetie. I feel like I haven't seen you in a day or more. How's it going?"

"Good," Amber said. "Missed seeing you this morning."

Lisa smiled. "I spent the night elsewhere last night."

"Of course you did. I hope that went well."

Lisa took a bite of her nectarine, then grinned. "It went extremely well, thanks. Hey, Will."

"Hey, Lisa."

Will moved over to talk to some of his friends, so Amber left her parka and bag with Lisa and went to get some food. She piled her bowl with greens and chicken breast, a side of raspberries and blueberries, then grabbed a drink and made her way back to the table and slid in beside Lisa.

"Did you eat?" she asked Lisa.

Lisa nodded. "As soon as I got here. I felt like I burned a million calories this morning."

"How was it?"

"Fantastic. The half-pipe was slick and sweet."

"I can't wait to watch you ride it."

"You know you could have watched me—or even snowboarded yourself, if you'd ever come up here and visit."

Amber started to eat her salad, her fork balancing on the bowl. "I feel such guilt about that, but at the same time I did what I had to do to work out this new program. My mom and dad went to Italy two summers ago. They invited me to go along and I said no to that, too."

Lisa's eyes widened. "Italy? Aww, honey, I'm sorry you missed that. Italy is amazing."

"I know. It's one of my favorite places. But in the end it was better that I didn't go. It made for a sweet second honeymoon for them, and since they rarely if ever take vacations, I wanted them to have that time alone."

"I'm sure they had a great time."

"Based on the photos they showed me, it looked like they had a great time. And they did not need their daughter coming along as a third wheel."

"I can see your point."

"Besides, I was busy working out my new routine."

Lisa smiled at Amber. "We haven't had any time to talk about that yet. Are you confident about it?"

She nodded. "I am. I think it's really good."

"I can't wait to see it. What's your music? Is it rock and roll?"

"There might be a little rock music. Then again maybe the only rock in there is Rachmaninoff."

Lisa narrowed her gaze. "You're not going to tell me what music you chose, are you?"

She slanted a sweet smile at Lisa. "Nope."

"Bitch."

Amber laughed. "I can't wait to see you kick some ass on the half-pipe. You get so high and it always makes me hold my breath, but you're so damn good at it that I end up screaming until I'm hoarse."

Lisa's eyes always brightened when they talked snowboarding. "You're so awesome to say that. And I'm so stoked about competing."

"What I'm excited about is to get the games underway."

"Me, too. Can you believe the opening ceremonies are tonight already?"

Amber took a long swallow of water, then laid her glass down. "When I decided to come back, four years seemed like it wasn't long enough, you know? There was so much to do. But after I finished my routine and practiced it over and over again, and then I made the team, I just wanted to perform. Suddenly, I wanted the games to get here and it seemed like the days went by so slowly."

Lisa laughed. "I know exactly how you feel. Part of me wants to soak all of this in and hope every second of these next two weeks lasts an eternity. The other part of me wants to get to it already so we can win."

She'd always loved Lisa's confidence. She didn't know if Lisa was ever nervous. If she was, it never showed. Then again, Amber was the same way. Whatever nervousness she felt she kept it bottled up inside so no one ever saw it. The minute your competition picked up on any flaw or nervousness, they'd pounce and use it against you. So outwardly, Amber was always the epitome of confidence.

"So what hot guy are you seeing tonight?" she asked Lisa.

Lisa shrugged. "Haven't decided on one yet. It depends on what parties develop after the opening ceremonies. You get to see everyone there so it's a perfect time to scout out the goodies."

Amber shook her head. "You're something, Lisa."

Lisa picked up an apple and waggled her brows. "Not the first time I've heard that."

Amber laughed. "You are so bad."

"Not the first time I've heard that, either."

Will came over. "What are you two talking about all huddled together?"

Amber looked up at Will. "We were discussing the opening ceremonies tonight."

"Oh, right. I've already got a line on some parties going on after the ceremonies."

Amber looked over at Lisa, who slanted a knowing smile at her. "Told ya."

"What did you tell her?" Will asked.

"That there'd be parties after."

"There are always parties. Lots of them."

"And no doubt you'll hit all of them?" Amber asked Lisa.

"Probably. I might drag you to all of them with me."

Amber shook her head. "Not a chance. And you shouldn't, either. Don't you have practice tomorrow?"

"Hey, I didn't say I'd be drinking. I just said I'd be partying."

Will laughed. "If anyone knows how to do that, honey, it's you."

Lisa nudged Will with her shoulder. "Spoken by a master partier himself. I'll take that as a compliment."

Amber watched the easy way that Will and Lisa interacted. She wondered if the two of them had ever hooked up. She wanted to ask Will, but she knew she'd come off as jealous and possessive, and since she had no claim on Will, it would be foolish to attach any emotion to whatever it was going on between them.

She just found him attractive and trustworthy. So why should she care if he'd ever had sex with Lisa?

Still, she was curious. So after they all split up to head back to their apartments to get ready for the night's events, she decided to satisfy that curiosity while she and Lisa were in the bathroom doing their hair.

"Did you and Will ever hook up?" she asked.

Lisa looked over at her. "No. We hung out at a lot of the same parties four years ago, but just as friends. There was never an attraction between us. I was getting busy with someone else at the time. So was he. Will became more of a big brother to me."

Relief washed over her, which was ridiculous because she had no claim on Will. "I see."

Lisa laid the flat iron on the bathroom counter, then leaned against the counter, giving her a curious look. "Would it have made a difference to you if we had?"

She thought hard about it, because she wanted to give Lisa an honest answer. "No. I like both of you. I was mainly just curious."

Lisa smiled. "Because you thought I might give you some advance intel on how good he is in the sack?"

Amber laughed. "Uh, definitely no."

"So you want to go into it blindly and be surprised?"

Amber had just finished applying mascara. She set down the wand and turned to face Amber. "Actually, I do. That's what exploration and sex with someone for the first time is all about, isn't it?"

"Mmm, definitely. All the new sensations and scents and what is he going to do, how is he going to do it? Is he going to be any good at it?"

"I imagine Will is very good at it."

Lisa laughed. "Because he's good-looking? Honey, I've known several great-looking guys whose looks don't match their skills in bed."

Amber picked up the blush. "That's disappointing."

"Tell me about it."

Now she wondered if Will would be good at sex. Despite what Lisa said, Amber had a feeling he knew what he was doing.

And she couldn't wait to find out.

ELEVEN

OPENING NIGHT CEREMONIES WERE ALWAYS THRILL-ing. Sure, it was a lot of standing and waiting around for your country's turn to go out, but it was also a chance to meet up with fellow countrymen you hadn't had a chance to see yet.

Will was up and ready for the moment. There was nothing like a huge arena packed with people cheering for you. That kind of momentum would carry him all the way through the games.

Tonight all the US athletes would wear matching clothes. Typically, he'd think that was stupid, but not here. Not for this. He felt that sense of cohesion tonight. They'd walk together as a united country. He'd walk with people he'd never met before, but after tonight they were all one nation. And before and after they'd cheer on all the other nations competing.

At least until he faced some of them on the ice.

They had a specific place they had to be, so he met up with Drew, Adrian and Jimmie and they walked to the arena together.

They found their designated area along with their coach and other teammates. Now there wasn't much to do except wait and talk with the other US athletes.

He spotted Amber coming in with some of the other figure skaters. She wore the dark navy pants and the red, white and blue jacket just like all the other US athletes. But she stood out, her golden blond hair pulled into a high ponytail that swung back and forth when she walked. She and a young, dark-haired woman had their heads together, talking as they came into the US athlete's area. When she looked up and saw him, she smiled.

Damn if her smile didn't punch him right in the gut. It was genuine, not practiced, as if she was surprised and happy to see him. He'd noticed it every time he saw her.

Will had dated a lot, and the one thing he'd noticed often was a well-practiced smile, the kind you knew damn well a woman spent time perfecting in front of a mirror.

Amber's wasn't like that at all. It was sweet and wide and the kind of smile that reached all the way to her sparkling blue eyes. She had the kind of smile that made a guy feel like he was the only guy in her orbit.

He made his way over to her, at the same time she said something to her friend and started walking toward him. When they met in the middle, she grabbed both of his hands and squeezed them.

"I know this is my third time to do this, but it's also going to be my last time. I'm so excited I can't even breathe."

That was another thing he liked about her. She truly loved being a part of the team. She never took any of this for granted, or felt that it was her right to be here.

He felt the same way. This was such a privilege and he intended to appreciate every second of being here. Especially tonight. So he lifted one of Amber's hands and brought it to his mouth, pressing a kiss there.

"You ready for this?" he asked.

"So ready."

There were televisions backstage in the waiting area, so they got to watch the other nations who went before them.

"I love seeing the other countries." Amber grabbed his arm and leaned against him. "Oh, look, there's Lisa. Aren't Canada's sweaters amazing?"

"Yeah." Will grinned seeing so many guys he played with walking on the Canadian team.

"There's Tim McCaffery right behind Lisa," he said, pointing to his teammate. "He plays on the Ice."

And through it all, with every nation making their appearance, the crowds cheered and applauded.

So when it was their turn, and the US walked out in full force, Will soaked in the clapping and the roars from the audience.

Somehow Amber ended up two rows ahead of him, which was okay because he walked with the hockey team. For many of the guys this was their first time, and he soaked in the looks on their faces as they saw the size of the crowd in the arena. There was nothing like it, because it was so much bigger than anything they'd ever experienced.

"Wow," Drew said as they rounded the turn on the track. "This is crazy."

"Yeah." He remembered exactly what it had been like when he'd stepped out with the US athletes four years ago. Utter exhilaration and the drive to bring home a medal for his country.

When they finished their walk, they stayed to watch the rest of the opening ceremonies. It was always such a thrill to see everything the host country had put together. Canada had done a spectacular job and the arena was filled with color and light and feats of spectacle. Will would never forget it.

After the opening ceremonies concluded, several of them got together to decide what to do. Some were tired and heading to their rooms, while others were hitting the club or some of the parties. Hard practice was coming up starting tomorrow, so they knew after tonight they'd have to buckle down. Will knew a lot of them would enjoy one last night of going out—although no one would go too hard with the competitions looming.

Will ended up circling around with Amber, Lisa, some of the snowboarders and a few of his hockey teammates.

"Claude is having a party," Lisa said. "We have to go."

Claude was a downhill skier, and this was his third trip to the games. He was also well-known for having legendary parties. Great music, awesome liquor. Claude's parties were always lit. Will had gone to a few of them his last time at the games, one after his team had won the silver medal. He'd partied so hard he could barely get out of the bed the next day.

He sure as hell wasn't going to go to that extreme—at least not this early in the games. But it would be a great kickoff to the games.

He circled around and found Amber. "You ready to let loose before we all have to settle in and go for those medals?"

She lifted her gaze to his. He loved her eyes. Her lashes were so long they brushed the top of her brow. "I'm game for whatever you have in mind tonight."

He felt that gut punch of desire. He was going to have to decide soon whether to take her to bed or turn her down, because he knew it wasn't fair to leave her hanging. And he sure as hell wasn't going to leave his balls in a twist when he had hockey to focus on.

"Then let's hit it," he said.

"Yes. Let's."

They all went to one of the restaurants and grabbed something to eat, everyone talking over each other about the games officially beginning tomorrow. It obviously wasn't just Amber who was psyched about competitions beginning. All the athletes were more than ready to compete, and she loved listening to them talk about how they were going to win.

It was kind of sad that everyone couldn't win, but that was the nature of competition. This wasn't a place where you got a participation trophy. You fought hard, and you either won or you lost. And everyone here knew that. Some would go home winners. Many of them would go home empty-handed.

That part was awful, because everyone here was loaded with talent.

"You've been quiet," Will said.

She had finished her dinner of filet of sole and asparagus, so she emptied her glass of water and nodded. "I was thinking about all these amazing athletes, and how many of them will go home without a medal."

Will scanned the restaurant. "Yeah. I've lost plenty of games. It sucks. And especially here, where you prepare for so long, and you gotta have that level of confidence, positive you're gonna be the one to win a medal."

She nodded. "We're all here to compete. It's the highest level, you know? Everyone is talented and prepared. And yet some of the best athletes in the world will still go home with nothing."

He put his arm around her, using his thumb to caress her jaw. "I don't know about nothing, Amber. The experience, the people you meet, the memories, the opportunity to say you were here. Those aren't a pile of nothings."

She lifted her gaze to his and offered a faint smile. "Oh, come on, Will. If your team doesn't medal, will you be satisfied to go home with just great memories?"

He paused a few beats before answering her. "Hell, no."

"That's my point. I just feel bad about so many people being disappointed."

"Nothing you can do about that."

"I suppose you're right."

"And besides, when you're out there on the ice doing your thing, are you worried about all those other skaters you're going to leave in the dust?"

Her lips curved. "No."

"You want to kick the shit out of them, don't you?"

"Figuratively, of course."

He grinned. "Of course."

"Yes."

"Then don't worry about it. We all know the risks we're taking. And we all intend to be standing on that podium."

He was right. She absolutely planned to be standing on the podium. In the center. Wearing gold around her neck.

After they ate, Amber followed the group that went to one of the luger's apartments. She'd heard of Claude. Everyone knew about Claude's parties. They were renowned, tended to go all night and no one on either side of Claude's apartment ever complained. Some thought he paid them off, or they got standing invitations and free booze, or maybe Claude invited them to Germany for vacations. Even the stories that weren't about the parties themselves were legendary.

Either way, Amber had heard the parties were always no-holds-barred fun.

But she'd never attended one. Lisa had invited her last time she was at the games, but it had been the night before her long program and there'd been no way she was going to a party when she had to skate the next day.

When they arrived at Claude's apartment, she could already

hear the loud music. It was as noisy as being at the club, which had to be insane for his neighbors and everyone on the floor.

Then again, maybe everyone on the floor—as well as above and below—were in the apartment, because the place was packed, people spilling out into the hallway.

"You're here! Welcome!" A tall, very lean, bald dude wearing a sleeveless T-shirt and loose white pants came out of the apartment and pulled Will into a bear hug, and then proceeded to hug everyone else, including Amber.

His hugs were fierce. He had a German accent and an effusive, welcoming smile.

"Claude, this is Amber," Will said.

"Of course you are," Claude said. "You're beautiful, honey." He kissed Amber on the cheek, then nudged Will. "Food and booze are inside. Have a great time."

Claude was clearly a force of nature Amber noted as he turned his back on them and exuberantly hugged the next group of arrivals.

It was an interesting mix of partygoers, too. Some people had on the standard athlete outfit: track pants and jacket with the logo from the games. Some wore shorts and tank tops, and there was a guy dressed only in a long-sleeved button-down shirt and his underwear, dancing with a girl in her bra and panties. Then again she also sported a tiara. They were getting down to a hard-driving dance beat in the hall.

Amber couldn't help but gawk. It wasn't even ten p.m. yet. A few of these people were utterly toasted.

She sure hoped they wouldn't be competing tomorrow. Then again, who was she to judge? Maybe those were the types of people who did their best competing hungover.

She just wasn't that type of person.

"Come on," Will said, grabbing her hand. "Let's go inside."

The noise was earsplitting. She leaned into Will. "Why doesn't anyone complain about the noise?"

"Everyone loves Claude. He invites all his neighbors to come visit him at his villa in Italy. He provides free alcohol and food. Plus, his apartment has an open-door policy. Who doesn't love that?"

"Someone who might want to sleep?"

Will squeezed her hand. "You need to get into the party mindset, Amber. It's all good."

She supposed if no one was complaining, she shouldn't care. Though if it was the night before her performance and this was her apartment building, she would definitely care.

"There are certain people who ask to be in Claude's building," Will said. "So, trust me, no one who's staying nearby will complain."

"Oh, I see. The party types."

Will nodded. "So don't worry about athletes losing sleep. Chances are, they wouldn't be sleeping much anyway, or they're the types that would sleep through all this."

The bass was so loud it thrummed along with her heartbeat.

She shook her head. "I could not sleep through this."

"You like quiet, huh? Or maybe some noise machine to lull you to sleep?"

She nudged him with her shoulder. "I'm not that bad, asshole. I just enjoy a full night's sleep, especially before a performance. That doesn't make me a party killer."

He slung his arm around her. "You need to lighten up and learn to take teasing."

They made their way to the well-stocked bar, where there were two gorgeous women serving. Amber opted for a vodka with cranberry juice that she requested they fill with a lot more cranberry than vodka. Will asked for a beer. They walked around and it was obvious that Will already knew a lot of people from the waves and shouts he got.

No surprise there. She already knew from her last visit to the games that Will was a popular guy. Then again, he was outgoing and friendly, always stopping to talk to someone or introduce himself to people. But he never left her out of the conversation, making sure to introduce her to everyone he visited with.

She'd never remember all these people's names, and she was shocked that Will did. She felt so out of her element. The only crowds she was ever comfortable with were the ones cheering her on at the skating rink. There, she felt she was interacting with them via her skating, through the music and her performance.

Here, she had to speak to people, interact on a social level. While it was easy enough in a large group, one-on-one interactions still made her uncomfortable.

And suddenly she realized that Will had disappeared and she was alone, and some guy was making his way over to her.

Shit.

Then she realized it was Blake, that hot skier Lisa had hung out with the other night.

"What's up?" he said, offering her a friendly smile.

"Oh, uh, nothing. What's up with you?" She took a long swallow of her drink, blinking back tears as she realized the drink had a lot more vodka in it than she'd anticipated.

"I'm Blake."

"Amber."

"What do you do, Amber?"

"Figure skater. And you're a skier, right?"

He cocked his head to the side. "That's right. Alpine skier. How did you know that?"

"I'm Lisa's roommate."

"Oh, right. She told me about you. She said you're an amazing skater."

"Lisa's very kind."

"Lisa's very honest."

She felt the tinge of embarrassment from his compliment. "Thank you. So tell me about skiing. That must be so exciting."

"It is. I've been doing it as long as I could stand up. I love it. How about you?"

"Same. Only figure skating. Not skiing. Obviously, since I'm not a skier. I'm a figure skater. Which you already knew." She fought the cringe of embarrassment. She knew she was totally fumbling this conversation. Blake was incredibly attractive, with beautifully thick blond hair and a sweet crinkle to his green eyes when he smiled. Which he was doing right now.

"So, you're from the States?"

"I am. How about you, Blake?"

"Right here in Vancouver."

That was probably why he and Lisa had hooked up. "Oh, it must be so thrilling for you to have the games here."

He smiled at her. He had a great smile. She could see why Lisa would like him. "Pretty much. Hey, have you seen Lisa? She said she was gonna be here."

Oh, thank God. An out. "I haven't, but we came in together so I know she's here. How about we go look for her together?"

"Sure."

Relieved she now had something to do, Amber grabbed his hand and tugged him through the packed-in crowd. Lisa was always easy to find because she was typically surrounded by a group of people. She found her sitting by the sliding glass doors with the group of snowboarders they'd come over with.

"Here she is."

Blake let go of her hand, then kissed her on the cheek. "Thanks, Amber. It was good to meet you."

"You, too, Blake."

Blake made his way toward Lisa, and Amber backed away.

Okay, maybe that one-on-one wasn't as horrible as she'd thought.

"You aren't picking up another guy, are you?"

She pivoted to see Will standing there. Whereas Blake had been attractive, Will simply took her breath away. There was something about his eyes, the way he gave her all of his attention when he looked at her. It made her feel as if there was no one else in the crowded room.

"Oh. No, of course not. Blake was looking for Lisa and I helped him find her."

He swept his hand from her wrist up her arm, bringing her forward toward his chest.

Her heart started pounding erratically as it always did whenever she got close to Will. "I'm glad to hear that. I thought maybe you got tired of waiting for me and had decided to hunt down some other guy to take you to bed."

She arched a brow. "I mentioned I was picky when it came to men, right?"

He cupped her neck, bringing her closer, their lips almost touching. She wasn't sure she was still breathing. His thumb brushed the artery in her neck, teasing back and forth and making her crazy with lust. She felt the thump, thump, thump of her heartbeat against his thumb, each pulse firing up her desire for him more and more.

"Yeah. I like that you're picky. You should be, because you're worth it."

She had to get out of here. She needed to get him out of here, where she could touch him and do all the things with him that she'd been thinking about.

"Will."

"Yeah?"

"What are we doing here?"

"I thought you wanted to come to the party."

She shook her head. "I want to be alone with you."

She waited for his reaction, hoping he wouldn't walk away. If he walked away, she was going to be devastated and disappointed.

His gaze roamed her face as if he was searching for the honesty in her words. Then he gave her a quick nod. "Consider it done."

She barely had time to grab the parka she'd dropped in the massive pile at the front door before Will dragged her out.

Okay, then. Enthusiasm. She liked that a lot.

As soon as the elevator doors closed, Will backed her into the wall and covered her mouth with his. She whimpered against his lips, sucking on his tongue as soon as it invaded her mouth. She'd never felt so hungry, so desperately needy about a kiss.

Just a kiss.

But it was more than just a kiss, and when he unzipped her parka and his hand roamed over her breasts, she wanted to cry tears of desperation and need.

She grasped his wrist and jerked her gaze to his. "Don't."

He stilled and started to back away, but she held a death grip on his hand.

"Don't. Stop," she said.

He rubbed his lips against hers, then pulled away. She saw the raging passion in his eyes.

"Elevator doors opened."

She sighed. "Damn."

"Yeah."

She sucked in a breath and tried to clear the hazy fog of sexual need from her brain as Will took her hand and led her from the elevator.

It was a short walk to his apartment building. She waited for the hesitation to sink in, for her to change her mind. It didn't come. All she felt was impatience and the driving need to get Will naked.

They stepped into an elevator again, and she had thoughts of pushing *him* against the wall this time. But she was afraid once they started up again, there'd be no stopping.

She really hoped there'd be no stopping next time. Will pulled out his phone and sent a text, then slipped his phone back in his pocket.

"I sent a text to Elias, my roommate," he said, slanting a smoldering look that nearly melted her boots to the elevator floor. "I let him know I need the apartment for the night. He said he's already got other plans."

She could barely breathe, the anticipation filling her chest. "I'm really glad to hear that."

The elevator pulled open on the second floor. Will once again grasped her hand in his and they walked the short distance to his apartment. He put his key card in, opened the door and she walked inside. He shut and double locked the door.

Amber unzipped her parka and laid it over the chair in the living room, then turned to face Will, who'd already shed his coat. He came toward her, giving her that look, the one that made her feel like delicious prey.

He kissed her again, this time with more force, more passion, more of everything she wanted.

She was so happy they were alone and locked in for the night. She'd waited so long for this, and nothing was going to get in her way.

TWELVE

WILL COULDN'T GET ENOUGH OF KISSING AMBER. OR of putting his hands on her. Or breathing in whatever that amazing scent was that seemed to be all over her skin. What the hell was that, anyway? Something sultry, for sure, and it made him want to lick every inch of her, from behind her earlobe all the way down to her toes, and everywhere in between.

Right now he had ahold of her rib cage just under her breasts and her heart beat so fast he wasn't sure how she wasn't hyperventilating. He pulled his mouth from hers.

"You okay?"

She licked her lips. "I'm great. How about you?"

His lips curved. "Couldn't be better. But your heart is beating superfast. I was concerned."

"Kissing you and touching you does that to me. Trust me, I'm more than fine." She moved into him and grasped his forearms. "In fact, I'd really like it if we could get my heart rate up even higher."

"I just want to make sure you're really ready for this. It's a big step."

She moved into him and trailed her fingernail up and down his arm, causing his heart rate to jump. It wasn't just Amber who was into this. He was way into it, into her, in ways he didn't expect. But this was her night and he wanted to make this special for her.

"Will, it's just sex. We're not in love, and we're not in a relationship. I have no expectations other than you giving me a few outstanding orgasms. You can do that, can't you?"

She talked a good game about how this wasn't a big deal. He knew better. Hell, even his first time had been a big deal.

He tugged her close and cupped her butt, drawing her against his hard-on, to let her know what she did to him. "I can give you more than a couple."

Her body quivered in reaction. "I'll just bet you can. How about now?"

"Now? You mean right now? While you're standing in the living room?"

"Well, I meant we could move into the bedroom."

He curved his palm over her hip and squeezed, then teased his fingers inside the waistband of her pants. "I need to educate you about sex, Amber. It's not just for bedrooms. Let me show you."

Amber fought for breath as he sat her on the plush, wide chair. He kneeled between her legs and took off her boots and socks, then reached for her pants and drew them down her legs. She shivered when he swept his hands over her calves, taking the time to circle his fingers over her knees.

Oh, wow, that was amazing. Who knew that touching her knees would be such a turn-on? But when he touched her thighs, she quivered all over, especially when he kissed her inner thighs.

"These are pretty," he said, teasing his thumb over her pale pink panties, inching closer and closer to her sex. And when he rubbed his fingers over her clit, she arched and gasped and dampened and quivered and oh, God, it was everything.

She wished she could separate from her body and watch what was happening to her while at the same time still be inside of herself to feel all these amazing sensations. It was too, too good.

He reached up and drew her shirt off, and with deft fingers unhooked her bra, drawing the straps down her arms. He took her panties off, too, leaving her naked in the chair. Her breathing went more rapid and all she could think about was coming, coming fast and coming hard. And having Will do it for her. She knew it was going to be so, so good. Monumentally good.

Slow down, Amber. It's just sex and sure, Will's likely going to make you come and it'll be great. But it's not like you're going to medal in orgasms or anything.

The only thing that was going to happen was that she'd get to finally eliminate the stupid virginity label tonight, so she could feel more . . . normal. She needed to remind herself that her world wasn't going to exponentially change just because she was going to have sex tonight.

But the way Will looked at her, as if she was the most beautiful creature he'd ever seen, made her feel amazing. She'd never been naked in front of a guy before, and it felt weird and kind of awesome at the same time.

"You're beautiful, Amber. Your body is perfect everywhere, from your long legs to your lush hips to your incredible breasts to your delicate fingers." He kissed her fingertips, then used his hands to touch every part of her body he'd just mentioned. His gaze lifted to her face as he cupped her breasts, circling his thumbs over her nipples. She'd long dreamed of what it would feel like to have a guy touch her like this, to feel a man's hands on her nipples. She'd touched herself plenty of times, of course, had even let guys feel her up over her clothes during make-out sessions. It had felt good enough.

Having Will's hands on her naked skin? Heaven. His hands were rough, his thumbs calloused and evoked quivering feelings that made her arch her back to silently ask for more.

He bent and put his lips over one nipple. She let out a whimper that turned into a moan when he gently sucked. And oh, that pleasure shot straight to her sex when he flicked his tongue over the bud. Her pussy quivered and she was afraid she might hyperventilate from all these sensations.

And he hadn't even made his way down south to all her good parts yet.

She hoped she didn't pass out when he did, because she'd hate to be unconscious during her orgasm.

He lifted up, bracing his hands on either side of her, then kissed her again, a deep, passionate kiss that left her head spinning.

Her whole world was spiraling and she wrapped her legs around his hips to center herself, but that only made things go more haywire because her sex made contact with his hard cock. And when he rubbed his jean-clad erection against her, she thought she might die. Or maybe climax just like that.

"Do you know how damn good that feels?" he asked, surging against her.

She raked her nails along his arms. "Yes. It would feel a lot better if you were naked and inside of me."

He smiled down at her. "Oh, we're not nearly ready for that yet."

"We're not?"

"No." He slid down her body, taking another taste of her nipples before kissing her stomach and hipbone. And when he kissed the top of her sex, nuzzling her pubic hair with his nose, she started heavy breathing again, the anticipation making her heart rate zip up fast.

She felt his tongue swipe up from her pussy lips and circle around her clit.

Oh, it was magnificent. Warm and wet and absolutely amazing. And when he put his lips around her clit to give it a gentle suck, it was everything she could have imagined, and more. He flattened his tongue against the bud, using slow, easy movements, easing her into the magnificent wash of his mouth and tongue, drawing her ever higher into ecstasy.

She felt like she was climbing, her orgasm right there, just out of reach. Will was in charge, holding her body like a master, taking her right where she needed to go. The higher she climbed, the more she moaned and whimpered, the faster his tongue and lips moved over her.

And suddenly she was there, crying out as her climax slammed into her, taking her breath, taking her sanity. She shuddered and said Will's name and maybe spoke in tongues. She wasn't sure, she didn't care. All she knew was it was glorious and exquisite and she wanted it to go on and on forever. This was nothing like giving herself an orgasm. It was so much better. It was a mind-blowing, perfect orgasm.

But finally, she came down from the euphoria, her senses returning to her. She realized Will was kissing her thighs, making his way up her body once again. And when his face hovered above hers, she cupped her hand around his jaw and brought him close for a kiss.

He tasted of her, and it left her in awe that he would do that for her—to her.

"That was amazing," she said. "Thank you."

He was still touching her, and despite that body-rocking climax, she still reacted to the movement of his hands on her. Her nipples hardened—again.

"You were amazing. Your body is amazing and you taste so damn good I could suck your pussy over and over again."

She shuddered out a sigh. This was just the beginning, and there was so much more to explore. "Now let me do that to you."

"Seriously?" He sat back on his heels.

She slid off the chair and straddled his thighs. "Of course. I want to learn how to do everything, Will. Not just fucking. And we have all night. Now off with your clothes."

THIRTEEN

WILL HADN'T EXPECTED THIS. HE WANTED TO MAKE this a good night for Amber. What he hadn't expected was to find a sensual, wild woman who just happened to be a virgin.

And now she sat on his thighs and said she wanted to give him a blow job.

Maybe he was dead and this was heaven. If so, he was a damn happy dead man.

She tugged at his shirt. "Let's start by getting this off. You're wearing way too many clothes."

He liked that she wasn't shy. He'd never been with a virgin before, and he supposed he had an expectation that a virgin would be shy.

Amber wasn't. She helped him pull his shirt over his head. He tossed it onto the chair.

"Oh. My. God," she said, smoothing her hands over his shoulders and chest. "You have tattoos."

"Yeah."

"I mean, I saw the ones on your hands, but I never—" She stared at them, then lifted her gaze to his. "They're beautiful, Will. Tell me about them."

He had a rocking hell of a hard-on and she wanted to talk about his tattoos? Now?

He brushed his thumbs over her nipples. "How about I give you the tour later?"

"Oh, right. Sure." She paused, letting her fingers map a trail down his right arm before bringing her focus back to his face. "Promise?"

"Absolutely promise."

"Okay, then." She slid off his lap. "Get on the chair. Oh, and lose your pants."

Now they were back on track. He got up and unzipped his jeans, letting them drop to the floor. He drew down his boxer briefs, sucking in a breath as he watched the way Amber stayed transfixed on his erect cock. She didn't look away, didn't seem at all intimidated. Instead, her lips curved in a way that he took as one hell of a compliment.

"Wow," she said. "That's impressive."

He took a seat on the chair. "Thanks."

She grabbed a pillow from the sofa, came over to the chair and dropped the pillow on the floor between his feet, then kneeled on it. She slid her hands over his thighs, using the tips of her fingernails to tease his skin. She moved between his legs, and when her belly brushed against his cock, he shuddered in a breath.

Man, he enjoyed that body contact.

She rubbed her breasts against his chest, then kissed him. He grabbed a handful of her hair and held onto her head, making sure she wasn't going anywhere as he explored the inner recesses of her mouth with his tongue. Her answering whimper infused him with the need to explore her all over. He wanted to push her to the floor and lick her again, then slide inside of her and pump until he released all this need he felt for her, until he came, hard.

But it was her turn to explore, to learn about his body, so he was going to have to wait.

She smoothed her hands down his arms, over his chest, lingering at his nipples. He sucked in a breath as she teased them a bit before snaking her fingers over his abs.

She lifted her gaze to his.

"You have an amazing body, Will. You must work very hard to keep it in shape."

"I skate a little now and then."

She laughed, and the low, throaty sound she made shot right to his balls. "Skate a little, huh? That must be how you ended up with these powerful thighs."

Her exploratory trek continued over his legs. He liked her hands on him. They were soft, smooth and a little bit of torture having her touch him everywhere but his cock.

But when she slid her hands between his thighs, his cock twitched. She wrapped her hand around it and damn did that ever feel good.

"Yeah, I like that," he said.

"Tell me how."

He showed her how to grab it at the base and stroke upward. "Like this. Don't be afraid to squeeze hard. You won't hurt me."

She gave him some pressure, and he cupped his fingers around hers, showing her exactly how much he wanted and how.

"Oh, yeah, that's good. So fucking good."

He wanted her mouth on him, but he let her have the lead. It wasn't long before she bent and took a swipe across the head of his cock with her tongue, then lifted her head and smiled up at him.

"Salty. Did I ever mention I love salty things?"

He gripped the arms of the chair and tried not to shoot his load right then.

She had such a sweet innocence, but there was fire and desire in her eyes. And when she put her lips over his cock head and flicked her tongue over it, he thought he might die.

She was making sounds as she slid her mouth down the shaft, and Christ, he might not survive this.

He thought she'd be clumsy, maybe even turned off or quit halfway through, but in reality she was killing him. She was eager and a goddamn expert at blow jobs for someone who'd never done it before. Her tongue was everywhere, she included her hands, and even played with his balls. It might be a learning experience for her but to him it was fucking torment. She had great hands and the sweetest mouth he'd ever felt on his dick.

"That's it," he said, giving her guidance. "Squeeze my cock with your mouth. Suck it, Amber."

She also took direction really well because she squeezed his cock head between her tongue and the roof of her mouth, then drew his shaft in slowly until he thought he might die.

Sweat beaded down the side of his face as he fought to keep from exploding in her mouth as she expertly wound her tongue around his cock head before engulfing him once again.

It was all he could take.

"Amber, I'm gonna come."

She lifted, released to stroke him while she smiled at him. "Let's find out what that's like."

And then she took him deep in her mouth again, using her hand to wind around the base of his shaft as she pumped him deeper.

"Ohhh, fuck." He exploded, spurts of come jettisoning from his cock. It was the best fucking orgasm, releasing into the soft recesses of her mouth.

She held on to him, taking in everything he had until he lay back, spent and empty.

When he'd gone soft, she released him and licked her lips, then sat back on her heels. "Well. That was fun."

He shook his head. "Woman. You kill me."

"Was it good for you?"

He reached for her and pulled her onto his lap. "Any more 'good for me' and my brains would have leaked from my ears. You get any better at that and you could kill someone."

She smiled, then brushed her lips across his. "I'm so glad you enjoyed it. What you did to me felt the same. It was an out-of-body experience."

"Good. I like making you come."

"Once you rest a little, we'll make each other come again."

He got the idea she wanted to make up for lost time. He didn't have a problem helping her experiment. He ran his hands over the soft skin of her back. "I'm down for that."

"This part was so fun," she said. "Imagine how great fucking each other will be."

She blew him away with how open she was to talking about sex. He'd been with plenty of women, a lot of them way more experienced than Amber. Some of them could barely even talk openly about sex. Yet Amber was more than willing to explore, and to voice what she wanted.

He liked this woman. And like her, he couldn't wait to see what else they could do together.

FOURTEEN

SO FAR, AMBER'S SEXUAL EDUCATION HAD EXCEEDED her expectations. It didn't hurt that Will was patient enough to not only teach her, but to let her explore at her own pace.

It also didn't hurt that he had a slamming body that was nearly irresistible and she wanted to touch him constantly.

After he got them glasses of water, they made their way to the bedroom.

It felt so odd to be wandering around naked with a man. This would be something she'd have to get used to. Not that she had any issues with her body. She liked the way she looked. Not that she thought she was perfect. She pretty much had no boobs and wide hips, which her mother always criticized.

No. You're not going to think about your mother. Not tonight.

She worked hard as a figure skater, and she was strong and it showed in her body. And she was damn proud of that.

Though at the moment she was way more interested in Will's body. There were definite advantages to being able to ogle a naked man up close, especially when said naked man had such amazing tats.

They lay on the bed facing each other. She appreciated he wasn't in a hurry to fuck her and get it over with, that he allowed her to inspect all his amazing tattoos. She asked him questions about their origins and his reasons for getting them. He patiently answered all her questions.

"I like this one," she said, trailing her fingers over the beautiful rose above his left wrist. "And the word 'Love'? Did you have that done when you were in love with someone?"

He shook his head. "No."

"Then why the word 'Love'?"

"Because I believe in it."

Her heart swelled. She rolled over onto her stomach, raising herself up on her elbows. "Why?"

"Why what?"

"Why do you believe in love?"

He trailed his fingers over her hip. "My parents. They've been together since grade school. They got married right after high school. They've been married for thirty years and they still look at each other like they're on their first date. And it hasn't always been easy for them, either. They've weathered some rough times, raised two boys, and still, they've always loved each other."

Amber saw a light shine in Will's eyes when he talked about his parents, about the love they had for each other. It made her heart squeeze to realize how much he cared for his family.

"It must be amazing to be surrounded by that kind of love."

He nodded. "Yeah. They have plenty of love for my brother and me, too. They're pretty amazing people."

"I can imagine."

He swept her hair behind her shoulder. "What about you? Do you believe in it?"

"In love?" She shrugged. "I don't know. My parents are more like roommates than lovers. They're polite to each other, but work is everything to my dad. And my mom's focus has always been on her dance studio. Plus me, of course."

"You don't think they love each other?"

She shrugged. "I don't know. I don't ever see them being affectionate with each other, like touching or kissing each other, you know? I'm not sure I've ever seen that. Maybe they are when they're alone, but they're not the kind of people who are outwardly demonstrative with affection."

"Even with you?"

"Even with me."

"Then that sucks, babe. Everyone needs love."

"Oh, I know they love me. They just don't show it outwardly."

"I guess your way and my way are different."

Her lips curved. "Like figure skating and hockey."

He laughed. "Yeah, like that."

He rolled her over onto her back and kissed her, and she soaked in the way his lips were so tender, yet insistent.

The man could take her breath away in the best way possible. She tangled her fingers in his hair and clutched, as if those luscious strands were a lifeline. He answered with a groan that made her pussy quiver.

She gasped. "Will."

"Yeah."

"Let's do this now."

He lifted above her. "You sure you're ready? Because I can get you more ready."

He moved his hand over her breasts, brushing her nipples before diving lower to cup her sex. She arched into his hand.

"I'm so ready I could come without you touching me. But keep touching me, okay?"

"I can do that."

He caressed her into a frenzy, until she was writhing into his hand and felt beyond the ability to comprehend anything other than his touch. She came with her entire body feeling as if it had been shocked with bolts of electricity, her breath leaving her body as she gasped for air.

Will was hard as he left the bed, and as she floated on a cloud of euphoria, she watched him grab a condom from his bedside drawer and put it on. She couldn't help but admire his hard cock. Like his tattoos, it was a work of art, too.

She hoped he could do magical things with it.

He climbed onto the bed, using his knee to spread her legs.

He gripped her thighs, the feel of his fingers so close to her pussy revving her up all over again. How could she still be so jacked up by him again after two mind-blowing orgasms?

"You ready?"

She was still pulsing. "More than. How about you?"

She saw his chest rise as he took in a deep breath, then dropped down over her body. "Amber, I'm so hard right now I could explode. I can't wait to slide my cock inside of you and feel your hot pussy squeezing around me. I'll make this good for you, I promise."

His words made her heart do leaps. She reached up and swept her hand across his jaw. "I believe you. Let's do this, Will."

He fit himself at the entrance to her pussy, then paused. "If at any time you want me to stop, you tell me."

She smiled up at him. "You know, this might be my first time with a cock, but I've used toys before. I'm a virgin only in that I've never been with a guy."

His smile heated her from the inside out. "I'll want to hear stories about what toys you've used."

She laughed. "And I might tell you sometime."

"Good. Until then, I'll still take my time with you."

This guy. He was so amazing he couldn't be real. And as he eased into her, she realized his cock felt nothing like the toys she'd used before. Will was real, and his cock was warm and pulsing with life. It swelled inside of her as he fit himself completely within her. Her sex responded in quivering delight.

"Oh." Amber wrapped her legs around Will's hips to draw him in closer.

"You okay?" he asked.

She raked her nails down his arms. "I'm more than okay, Will. You feel . . . amazing inside of me. I was just thinking that you're nothing like a dildo."

He laughed. "Good to know."

"I meant that as a compliment. I mean your cock is hot and I can feel it pulsing inside of me. It's an incredible sensation. And the way my pussy reacts. It . . . quivers."

He drew in a deep breath. "I feel it. You feel good, Amber. So damn good. Tight and warm and squeezing my cock so hard."

His words made the room feel hot. They made *her* feel hot—and achy all over. But it was a good kind of ache. She couldn't get enough of these sensations, as if every part of her tingled.

And when his pelvis rubbed against her clit, those tingles shifted to sharp, delicious shocks of pleasure. She wanted a lot more of that so she lifted against him.

"Oh, fuck yeah," Will said, grinding against her, deepening his thrusts, until she felt him both inside and out.

She was losing her mind, lost in the way his hands seemed to be everywhere, touching her breasts, snaking along her hip and grasping her butt to draw her closer to the center of him.

He'd occasionally slow down to lift and look at her, as if he wanted to make sure she was still there with him.

She reached up to smooth her fingers over his jaw, to feel the prickles of his beard, which sent goose bumps along her nerve endings. And then, his gaze fixed on hers, he thrust into her, making her gasp.

"Will," she whispered, no longer capable of rational thought other than his name.

"Yeah, babe. I'm here with you."

That was all she needed to know, because these feelings, these sensations, had become overwhelming. She felt as if she was deep within the center of him, and when he took her mouth in a kiss that blasted her senses, she tumbled into orgasm, grasping onto him and rocketing through shock waves of the sweetest pleasure.

"That's it," Will said. "Oh, fuck yeah that's it." He dug his fingers into her skin, grasping her closer. He held her so close she felt pain, but this pain sent tingling pleasure down her spine.

She thought she'd be the only one losing control when she came.

She'd been so wrong. He groaned against her and shuddered, and she felt every part of him as he came. She closed her eyes and absorbed every tumultuous quake, taking in his groans and the movements of his body within her.

She let out a breath, overcome by the experience. It had been magnificent, exceeding her expectations.

And, instead of immediately rolling away from her, Will cupped her behind and gathered her close, kissing her neck and nibbling on her skin, making her feel as if she had been anything but a fuck to him. She felt cherished and protected.

Oh, she knew she wasn't a girlfriend, that this had been just sex and nothing more for both of them.

But for her first time, it had been memorable and glorious and wonderful. And she had Will to thank for that.

He finally disengaged from her, but not before giving her a gentle kiss and smoothing his hand over her hair. "I'll be right back."

He left the room and went into the bathroom. Amber stretched her arms over her head and wiggled her toes, then smiled.

She wasn't a virgin anymore. Finally. And her first experience with sex had been outstanding.

When Will came out, he climbed onto the bed next to her and laid his hand on her stomach. "Feel okay?"

She leaned into him, needing his touch on her skin. "I feel great. That was amazing. You were amazing. Sex is amazing. Did I say amazing too many times?"

He gave her a smile. "I'm okay with amazing, especially if you're going to say it about me."

She grinned, then rolled over onto her back. "Not that I have anyone to compare you to, of course. But it was really good."

"Want me to call up a few guys to come in so you could have your way with them for comparison purposes?"

She shoved at him and laughed. "No. Jerk."

"Good answer. I don't really want to share you with anyone."

Her heart squeezed. "You don't?"

"Hell, no. You're beautiful, you're smart, you give amazing blow jobs and you're great in the sack. Why would I give you up?"

If he kept talking like that, she might get all emotional about him. And that couldn't happen. She needed to remind herself—continually—that this thing she was doing with Will was just for fun. And for her sexual education.

"You're pretty damn good at it yourself. I wouldn't mind a few more lessons."

He swept his hand upward, over her breasts. "It's a big hardship, but I'd be willing."

She moved her hand down and circled his erect shaft. "Yes, it's big and hard all right."

He laughed and pulled her on top of him. "Lesson one. How to ride a man like a cowgirl."

She pressed her nails into his chest. "I can already tell I'm going to enjoy these lessons."

FIFTEEN

AMBER GOT BACK TO HER ROOM ABOUT SIX-THIRTY IN the morning. She and Will had fallen asleep about four.

She finally rolled out of bed, got dressed and bent over to brush her lips against his temple. He reached for her.

"Leaving?"

"Yes. I have practice."

"I'll get up."

She sat on the edge of the bed. "Don't. I'll make my way back to my place."

"No. I'll walk with you."

He ended up putting on clothes and his parka and boots and walked her to her apartment, which was totally unnecessary, but also incredibly sweet. He pulled her against him and kissed her. It was a delicious kiss that warmed her from her hair to her toes.

"I'll see you later," he said.

"Have a good day."

She smiled all the way up to her room, yawning the entire time.

It was going to be a long day. She had enough time to shower, dress and make it to the dining hall to grab coffee and down an egg-white omelet before she had to get to the ice rink for practice.

At least she didn't have a performance today, for which she was supremely grateful.

"YOU LOOK TIRED," VALERIA SAID. "THERE ARE DARK circles under your eyes."

"Yes, I'm a little tired this morning."

Valeria massaged Amber's hamstrings to loosen them up before she took the ice. She also gave Amber a critical look. "You party last night?"

Amber trusted Valeria more than anyone. "Define *party*."

"Drinking?"

"No."

"Out with a boy?"

To Valeria, any man under the age of thirty-five was a "boy." "Maybe."

Amber winced when Valeria gave her a hard stretch.

"You spend the night with him?"

"I did."

"Who is this boy?"

She absolutely wasn't going to give Valeria his name. Not yet, anyway. "A hockey player. He's very nice."

"Hmph. You should not trust boys."

Amber fought the smile. "I'm not planning on marrying him, Valeria. I just want to have some fun."

"Fun is good. Don't get your heart hurt."

She knew Valeria cared about her. Amber had been with Valeria and Yegor since she was ten years old. They were like her second parents. She spent more time with them than she did with her own parents. "I'm being very careful, and my heart isn't involved."

Valeria just huffed. "Your mother will not be happy about this."

"I don't plan on telling my mother anything about my sex life."

"Good. The less she knows the better. You know how she is."

"Yes, I know how she is. She thinks my entire life should be about skating forever until I die."

"She's not that bad."

Amber looked backward at Valeria. "You know she is."

Valeria continued to stretch her for several more minutes. Amber could tell she was thinking. When she finished, she helped Amber down from the table.

"I change my mind. Go, have some fun. But don't let a boy break your heart."

"I'm in charge of my heart, Valeria. I promise to be careful."

Valeria cupped her face with her hands. "You're like my own child. I never want anyone or anything to hurt you."

Amber's eyes filled with tears. "Hey, where's my tough Valeria? I can't skate if you make me cry."

Valeria's eyes were teary as well. She blinked and straightened. "Bah. Making you cry is Yegor's job when he tells you you're doing everything wrong."

Amber laughed. "So true."

As she took the ice for practice, she realized how very lucky she was to have someone who cared so much about her. Valeria had always been there for her, to give her advice, to take care of her body, but also to listen. She never lectured her or told her what to do, other than whatever it took to keep her body healthy.

When it came to her emotions and her feelings, Valeria always made time to listen to her. Her mother never wanted to hear about what she wanted or how she felt. If it affected her skating, her mother had always told her that skating came first, everything else was secondary.

As she bent forward to stretch, she was reminded of a party she'd wanted to go to when she was seventeen. They were in London for a competition, and all the skaters from all the countries had been invited. Coaches would be there, so it would be chaperoned. The first thing her mother wanted to know was if media would be there. Since it was closed to media, her mother said there was no reason for Amber to go and the only thing Amber would find there was trouble.

She hadn't been allowed to attend and she'd been devastated. While every other skater had attended the party, she'd stayed in her room and cried.

Valeria had come into her room and Amber had vented to her about how unfair her mother was. Valeria hadn't said a word, just allowed Amber to cry and complain, and then she'd held her and comforted her and told her someday she'd be allowed to make her own decisions.

Like she was doing now. Her mother's voice still lingered in her head, and she knew her mother would never approve of what she'd done with Will, certain that it would somehow affect her skating performance.

Instead, as she went through her practice routine, she felt invigorated and alive in ways she hadn't felt before. Her music infused her and her jumps hit the mark. Even Yegor commented that she looked good out there.

Of course, she looked good out there. Because she felt good.

She felt damn good. And not because she was swooning over some guy.

But because she'd made a decision she felt good about. Because she'd made her own choice for once in her life.

And that was the part that felt really damn great.

After practice, she went back to her apartment. She grabbed a tall glass of water and sipped on that while she checked messages on her phone.

There was a text from Lisa.

What's up? Watch skiing with me today!

That did sound like fun. It had snowed overnight and the fresh powder should make for a great day on the slopes. She sent a text back to Lisa letting her know she wanted to go.

She had another message, this time from Will.

Practice at eleven, then I'm free. What are you up to?

She let him know she had plans to watch skiing with Lisa and invited him along.

He texted back a short time later. I'm in.

She also had a missed call and a voice mail from her mother. She sighed. Why couldn't her mom just text her?

She punched the voice mail button and listened.

"Hi, Amber, honey. I just wanted to check in with you and make sure you were settled in. I watched you in the opening ceremonies. Your face looked a little full. You're not eating too much, are you? Are you getting to bed at a reasonable hour? I hope you're practicing a lot. Call me. Love you."

Amber rolled her eyes and deleted the message, then slid her phone across the kitchen counter, glaring at the phone as if it were the evil representation of her mother.

She got up and wandered into the bathroom, inspecting herself in the mirror.

"My face looked full. Thanks a lot, Mom."

Her face looked like it always did. She always thought she had a cute face. Heart shaped, with prominent cheeks and full lips. She pressed on her cheeks to see if they appeared any fuller. She pressed in again.

She looked okay, but then again—

"What the hell are you doing?"

She jerked, her heart pumping full blast as she turned around to see Lisa leaning against the door frame.

"Nothing."

"Didn't look like nothing."

She sighed. "My mother left me a voice mail and told me that during the opening ceremonies my face looked full."

Lisa rolled her eyes. "Your mother is a hypercritical bitch and she's full of shit. You're beautiful."

Amber laughed, leaning her butt against the bathroom counter. "Don't hold back, Lisa. Tell me how you really feel about my mother."

"I've already told you how I feel about your mother. I think she picks on you unnecessarily about every invisible flaw—that you *don't* have by the way. And she goes out of her way to make you feel bad about yourself. Don't let her do that to you, Amber. You have a banging body, and your face is perfect."

"I wasn't fishing for compliments, but that sure felt good and I needed it. So thank you."

"You're welcome. Feel free to return the favor."

"You're tall, blond, blue-eyed and breathtaking. And you're a stud on a snowboard."

Lisa grinned. "Too bad we're not gay, honey. We'd be perfect together."

Amber laughed. "We would, wouldn't we?"

"Yes. But alas, I like dick."

"So do I."

Lisa cast a critical look her way. "How would you know unless you tried one out?"

"Well, as it happens . . ."

"No. You didn't." Lisa's eyes widened. "You did? With Will?"

Amber nodded.

"Oh. My. God." Lisa grabbed her hands and dragged her out of the bathroom. "I want to know everything. Come on."

They went into the kitchen and pulled up the chairs at the kitchen island. Lisa fixed them glasses of iced tea, then slid one across to Amber.

"Okay, spill. Was it last night?"

Amber nodded.

"The party at Claude's was so crowded and I sorta got—uh—distracted with Blake."

"You? Distracted with a guy? That's so unlike you."

Lisa laughed. "Shut up. Anyway, I did go looking for you and figured you had left. But I thought you'd come back here. I didn't come back to the apartment last night."

Lisa was actually blushing. She never blushed when she hooked up with a guy. That was interesting.

"I didn't come back here, either."

"Ohh, so you stayed at his place. The plot thickens. So was it good?"

"It was very good. Like all-night-long good."

Lisa grabbed her hand. "Oh, honey I'm so glad. I was hoping the first time you hooked up it would be great for you."

"Thank you. It . . . exceeded all my expectations about sex."

"So even better than great, huh?"

"Well, I have no basis for comparison, but it was pretty mind-blowing."

"Awesome."

"Now about you. What was that blush on your cheeks when you were talking about Blake?"

"Oh, that? Nothing. You know, just another dick in a long line of dicks. They're all pretty much the same. As long as I get off, it's good."

Amber wasn't buying Lisa's casual brush-off. She knew her friend.

Last time she really had brushed off guys. This time was different. "Uh-huh. This is me, Lisa. You know you can tell me anything."

Lisa hesitated and took a couple of sips of her iced tea. "Okay, fine. So I've been kind of hanging out with Blake."

"Obviously."

"He's from Vancouver like me, and he's on the ski team. And he's adorable and sweet and we've been kind of seeing each other."

Now it was Amber's turn to be shocked. "You mean seeing each other before the games?"

Lisa nodded. "Yes. For almost six months now."

This was a new side to her friend. "Wow. You never date."

"I know." Lisa slid off the barstool and slid her fingers through her hair. "It's bizarre. We met through someone on my half-pipe team. There was a get-together one night after a competition and we were all hanging out at a lodge. Blake and I just talked. I mean . . . we just talked, Amber. All night long."

"So what you're saying is you didn't hook up?"

"No. Not for like two weeks. He said he never wanted me to think he wanted me only for sex. He said he liked me and he thought we should get to know each other first. Which, you know, is so unlike most guys I've been with."

"Wow."

"Right? So anyway, we've kind of been together ever since."

Amber understood. "You like this guy, Lisa."

"Of course I do."

"No, I mean you really like this guy."

Lisa climbed back onto the barstool. "I don't know. He's so nice and, oh my God, so incredible looking. And he takes me out to dinner and we ski and snowboard together. He's like . . . perfect. Almost too perfect."

"So you're waiting for something awful because you don't think it can be this good?"

"Yes. I haven't had the best luck with relationships in the past. Which was why I decided to just use guys for sex."

Amber shrugged. "I'm the last person who would know anything about relationships, but maybe Blake's a nice, great-looking guy who likes you. Would that be so bad?"

"It wouldn't be bad at all. But you know me, Amber. I'm a free spirit who doesn't want to settle down."

"Except?"

Lisa laid her elbows on the table, then rested her face in her hands. "Except I might be in love with Blake. Which would be the worst thing ever."

Amber's heart squeezed. "Oh, honey. Would that be the worst thing that could happen to you?"

"What if he breaks my heart?"

She read the uncertainty and anguish on Lisa's face. They'd done a lot of talking four years ago, so she knew Lisa had gone through some bad relationships and equally rough breakups in the past. Trust was a big issue for her. "What if he doesn't? What if he makes you incredibly happy?"

Lisa opened her mouth to speak, then shut it again and stared at her. "I don't believe that'll happen."

"Maybe you should think about changing your belief system."

"It scares me. I've never felt this way about someone. I've never truly been in love before, Amber."

"Neither have I, but I can't imagine I'd run away from it if it happened."

"I just don't know. It might be the stress and pressure from the games, but the flight-or-fight syndrome feels like it's kicking in at the moment, and my first instinct is flight."

Amber rubbed Lisa's back. She'd had enough conversations with her friend to understand her fear. "I don't think awesome guys and love come around all that often, Lisa. Maybe you should try shoving down that instinct to flee and stick around to see what happens between the two of you."

She nodded. "I guess. Maybe you could spend some time with him and tell me what you think?"

Amber smiled. "I'd love to. We sort of had a very short conversation at Claude's place. He seems very nice."

"He is very nice. And he's skiing today."

"Yes, we'll get to watch him. I'm excited."

"Me, too. And nervous for him. I want him to do well."

This was so fun. She'd never seen Lisa this nervous about a guy before. She'd always been so chill about men. "I'm sure he'll do great. I hope he has a huge cheering section."

"He'll have us for sure. And his parents will be there."

"No pressure there, huh?" Amber said with a smile.

"I know, right?"

"Oh, I invited Will to go with us."

"Excellent. Now I'm even more excited. I'm going to finish getting ready."

They ended up side by side in the bathroom doing their hair and makeup. Lisa showed her how to work a smoky eye shadow and deepen her eyeliner game to bring out the blue in her eyes.

Amber tended to go light on makeup except for her performance makeup, which always had to be exaggerated. So whenever she wasn't performing, she tended to wear very little makeup. But as they worked side by side in the bathroom, Lisa told her she could put on makeup without it looking the same as when she was performing.

"You're so pretty, Amber," Lisa said. "You don't need much. But let's accentuate your stunning eyes."

Lisa had amazing blue eyes, too, and she never looked overly made-up, so Amber put her face in Lisa's capable hands.

"If I'd had a sister, I imagine it would have been a lot like this," Amber said.

Lisa looked down at her. "Probably. But then we'd fight over the same boy."

Amber laughed. "You think so?"

"Oh, I know so. I mean, look at us. Both head-turning stunners, you know we'd attract hot guys. And then you just know we'd like the same one."

Amber shook her head. "I don't think so. I've met Blake. He's tall and blond and Will is tall and dark."

"So you think we have different tastes in men?"

"You didn't have sex with Will four years ago."

Lisa nodded. "This is true. I friend zoned him right away. He's just not my type. I mean he's incredible looking of course. But he and I just hit it off in a friendly way almost immediately."

"See? We'd never fight over guys."

Lisa laughed. "You're right. We'd be amazing sisters, Amber."

She missed hanging out with Lisa. It was times like this she realized how much she wrapped herself up in her work, in training and performances, and how little she allowed herself to have fun.

That was all going to change after these games.

After hair and makeup, they went into the bedroom and got dressed. Lisa chose black ski pants and a beautiful white sweater. Amber chose red leggings and a black sweater. They slipped on their insulated boots, put on their parkas, then made their way to the shuttle that would take them up the mountain to the ski slope.

They got out at the bottom of the slope and fortunately got to bypass the entry line by using their badges.

They found seats with several other athletes from the US, Canada and other countries. It was great to see so many athletes here to cheer on their teammates.

It was cold today, but bright and clear, which would be perfect for the skiers.

Today was the downhill. Amber had skied plenty of times before, but these competitive events went beyond skiing. It took skill and strength to make it down the mountain fast without wiping out.

"Blake qualified well on this," Lisa said. "I think he's got a decent shot to medal, depending on how well Marco and Jean do. They're his top competitors."

"They're fierce competitors, too. I watched Jean ski in the French competition last year. He's formidable."

Lisa nodded. "He'll be difficult to beat, for sure. But Blake has been training so hard, and his coach has a great deal of confidence in him. So do I."

"Then we'll cheer him on so loudly he'll be able to hear us from the top of the mountain."

Lisa laughed. "You bet your ass he will."

Amber's phone buzzed. It was a text from Will. "Will's here. I'm going to go meet him and bring him up here."

"Okay."

She made her way across the aisle and down the stairs. Wow, it had gotten so crowded. No surprise since so many people had arrived in the past couple of days, in addition to all the athletes who wanted to watch the competitions. It didn't hurt that downhill skiing was a popular sport.

Of course, to Amber's way of thinking, all the winter sports were popular.

She spotted Will at the bottom of the risers. He saw her, too, and made his way up the stairs. They met halfway.

"Hey," he said, grabbing her hand. She thought he might kiss her, which could be awkward.

But he didn't. He squeezed her hand, then let go of her. She sighed in relief.

The sex had been fun and she liked Will, but she didn't want to go parading around in a large crowd hand in hand with him, either. Yet.

"How was your practice this morning?" she asked Will.

"We're looking fierce. We're all ready to play actual games, though."

"I know the feeling."

She led him up the steps to where she'd been sitting with Lisa, who fortunately had held the space on the bench for them.

Will hugged Lisa and they took their seats.

"I'm so nervous for Blake," Lisa said.

"That your boy?" Will asked.

"Yup."

Will nodded. "I've watched him ski before. He's damn good and has a great chance at making the medal stand."

"I'm so hopeful," Lisa said. "And so nervous."

As Lisa stood and looked up the mountain, Will turned and whispered in Amber's ear. "She's got it bad for this guy, doesn't she?"

Amber nodded. "Yes. It's very sweet."

"This is a different side to her. I like it."

"So do I."

The announcer came on so everyone settled. When the first skier came down, an Austrian, Amber could feel the tension fill the entire spectator area, herself included. She wanted Blake to do well, but she wanted all the skiers to do well. She couldn't help it. As a professional athlete, she knew how hard everyone worked to prepare for the games. She wouldn't wish ill on anyone, including her own competitors.

The Austrian came in with a decent score.

Two more came down after him, and they were good as well. Not that she was surprised. All the athletes that were here at the games were exceptional.

Blake would ski third to last, followed by Jean, then Marco.

"I've skied down mountains tons of times," Will said. "You know, for fun. But this, doing it with the incredible speed and the turns. This takes a level of skill that rocks so damn hard."

They all understood what it took to become an expert in your field. That it wasn't just sliding down a mountain on skis. There was a skill level that took years of practice, of hard work and spills and spending hour upon hour getting every twist and turn just right. And then being just a bit better than everyone else.

When it was Blake's turn, Lisa grabbed Amber's hand and squeezed it so hard she winced.

"He's going to do great, you know."

She wasn't even sure Lisa heard her. Her friend's focus was on the top of the slope where Blake was poised to take off.

"Come on, dude," Will said. "You got this."

The buzzer sounded and Blake pushed off. It appeared to Amber as if Blake's skis were on fire as he soared down the slope like a lightning-fast blur, shushing past the gates in perfect motion. She barely breathed during the minute and a few seconds it took for him to reach the bottom. Lisa and Will were both screaming, the cheers around them were incredibly loud, and when Blake got to the ending gate, Amber knew he had to be in first place.

The score showed he'd beat the previous first-place competitor by three whole seconds.

"Three damn seconds," Lisa said, turning to hug Amber. "Three seconds."

"That's amazing," Amber said. "He was awesome."

Lisa was grinning. "Wasn't he? I need to go hug him."

"Yes, you do."

Amber was so happy for Lisa—and, of course, for Blake. She watched as Lisa fought her way down the risers and over to the fenced area. After Blake did a few media interviews, he caught sight of Lisa, went over and gave her a kiss and a hug.

"That's sweet," Amber said.

"They look good together."

She leaned into him. "We look good together."

Even though she'd started the lean in, he hadn't moved away yet. "You know, I'd really like to kiss you right now."

Now she was plenty warm, and it all had to do with the hot man who stood next to her and the way he looked at her. "Kind of crowded here for a kiss. Plus, TV cameras."

"The crowd is watching the skiers. And the TV cameras aren't the least bit interested in the spectators."

"But the spectators have cameras."

He cocked his head to the side. "There you go, being all logical, Amber."

She laughed. "We'll make some alone time later."

"Now I feel like your dirty secret."

"I know." She wiggled her brows. "Naughty, isn't it?"

They watched Marco and Jean, who, as expected, skied flawlessly. They were first and second after their scores were put up.

Lisa finally made her way back through the crowds and up the stairs. When she met up with them, she threw her arms around Amber. "Wasn't Blake amazing?"

"Totally amazing," Amber said.

"Of course, Jean and Marco skied better so that puts Blake in third after his first run."

"Yeah, but he still has a shot at beating them," Will said. "Their times were all close."

Lisa looked up the slope. "This just makes me more nervous."

"He'll do fine, honey," Amber said.

The second runs began, all based on first-run scores, which meant Blake would ski third to last again. As every skier came down the hill, the scores—and standings—changed. This was expected, but it left Blake in limbo, because many of the second runs were better than the firsts. Which put Blake's standing in jeopardy.

"He's going to have to have a good run," Lisa said. "Hans's second time down was excellent and now he's in third place."

"Trust me," Will said. "He's fully aware of what he's got to do to secure a spot on the podium. He'll get it done."

Amber hoped so.

Blake was up next. With two skiers behind him, and this being the last run, he had to do it now to secure a medal.

They were all leaning forward as Blake shot out of the gate. Not only could they see him come down the slope, but there were also big-screen TVs set up at the bottom of the slope to show the action up close.

Amber's nerves were shot. She wasn't even this nervous when she skated. Then again, she knew her own skill set and what she was capable of. With someone else, she had no idea, and now that she knew how close Lisa was to Blake, she wanted him to succeed.

He blitzed down the slope, seemingly faster than his last run. Amber wanted to watch the clock, but she wanted to keep her eyes on Blake, too. He slid his skis past the finish line three one hundredths of a second faster than the athlete currently holding first place.

They all erupted in cheers. Amber hugged Lisa.

"He's going to medal," Lisa said. "No matter what happens with Marco and Jean, he'll be on the podium. He'll be stoked about that."

"I'm so happy for him," Amber said.

"Now we have to watch these last two guys and see what medal he'll end up with," Will said.

Marco came down next, and his run was flawless, putting him

ahead of Blake, which wasn't unexpected. He'd won gold in many competitions, from the international games to world competitions.

Lisa stood. "I'm heading down to be there with Blake at the end."

"Okay," Amber said.

After Lisa left, Will leaned over toward her. "I like seeing her this excited for a guy."

Amber smiled. "Me, too."

Jean was the one to beat, and the crowd cheered wildly for him. He was incredibly popular—and ridiculously talented. But he wavered on one of the turns and missed a gate. It cost him time and points. Amber's heart was in her throat as she waited for him to finish.

He finished in third place, a shocking finish for the previous gold-medal winner.

Which meant Blake would take the silver medal.

"Oh, my God," Amber said. "Lisa is going to go crazy."

Will grinned. "Blake's going to go crazy."

Amber scanned the waiting area. Will was right. Blake was pumping his fists and hugging both Jean and Marco. Then he walked over to the fence where his parents were waiting to give him a hug, before finding Lisa to kiss her.

"Aww. That's sweet."

"Yeah. Makes me wish my parents were going to be here."

She looped her arm in his. "I'm sure it does. I'm sorry they can't be."

He shrugged as they followed the rest of the spectators down the stairs to exit the venue. "I'm used to it. And their business is more important than this. They'll have it on TV in the bar and draw a huge crowd, which will be great for the business."

"You're so . . . understanding."

He laughed. "About what?"

"About doing this on your own, without a support system."

"I have plenty of support here. My coaches, my friends, my teammates. Trust me, I'm not alone."

Amber supposed that was true, though she didn't know from experience. She'd had her mother at every event from the very beginning, from the time she was a child skating at her first amateur event. Her father had attended as well, but only the major competitions. She couldn't imagine her mother missing even one. Despite being at odds with her mother, despite her mom's constant criticisms, she'd never been alone. She'd always felt a sense of comfort knowing she was sitting in the stands.

Clearly, she and her mother had a twisted relationship.

"Hungry?" he asked.

She shook off thoughts of her mother and smiled up at him. "Yes. What did you have in mind?"

They'd arrived at the village. Suddenly they were surrounded by a bunch of Will's teammates.

"Hey," Drew said. "Where've you been?"

"Alpine skiing."

"Observing, and not participating, I assume," Adrian said.

Will laughed. "Yeah, a friend of ours was competing."

"He medal?" Drew asked.

"Silver medal," Amber said, still feeling the thrill of watching Blake compete. She barely knew him, and yet it had filled her with anticipation for her own competition.

"Awesome," Drew said.

"What about you?" Will asked. "What have you guys been up to?"

"We watched bobsledding," Eddie Gannon said. "Now we're hungry. You all hungry?"

Will looked at Amber. "Are you up for eating with the guys?"

"Of course." Lisa hadn't rejoined them yet. It was possible she'd decided to hang out with Blake and his family, but Amber sent her a text message letting her know they were headed to the dining hall to eat, in case she wanted to catch up with them.

Lisa texted her back a short time later to tell her she was going to hang out with Blake and his family for the medal ceremony, and she'd catch up with them later.

The dining hall was busy, but then again now that the games had started it would stay that way until the end.

They found a table that would fit them all. Amber wandered around, checking out all the amazing international foods. She decided on chicken curry and coconut rice, along with a cabbage salad, mangoes, watermelon and papaya.

Since the dining hall was ridiculously huge, she almost lost sight of their table. Will must have seen her wandering, because he stood up and waved his arms.

She slid into the spot next to him. "I swear, I get lost every time I'm in here."

"I'm the same way," Drew said. "I swear, it's like first day of high school all over again."

She laughed. "Thank you for making me feel better about looking like a moron."

"Honey, you could never look like a moron," Drew said.

She decided right then that she would like Drew forever. "Thank you for that."

"Quit hitting on my lady," Will said in between bites of his chicken.

Drew laughed. "Not hitting on your woman. Just being friendly. Besides, you've met my wife, right?"

"I haven't. Is she here?"

Drew shook his head. "No. Unfortunately she couldn't make it because she has fashion week."

Amber perked up at the mention of fashion week. "Oh, she's a designer?"

"Yeah. Carolina Preston."

Amber's eyes widened. "I know her line. I love her clothes. And your wife is gorgeous, Drew. You're a very lucky man."

"Thank you. And yeah, I'm really lucky."

"I'm sorry she couldn't make it."

"Me, too. So is she. But it's just the timing. Fashion week keeps her busy twenty-four hours a day for several months. And then the week before and the entire month of February? I barely see her at all."

"Must be rough on both of you."

"It's actually okay. It's her work and it's important. Plus, she's damn good at it, so I want her to put her attention where it belongs. So yeah, she felt awful, but I told her that was her job, and this was mine, and she needed to focus on doing hers. Besides, she'll have the TV on at the design house whenever I'm playing."

Amber felt the love—and pride in his wife—with every word Drew spoke. It was so sweet. "So when you're in New York during fashion week, do you go watch her show?"

"As long as I'm in town I do. I've only missed one so far."

Will leaned over. "He told us that one year, when they were first dating, Carolina got him to walk in one of her shows."

Amber's brows rose. "Like a fashion model?"

Drew laughed. "I'm no fashion model, but yeah, I walked in one of her shows."

"Oh my God. That must have been so exciting."

"More like terrifying. But I got through it."

"And after she made him do it he still married her," Will said.

Amber laughed. "I would hardly call walking the runway in a fashion show a form of torture, Will."

"When you're a hockey player, it is," Will said.

Drew raised his eyebrows. "But my wife can be persuasive."

"You are so sweet, Drew."

"Stop telling him that," Will said. "You'll get him all mellow and mushy and then he'll suck during the games."

Drew glared at Will. "I never suck at hockey."

"I seem to recall the Ice jamming up the Travelers a time or two." Will said slanting a grin in Drew's direction. "Or maybe five or six. Ten or twelve."

"I think you have a faulty memory, because our defense kicked your ass the week before we flew out here."

Will gave a thoughtful look to Drew. "Buddy, did you take a stick to the head in our last matchup? Because I'm pretty sure we won that game."

"Yeah, and I think Kozlow slammed your head against the boards too hard, because you're suffering from amnesia."

Amber rolled her eyes and ate her lunch while she listened to the two of them argue it out. It was a good thing figure skaters didn't trash talk each other like this.

Then again, it might fire them up if they did. Though their competitions weren't one-on-one and they didn't occupy the ice at the same time. Still, they were all adversaries.

Amber couldn't imagine trying to skate against one of her competitors, on the ice at the same time.

Since Will and Drew had decided to forego their argument in favor of devouring their food, she turned to Will. "When I compete, I'm all alone on the ice. It's my performance that will win or lose for me. What's it like, fighting it out on the ice against a competitor?"

Will looked at Drew, and they both grinned.

"It's the biggest adrenaline rush there is," Will said.

Drew nodded. "It fuels a fire inside of me like nothing else ever has."

Will half turned to face her. "You know that with every game the other team is going to be good. Sometimes even better than you. You have to find the fight inside of you, that fire that burns deep inside, like Drew said. You have to want to win more than they do, and fight as hard as you can, because you know they aren't going to make it easy for you."

"It helps if you're good at what you do, too." Drew shot a confident grin at Will.

"Yeah, that part helps," Will said. "But when you get to the level of a professional player, it's a given that you're good."

Will looked at Amber. "We know we're playing at the top of our game. We've been at this for several years now. We're not rookies just learning the ropes anymore. Our team counts on us to know what the hell we're doing."

"And to be the best at it," Drew added.

"I love hearing both of you describe playing. There's such a passion that comes out of you when you talk about it, as if you were born to do this."

Will laughed. "I don't know about Drew, but I *was* practically born playing hockey. I don't remember a time when I wasn't playing."

Drew cocked a smile. "Same."

She finished up her chicken, then set her bowl to the side.

"You're the same way about figure skating, aren't you Amber?" Drew asked.

"You mean that competitive passion?"

Drew nodded.

"I'm here for the third time, one of the oldest figure skaters competing. If I didn't feel that fire to win, I wouldn't have subjected myself to another grueling four years of practices and competitive events. So, yes, I feel that passion."

"I know it's not the same as what we do," Will said. "But I know you have that fire inside of you. I've seen it just in your practices."

"You watched her practice?" Drew asked.

"Yeah. She's beautiful on skates. She has amazing power. And those jumps. Man, you gotta see those jumps. She gets high and does these circles in the air that seem to defy gravity. Then she powers through like nothing I've ever seen. And yet there's this beauty in the way she moves that I can't even describe. It's like—you know when you go to a museum and see something like a painting or a sculpture that makes you stop and stare? You don't know what it is that's getting to you about it. It's just so goddamn beautiful you can't help yourself. You have to stare at it. That's Amber."

Amber could barely breathe. She'd never heard someone describe her skating like that.

"Hell, Madigan, that's fucking poetic," Drew said, slapping him on the back. "I didn't know you had it in you."

Will grinned, then turned to Amber, his lips softening into a tender smile.

"Thank you," she said, reaching out to squeeze his arm.

"You're welcome."

Drew stood. "If you two are going to get all gooey romantic, I'm gonna go call my wife."

Amber smiled at Drew. "It was great having lunch with you, Drew."

"You too, honey. See you on the ice," he said to Will.

"Later, Hogan," Will said.

"I like him," Amber said after Drew walked away.

"I do, too. He's a great guy. But don't tell him I said that since he plays for a competing team."

Amber laughed. "Your secret is safe."

"Does that mean you'll keep all my secrets?"

"That depends. You're not an international spy, are you?"

"Oh, now you're putting conditions on keeping my secrets."

"Hey, I'm a law-abiding citizen. Besides, we're in Canada. I'd like to be able to get back home."

He shot her an incredulous look. "You'd throw me under the bus, sell me out, feed me to the wolves, all just to get back into the US?"

"You bet your ass I would. Who'd feed my cat otherwise?"

"You have a cat?"

She leveled a smile at him. "No."

"I didn't think so. You don't strike me as a cat person."

"I love cats. And what does that mean?"

"I love cats, too. I just picture you walking some retriever-Labrador mix down the streets of Manhattan."

She laughed. "I live on Long Island, not Manhattan."

He shrugged. "I still have this mental picture of you walking some big dog in Manhattan."

"Are you telling me you've had some psychic vision that I'm going to be moving to Manhattan?"

He leaned forward and teased his fingers up her forearm, giving her delicious chills. "I don't know. Maybe. Why? Do you have some secret desire to live in Manhattan?"

"No. I'd like to move somewhere outside of New York."

"Yeah? Any idea where?"

"I don't have a clue."

"And what would you do in this unknown place?"

"Teach figure skating to kids who can't afford it."

Drew leaned back, as if he was trying to figure out if she was on the level or not. "Really. Got it all figured out, huh?"

"Yes."

"Why?"

She shrugged. "I was always skating with the privileged kids when I was younger. And then in competitions I'd hear stories of community fund-raisers and how much work went into getting some of these kids to competitions. It seemed so . . . unfair. It made me wonder how many more never even have the chance to learn how to skate, let alone get to the point where they could compete. There have to be amazingly talented kids with so much potential who only need to be given the opportunity to learn."

He didn't say anything.

"What?" she asked.

"That's a kick-ass idea, Amber."

She smiled. "Thanks. It's a passion. I hope I get to do it."

"No reason you can't."

"Plus, my mother will hate it. She wants me to be famous."

"No shit?"

"Yes. She thinks when my career is finished I can use it as a stepping stone to bigger things."

"What kinds of bigger things?"

"I have no idea. A book? Product endorsements? Knowing her, she already has a plan for me."

He shifted in his seat, turning his chair so he faced her. Then he leaned forward. "Have you ever told your mom *your* plan for your future?"

"God, no. I'd have to endure endless lectures about how I have to use my talent to climb the ladder to success and fame."

Will grimaced. "Seriously?"

"Oh, yes. I've been hearing that speech since I was five."

"No, you haven't."

"I have. Which is why I keep my plans for my future to myself."

"I can see why. Sorry, Amber."

"Don't be. I'm used to her. Besides, I know in her heart she wants what's best for me, but sometimes I think her ambitions for herself when she was younger get mixed up with what she wants for me."

"You should talk to her."

She shook her head. "I tried, twice. Once when I was a teenager, and then again when I turned twenty-one. She argued that she knew best and I should trust her to manage my career. I gave up after that."

"I dunno. My dad put me on skates when I was little because he loved hockey. I took to it right away. I joined hockey clubs and played all through school, but I never felt pushed into it. I was always allowed to make my own choices. Fortunately for me, I fell in love with the sport and can't imagine doing anything else."

"You can't play hockey the rest of your life, Will."

"I can't?"

He grinned.

Amber laughed. "I mean, hockey players have a shelf life."

"True. I also have a degree in marketing and communication."

"Decent. What do you plan to do post hockey career?"

"I don't know. If my brother doesn't want to take over the family bar, then I will. I already have ideas for expansion."

"That sounds fun."

"You'd like the bar. It's rowdy and exciting, and if you like sports, it's a magical place. There's always a game of some kind or another on, though in Chicago it's typically going to be baseball, football or hockey. And when the international games are on, everyone comes to the bar."

"Even when you aren't playing in the games?"

He slanted a smile at her. "Yeah, even when I'm not in the games. There are regulars who've been coming to the bar for forty years. There's shuffleboard and pool, plus some video games we added a couple years back. Mom and Dad are always there working behind the bar. The customers love them. Now that he's in high school my brother comes in and buses tables on the weekends. I used to do that, too, when I was in high school. Whenever I wasn't playing hockey."

"I do like sports. And bars. And your family sounds amazing."

"They're pretty cool."

"It's very unlike my family."

"In what way?"

"Obviously your family does things together. They hang out together. They own a business together. My father is always at work. I can't remember ever hanging out at the office with my dad."

Will raised a brow. "So you've never seen where he works?"

"Obviously I know where he works, but no, I've never spent any time there. I've been to the dance studio often with my mother, of course, since I've taken dance lessons from the time I was three. Jazz helped with my endurance and with the artistic part of my program. Ballet helped my flexibility and was a benefit to skating."

"I could see that, I guess. I really don't know anything about dance, but I'd bet you look hot doing it."

She smiled. "Anyway, my parents' two careers don't really mesh. I don't know. I guess I just don't see my family as a traditional family unit."

"What's a traditional family unit these days, Amber? Every family is different."

She shrugged. "I know. I mean, mine has been . . . unusual. Since I often traveled, that meant I was on the road a lot, either with my mother or with Yegor and Valeria—they're my coach and my trainer."

"Are you close to them?"

"Very. They're like my second set of parents."

"That's nice to have."

"It is."

"But you've done things with your parents, right? Vacations and things?"

She shook her head. "No. My parents took a trip to Italy two years ago. I'm pretty sure that's the first vacation they'd had in—" She thought about it. "As long as I can remember. And my father complained about having to take time off work. But my mother insisted. In the end, they went, and they both seemed happy when they got back."

"But you didn't go?"

"No. I was in the middle of working up my new performance routines for the games, so I didn't go with them. Which at the time I thought was a good thing, because they needed some time alone together."

"Ah. A second honeymoon kind of thing, right?"

She nodded.

"When they came back, they both told me they had a great time. And within a week they'd gone their separate ways again, Dad to spend hours at his office and Mom to the dance studio, and life at home went back to normal."

"Define normal," Will said.

"Strained silences at dinner where Dad stares at his laptop while he eats and Mom works crossword puzzles and quizzes me about my practice that day."

"That sounds so fun. So you still live at home."

She nodded. "Since I work nonstop at skating, I have like . . . zero income. That's going to change after the games. I have to get out of there."

"Making you a little crazy?"

She laughed. "More than a little."

"So you've made a plan to get a job and relocate?"

"Not exactly. My only goal right now is to win gold. After that, I'll figure it out."

"One step at a time, right?"

"You got it."

"I think it's a good plan."

"You do? It's like . . . no plan at all."

"Look. You gotta focus on winning the gold first. You've spent the past four years doing that. You already know you want to get out of your parents' house, and you want to do something to make money, so you have a long-range plan."

"I . . . guess. But it's not like I have something lined up."

He shrugged. "The other stuff will fall into place after that. You don't wanna clutter up your head with 'what am I gonna do after Vancouver' nonsense. Focus on your skating and worry about the rest of it later. It's not like your parents are gonna evict you after the games, right?"

"No, they won't."

"I mean, it makes sense for it to be tucked into the back of your mind. It is your future, after all. But front and center? Gotta be skating for a medal. That's your focus right now."

It wasn't often that her opinion was even considered, let alone thought of as valid. "Thanks."

"For what?"

"For thinking I have decent ideas."

"I think you have a lot of good ideas, Amber. I can't wait to hear all about your plans for your life after the games. I also can't wait to watch you skate."

Just the thought of skating for a medal fueled her. "Thank you. I'm so excited. We both start tomorrow, don't we?"

He nodded. "Tomorrow's our first game."

"And I have the team competition beginning tomorrow."

"What time?" he asked.

"For me? I skate at noon."

"We're at three tomorrow afternoon."

"Excellent," she said. "I'll be there."

"I won't get to watch you," he said, giving her a disappointed look. "I have to report to the hockey arena at noon."

She laid her hand on his arm. "It's okay. You know we're going to have some overlap."

"But I like watching you skate."

"There will be other opportunities. And this is the short program. If I'm good enough—which I will be—the US team will move on to the finals for the team event. Then hopefully you'll be able to watch the long program. Which you'll be able to see again anyway, when I perform it in the individual medal event."

He grinned at her.

"What?"

"I love how confident you are."

"I wouldn't be here if I wasn't sure I'd win."

"But there's no ego in it, no arrogance. You just know you have the skills."

She felt her cheeks go warm. "Thank you. You always say the nicest things."

"Nah. Just the truth. You ready to get out of here?"

"Yes. I'd love to get some fresh air."

They put on their coats and hats and went outside. It was cold, but there was no wind. The sun was still out which meant the day was perfect.

Will took her hand. "Come on. Let's go play."

She arched a brow. "Play? Where are we going to play?"

"Up the hill some."

He walked them up a fairly steep hill to the top. There was thick snow up here, but she was wearing tall snow boots so she didn't mind sinking in.

"Lots of snow here," Will said. "It's perfect."

She cast a sideways glance at him. "For?"

"Building a snowman, of course."

She stared at him. "You're serious."

"I'm dead serious about my snowmen. Come on."

He sank to his knees and started rolling snow into a ball. She hadn't moved yet, because she was still unable to believe he was actually doing this.

"You're really building a snowman?"

He cast a look at her over his shoulder. "I'm not frying bacon up here. You gonna join me or what?"

She walked bent over to get closer to him. "You do realize you aren't eight years old, right?"

Before she knew it, she had been flipped onto her back, buried in the snow, and Will was looming over her, his body covering hers. "We're always eight years old, Amber. Where's your sense of fun?"

"It's hard to have a sense of fun when your ass is freezing in the snow."

He laughed, jumped up and grabbed her hands, hauling her up. "Come on. Snowman time."

"Just so you know, I've never built a snowman in my life."

He paused. "You're lying."

She shook her head. "Not lying."

"You get plenty of snow in New York."

"Of course I do. But I was always at practice, either skating or ballet. And then there was school."

"Come on. You had to have been allowed to play."

"Play was structured. Reading time, piano lessons, educational films."

He wrinkled his nose. "That's not play. I mean, reading is fun, as long as you get to choose what to read." He stared at her.

She stared back.

He rolled his eyes. "We'll talk about that later. But how about playing outside in the snow? Climbing on the playground equipment, running around with your friends?"

She didn't answer him, because there was no point. Most people didn't understand the way she was raised.

"Okay, then. Today is building a snowman day."

She appreciated that he didn't press her about her screwed-up childhood. The less she had to delve deep into her past and think about it, the better it was for her own emotional health.

So instead, she knelt on the ground and rolled snow into a giant ball with Will. Turned out, building a snowman was some serious work. And also serious fun. They argued over how big his bottom half should be.

"We're not building the Bigfoot of snowmen here, Amber," Will said. "Let's keep his proportions reasonable."

"But you want his base to be stout enough to hold him up in stiff winds, especially on top of this hill."

Will laughed. "Okay. We'll make him a little bigger."

Once they had the base, they made the center, which went a little faster.

"How many snowmen have you built?" she asked.

"I don't know. A lot. Mostly in the front yard of our house or at friends' houses."

"Did you build them with your dad?"

"Yeah. A few times. With both my parents. And Ethan—that's my brother—and I would build snowmen together after the first snow of the year every year."

She could picture a young Will hanging out with his mom and dad or his little brother building a snowman in his front yard. It made her heart ache to think about how much fun that must have been.

She could never picture her father or her mother getting knee-deep in the snow with her. It just wasn't their thing.

Which didn't make them bad parents. They just weren't fun and playful.

Enough, Amber. Don't compare.

She went back to the task. They finished the middle. The head was the easiest. But then it occurred to Amber that their snowman would have no face.

"We have a faceless snowman," she said to Will.

"Oh, I took care of that when we were in the dining hall." He unzipped his parka and pulled out a carrot and several small dark round cookies that they used for his eyes, his smile and the buttons on his coat.

"Now he needs arms," Will said. He found some sticks on the ground and broke them into the appropriate sizes to use for his arms.

Amber surveyed their creation. "He's adorable."

"Kneel next to him, Amber. I'll get a picture."

She knelt next to the snowman, put her arm around him and pressed her lips to the side of his face.

Will laughed. "Cute. And now I'm jealous."

She got up and went over to Will, kissing the side of his face.

"Your lips are cold."

"Blame Snowman."

He pulled her against him and wrapped his arms around her. "Are you cold?"

"Getting there."

"We'll go inside in a minute. But first."

Will dropped them both to the ground. Amber laughed. "This isn't warming me up."

"Oh, come on. You have to make out in the snow. If you haven't built a snowman, I'll bet you haven't kissed in the snow."

She pressed her hand to his chest. "How do you know? I might have done this a hundred times."

He searched her face. "Have you?"

She laughed. "No."

He rolled her on top of him and cupped her neck, bringing her face to his for a kiss that warmed her more than being in front of a fire would have. She no longer felt the cold or the snow. Not with warm lips and a hot male body against her.

But then he lifted. "Ready to go?"

"If by 'ready to go,' you mean to your room or mine, then yes. I'm more than ready."

He grinned, got up and pulled her up as well.

"Turn around," she said. "You have snow all over you."

He did, and she brushed all the snow off his back. Of course, he had some on his butt, and it was no hardship to run her hands over his very fine ass and down his legs.

"You're lingering," he said.

"You noticed that, huh?"

"I did." He pivoted to face her. "Your turn."

She turned and he brushed the snow off her back, then bent and cupped her butt.

"I don't think there's snow there."

"There isn't. But you're not going to deny me the chance to touch your amazing ass."

She smiled. "No, but shouldn't we go somewhere to be alone before you do that?"

He peered over her shoulder. "Why? You grabbed my butt here on top of the hill."

"That's different."

"It is? How so."

"I—" She realized she had no answer. "Okay, my entire thought process is sexist, so I'm not even going to finish that statement."

He laughed. "Good." He cupped her butt and kissed her, a long, lingering kiss that made her forget all about their location, or who had grabbed whose butt. The only thing it made her think about was being alone with Will.

Naked and alone.

She clutched his coat with both hands. "We need to go. Now."

His lips curved. "Something you want?"

"Yes. You. Naked. Inside of me. Now."

"Then why the hell are we standing out in the cold on this hill?"

She offered up what she hoped was a sexy smile. "I don't know, Will. What are we doing out here?"

He took her hand and led her down the hill. She wasn't sure, but she thought maybe he had quickened his step as they made their way back to the village. When they got to the main quad, he turned to her.

"Your place or mine?"

"Lisa texted that she was leaving the village to eat with Blake and his parents. My guess is they'll be occupied. Let's go to mine. I'll be sure to text her and let her know you and I are going to be at our place, so she'll steer clear."

"Perfect."

They headed toward her building, and again he quickened his step.

"You in a hurry?" she asked.

As they stepped inside her building, he looked at her. "Already envisioning you naked."

She liked that he was as eager as she was. No doubt he'd had plenty of sex in his lifetime, but for Amber, this was all still new to her.

New and exciting and exhilarating and she wanted a lot more of it.

With Will.

So when they got to her apartment and she opened the door, she had already unzipped her parka and taken off her hat and gloves. Will had shrugged out of his and had taken off his hat. His hair stuck up in places. Hers probably did, too.

She didn't care. She took off her parka and dropped it on the table near the door. When Will drew her into his arms, she reached up to slide her hands into the thick softness of his hair.

Their lips met and it was like an explosion of all the pent-up passion that seemed to be constantly boiling inside of her, ready to erupt. She moaned against his mouth, and when his tongue slid across hers, everything in her body quivered in response. He reached across her rib cage and cupped her breast, teasing her nipple through her sweater.

She fought for breath as he lifted her sweater and palmed her skin. Just the contact of his hand on her bare flesh caused a sexual response, and he was only touching her stomach.

He lifted her sweater over her head, and when she searched his face, the passion she saw reflected in his eyes matched what she felt coursing through her veins. Need sparked within her, and she unhooked her bra, letting it fall to the floor. She reached for his hands, placing them on her breasts.

"Touch me."

He swept his fingers over her nipples, then bent to take one in his mouth. The brush of his hair across her breasts tickled, but also turned her on in ways she hadn't expected.

Everything was a new experience for her, something she never knew would be so exciting.

She pushed him to the sofa. He sat, and she straddled him, sliding against his erection. He gripped her hips to help her.

"Feel good?" he asked.

"I think I could come with all my clothes on." She laid her hands on his shoulders. "But I'd rather not. I want your cock inside of me."

"Then take your pants off."

She climbed off, shrugged out of her pants and underwear while Will undid his jeans. She went into the bedroom to grab a condom and came back. Will had undressed and sat on the chair, naked.

"I have to admit," she said, "that seeing you naked does things to me."

He drummed his fingers on the cushion of the sofa. "Yeah? What kinds of things?"

She straddled him again and unwrapped the condom, rolling it over his cock. "Things like making my nipples hard and my pussy soft and quivery and damp."

He traced her nipple with his finger. "Huh. It just so happens those are all my favorite things."

"That's good to know. How about a woman who screams when she comes? Is that a favorite, too?"

He held onto her while she lifted, then settled on his cock. "Might be my number-one favorite thing."

She gasped out a breath as she seated herself fully on top of him, her pussy quivering as his cock swelled inside of her. "How about we make that happen then?"

He dragged her hips forward, then back again, raking her clit along his flesh. "I'll give it my best shot."

His best shot was damn good, because she could already feel the tension rising inside of her. The pleasure was intense, and in this position she had all the control.

She liked that sense of power, and used it to lean forward, to rub her breasts against his chest as he arched into her.

"Oh," was all she could manage to tell him he was hitting all the right spots. She held onto his shoulders and slid back and forth, giving them both what they needed.

"Fuck, yeah, that's good," he said.

He gripped her hips and dug his fingers into her flesh, which only heightened her sense of pleasure. And being able to see the look on his face, the passion in his expression every time he thrust into her, enhanced her pleasure in ways she hadn't expected.

Her breathing increased with every movement. Whirls of need rose within her, a steamy promise of the orgasm that hovered just beyond her reach. She dug her nails into Will's skin.

"That's it," he said. "I feel you tightening around me. Come on."

His voice was a balm in the wild maelstrom of the sensual storm that rocked around her. Sweat beaded between her breasts as she moved faster, seeking the climax she wanted so badly.

And when it hit, it rocked her with deep pulses that made her cry out. She looked at Will, his gaze riveted on hers as she let go.

It was unimaginable pleasure and she gave into it, into him as he thrust harder and faster into her until she wasn't sure where she ended and he began. And when he shuddered, his features tightening with his own orgasm, she soaked it all in, lying on top of him to hold him through it.

It took her a while as she regained her balance to realize they were stuck together. Like . . . literally stuck together.

"We're sweaty," she murmured as she swept her finger down his arm.

"I could for sure use a shower."

She lifted and smiled down at him. "That was intense."

He grinned. "That might be an understatement."

They disengaged, then headed for the shower to rinse off. Amber felt a lot better after they showered the sweat off. They towel dried and got dressed.

Amber went into the kitchen and Will followed.

"Something to drink?" she asked.

"What have you got?"

She opened the refrigerator. "Water and juice and energy drinks."

"An energy drink will work. I need one after that workout."

She laughed. "It did feel like a workout, didn't it?"

He popped open the top of the drink and took a couple long swallows. "Did to me. Though I think you did most of the work."

She leaned into him and brushed her lips across his. "I enjoyed that position very much. We'll have to do that again."

He wrapped his arm around her and tugged her against him. "Anytime."

She hopped up on the bar stool and took a sip of her water. "You know what I like about you, Will?"

"Many things, no doubt."

She laughed. "True. But I like how agreeable you are. Especially about sex."

"Hey, you wanna do it, I'm your guy."

"See? Agreeable. We're a good match."

He tipped his energy drink can to her bottle of water. "I'll drink to that."

Amber had thought this trip to the games was going to be all about practice and performance. She couldn't have imagined how different it was turning out. So far, she was having a wonderful time.

But now the real work was beginning. And it was time to focus. Still, she could focus and still have fun, right? Not that she'd ever tried it before, but she was certain she could make it work.

Because she liked Will and there was still plenty of fun to be had.

SIXTEEN

IT FELT SO DAMN GOOD TO BE ON THE ICE AGAIN, THIS time in an actual game. This was what Will had come here for. Adrenaline fueled him as he waited for the two teams' national anthems to play. The arena was filled to capacity. The one thing Will could always count on at the games was hockey-loving crowds.

They were playing Latvia today, and Will knew there were more than just US and Latvian fans in the arena.

Not surprising. Who didn't love hockey?

He intended to draw fuel from all that noise.

They skated to center ice for the face-off. Will crouched down, his breath coming out white on the cold rink. His heart pounded, but not from anxiety. He was ready to get started.

The US team grabbed the puck at the drop. Will had his eye on Drew, and when the puck passed their way, Drew took it down to the Latvian side, moving to the interior. Drew smashed it toward Will, who took the shot on goal.

The goalie blocked it.

Damn. Would have been sweet to start the game with a goal, but Will shook it off, fighting the defender behind the net for the puck, coming away with it.

After that it was a fast-paced skate. Two players jammed him up against the boards as they fought for the puck, and Latvia came away with it, skating toward the US goal.

Will waited, not so patiently, for his turn at the puck again.

When the US defenders won the war on the US side, Will was there to pick up the puck as it was passed to him. He outskated the Latvian defender, his eye on the goal as he sailed the puck toward a waiting Drew.

Damn. The whistle blew for an off-side.

He'd had momentum going, and now they'd start over at the face-off.

Drew took the face-off and sent it down the ice toward Gannon, who passed it to Will. Will had a clean shot so he took it.

It slid right between the goalie's legs and lit the lamp for a score.

Will lifted his stick. Drew skated over to him and slapped him on the back.

"Damn good goal, buddy."

Will grinned. "Thanks."

They took their seats for relief and watched the action until it was their turn to get back on the ice. Will took a couple swallows of water, feeling confident in his team.

They had this.

By the third period, they were up by three goals. Will and Drew worked like clockwork. Their passes were on point and they were sailing through this game.

Will had two goals, Drew had one and Gannon had scored, too. Defense had been killing it.

With a breakaway, they made their way to Latvia's side. Will shot the puck to Drew, who slid it into the net and lit it up for a goal. Will raised his stick in triumph.

Heaving a breath, he went to Drew.

"Nice one."

Drew nodded and grinned. "Great pass. Let's do it again."

All they had to do was keep playing like this and they'd wrap up this one. They were deep in the third period, there were two minutes left in period play. They just had to hold out and not do anything stupid.

Latvia was hustling, and as Will took the puck he got slammed against the boards, two on one. The guy to his left shoved a fist in his face.

Fuck, that one hurt. He elbowed back at the defender. Suddenly helmets came off and he was double-teamed by two of them. He threw punches back. He knew he shouldn't, but he'd be damned if he was going to stand there and be a punching bag just because they were frustrated.

Then Drew was there and so was Gannon, and it felt like both teams were involved in the brawl.

It took a while to pull everyone apart. Will ended up in the penalty box along with the two Latvian defenders.

He finished the game in the penalty box. Fine with him, because they still won. He skated out and lined up to shake hands. The game was over and he never held a grudge, including with the two Latvian defenders he'd just fought with.

It had been a good, hard-hitting game.

And now they'd move on to the next one.

They made their way to the locker room.

"That was a damn good start," their coach said. "Keep up that kind of enthusiasm and game play, and we'll go far."

Drew looked over at him and grinned. "And try not to fight every team we play."

"Hey. I didn't start that one."

"You're just easy pickings," Eddie said. "Must be that pretty face. They think you're a puss."

"Fuck you, Gannon."

Eddie laughed. "At least you won't be so pretty for the next few days. That's a hell of a bruise on your cheek."

"I'm still prettier than you, asshole."

Drew laughed at both of them.

"Get some rest," their coach said. "I'll see you tomorrow."

Will showered, then got dressed at his locker.

"Starving," Drew said. "You wanna grab a bite?"

"Yeah. Let's do that."

They hit up the dining hall along with several of the other guys. Will went for trout and asparagus, along with a salad.

"We should watch the games that are being played tomorrow," Drew said. "Check out the competition."

Will nodded. "Not to mention, several of our teammates are on some of those teams."

Drew took a bite of his food, then nodded. "I know. It's weird that guys I play with all season long are now my competition. It's hard to wrap my head around that."

"Yeah. It'll feel odd when we play against them."

"It happens all the time in hockey, though," Drew said. "You play with a guy for years, then suddenly he's a free agent and signs with another team and now he's a competitor. You're still friends, you just play against each other."

"You're right. I'll have to think of it like that when I play against some of my friends."

"And then guys like you and me who always play against each other find ourselves on the same team."

"For a couple of weeks, anyway," Will said, then shot a grin at Drew. "Then we'll go back to trying to kick each other's asses."

Drew laughed. "True that. But for the next couple of weeks I'm glad we're on the same team, Will."

"Me, too."

Will's phone buzzed. It was Amber.

Saw your game. You kicked ass.

He grinned and texted back. Thanks! Where are you?

She replied with: Hanging with Lisa. Catch you later.

"Girlfriend?" Drew asked.

He was about to say no. But maybe that wasn't true. Hell, he didn't know what they were to each other, so he replied with, "It was Amber."

"I like her."

"Yeah, me, too."

Drew finished off the last of his noodles, then took a long swallow of juice before pushing his trash to the side. "So, is she a fling for the games, or something else?"

"I dunno. I mean, we're just having some fun."

"Fun is good. But she doesn't strike me as the kind of woman you fuck around with and forget."

That was an interesting observation. "Yeah? Why's that?"

"I don't know. Maybe she reminds me of my wife in some ways."

"You trying to move in on my woman, Hogan?"

Drew laughed. "No. Not what I meant. She doesn't even look like Carolina. But there's something about her that's familiar. She's smart and funny and sweet and beautiful. I don't know, Will. She's not throwing herself at a different guy every night, so she's not here to party. Not that there's anything wrong with that, since a lot of the guys here do that. And if the dudes can do it, the women sure as hell can. But Amber strikes me as a woman who's got that special something."

Will knew what Drew was getting at. "I know what you mean. She is special. I just don't have a definition for what we are to each other. I was being honest when I told you we're having fun right now."

"Because it's new for the two of you."

"Yeah."

"I didn't mean to push you into something you weren't ready for." Drew dragged his fingers through his hair. "Hell, I don't even know what I'm getting at. I think I really miss my wife."

Will would like to say he understood, but he really didn't since he'd never had a wife before. "I'm sure it's rough not having her here."

"Yeah, it is. You're lucky you have someone."

He supposed he was. He'd had fun making his way through different women last time he was here. He'd had no regrets, and the women he'd been with had been as on board with the freewheeling fun as he'd been. But he had to admit, concentrating on just one woman this time? It sure as hell was different. But, it was kind of nice, too.

He looked at Drew. "When you met Carolina, did you know she was the one?"

"You mean, the one I was gonna spend the rest of my life with?"

"Maybe not even that, but just, that one special woman for you?"

"When things first started out with us, I sure as hell wasn't looking for a relationship. But I knew there was something different about her. I kept finding reasons to be around her, and that had never happened to me before. So yeah, I guess even subconsciously, I knew she had to be in my life. Maybe the fates or destiny or something puts someone in your path and makes you pay attention, you know?"

Will nodded. "Yeah."

Will didn't know if he believed in fate or destiny when it came to meeting that one person you were meant to be with. Then again, he did believe in love and finding your soulmate or whatever the hell that person was called.

He'd have to pay closer attention to what was going on between Amber and him. He didn't know if she was the one or not, but he liked spending time with her. He also didn't feel the need to seek out anyone else.

He was happy. He was having fun. For now, that was good enough.

SEVENTEEN

"ARE YOU NERVOUS?"

Amber was lacing up her skates. She slanted a smile at Tia. "No. We're going to sail through the long program. You were spectacular in the short. All you have to do is keep that momentum going."

Tia drew in a deep breath. "Thank you for saying that. But China was so formidable."

Amber nodded, tightening up her laces. "They were a surprise. It's all because Hua skated tremendously well. But I don't know if their free skate is strong enough to beat us."

They were currently in second place in points. Amber knew Tia had a strong long program, and she knew her own was good enough to score high points for the US team. And because this was a team event, they could rely on the pairs and the ice dancers as well as the guys' individual programs.

Amber grinned.

"What?" Tia asked.

"We're going to wipe the floor with the other teams. Have you seen Telisa and Robbie's free skate program?"

Tia looked at her, then smiled. "Oh. Right. They won Worlds with that program. Not to mention Amaryllis and Andrew's ice dancing program, which is amazing. Oh, and I've seen Rory's free skate. He is so good."

"Brandon's is excellent as well," Amber said. "I'm feeling pretty good about the US team's chances in the next round."

"And you skate last. Does that make you more nervous or less?"

Amber shrugged. "I don't get nervous. I just skate."

"You're like ice, Amber," Tia said. "I hope to be like you someday."

Amber laughed, then leaned in to rub her shoulder against Tia. "No, you need to be like Tia, and no one else. You're going to kill it."

Tia smiled. "You're right. I'll do that. Only a lot less nervously."

"There's nothing to be nervous about, Tia. You have a strong program and you have the skills. Remember that when you take the ice."

"I will. Thanks, Amber."

Amber recalled what it was like to be Tia's age. Everything was new and exciting—but also terrifying, because she'd had no idea what to expect. She'd had no one to mentor her back then other than her coaches and trainers. If she'd had an experienced skater to show her the ropes, to make her feel less nervous, this would have been so much easier. She'd vowed back then she would give back if given the chance.

And then she'd isolated herself from the other skaters for the next several years, mainly because of her mother's notions that other skaters were her competition—the enemy. Yes, they were competition, but the whole idea of them being the enemy was ridiculous. You only competed against yourself. You were only as good as your own talent. No other skater could take that away from you. You could only be defeated by your own insecurities and lack of preparation.

She felt a lot better about coming out of her shell. And since this was her first time participating in the team competition, she felt more a part of the US figure skating team than ever. And so excited about their chances, too.

While she waited for the event to begin, she grabbed her phone to check her e-mail and messages.

There was a voice mail from her mother. She scrunched her nose. She'd done a TV interview the other day. Her mother probably had something critical to say about it.

She'd check that voice mail later. The last thing she needed before a performance skate was something negative on her mind.

There was a text from Lisa.

Kick some ass, girl. I'll be there watching! Followed by several emojis, including skates and hearts.

She grinned.

Another text, this one from Will. I'll expect to see you in the center on the medal stand with the rest of the US team. You can do this. His text had been accompanied by a medal emoji.

She shook her head and smiled, but she loved his confidence in her.

She'd watched his game the other day against Latvia. He'd been relentless in his pursuit of the puck during that game. And then that fight. He'd definitely held his own against two defenders. She understood the "Mad Dog" moniker now, after watching him play.

The US team sat together to watch the competition. This would typically be the time that Amber would stand in the back, do her warm-ups, put her earbuds in and shut out everything—and everyone—until it was time for her to perform.

Not this time. She and Tia sat next to Rory and Brandon,

watching the performance of Darren and Christina, the Canadian pairs skaters.

"They are so good," Rory said. "Perfectly synchronized in their jumps."

"Did I ever mention I started out in pairs?" Brandon asked.

"You did not," Amber said.

Brandon nodded. "When I was ten, I was paired with Melissa Hawthorne. She was an utter perfectionist and had the worst mother ever. Everything that went wrong was my fault, according to Melissa's mom. And our coach was even worse. He favored Melissa and he thought everything that went wrong was my fault, too."

"Maybe everything that went wrong *was* your fault, Brandon," Rory said, then nudged him with his knee.

Brandon laughed. "I swear, I started to think that way, too. My parents pulled me out of pairs after a year and started me on individual skating."

"I'm so glad they did," Tia said. "You're a great individual skater."

"I agree," Rory said. "Pairs just doesn't seem to suit you."

"He's right," Tia said. "You shine as a single skater."

"Plus, I don't see Melissa sitting here with us, so who's the better skater now, hmmm?"

Brandon grinned, then leaned back and pulled Amber toward him so he could kiss her on the cheek. "Thanks for that, Amber. Thanks, all of you. I wasn't fishing, but my heart is full now."

"Sometimes we have to start out in the wrong place to find our right place," Amber said.

"You said a mouthful there, sister," Brandon said.

The Canadian pair scored a decent set of points. Sergei was up next for Russia. Amber watched him skate onto the ice. Sergei always exuded supreme confidence, as if to say, "I dare you to find fault with my program." She admired that about him.

"He's so formidable," Rory said.

"And so hot," Brandon added.

"Focus, Brandon," Rory said.

"I am focusing. On Sergei's fine ass."

Rory rolled his eyes.

"He *is* seriously fine looking," Tia said.

"See?" Brandon said.

Amber offered up a wry smile. "I can't disagree. It's the dark hair and those piercing blue eyes."

"The body isn't making me look away, either," Brandon said.

Amber admired how cleanly Sergei skated. He was totally without flaws, but if she were being honest, he lacked passion. She could appreciate the technicality of his performance, but she didn't feel any emotion.

"He was wonderful," Brandon said after Sergei finished his program.

Brandon, on the other hand, clearly felt a lot of emotion, and Amber knew it had nothing to do with Sergei's skating.

"You have it bad for him, don't you?" Amber asked.

Brandon offered up a sheepish smile. "Kind of."

"And . . . does he have it bad for you, too?"

Brandon looked over at Tia. "He might."

"I knew it," Tia said. "I saw you two over in the corner of the rink chatting it up at practice the other day, and I knew from the way you two were leaning into each other that you were talking about more than just skating. You're seeing each other, aren't you?"

"Mayyybe."

Amber laughed. "You are so cute when you're being coy and secretive, Brandon. But I totally understand if you don't want to talk about it."

Brandon leaned over her shoulder. "I want to talk about it so much it makes my stomach hurt. But Sergei has to be careful. His coaches are extremely restrictive about his extracurricular activities."

"You can handle keeping it on the down low," Rory said. "No reason his coaches need to find out."

"Exactly," Amber said. "Hang out in large groups, then the two of you can subtly disappear for some alone time."

"You speak from experience, Amber?"

If only they knew how little experience she actually had, but she wasn't about to reveal that. So instead, she just shrugged. "I might."

"And who 'might' you be cuddling in dark corners?" Tia asked. "Since I'm cuddling no one but my phone."

Amber laughed. "None of your business."

Tia just gave her a knowing smile. "Bet I can guess."

Amber wasn't going to give that suggestion any credence. Instead, they watched the French ice dancers compete. They were very good, but the Canadians had been better.

It wouldn't matter, anyway, since the US team was going to clear the ice with all of them.

Tia stood. "I'm up next. Wish me luck."

Amber was happy to see that Tia seemed a lot calmer now. "You don't need it, honey, but good luck."

"We're all rooting for you," Rory said.

Tia smiled and disappeared.

"It's nice you're hanging out with us," Rory said to Amber. "You've never done this at any of the competitions."

"I'm turning over a new leaf this time," Amber said. "Trying not to isolate myself."

Brandon nodded. "Isolation can kill you, competitively. I know some people like to stay in their own heads, but I can conjure up the worst scenarios if I do that."

"Me, too," Rory said. "And I won't give them voice by telling you what they are."

Amber had never done that. She'd just plugged into her music and shut everyone out. The only thing it had generated was loneliness. Her performance on the ice had never suffered, though. She'd been lucky.

Lucky and lonely.

But no more. She craved friendships and sex and romance and maybe even love someday.

As soon as she won gold. And every time she skated she moved closer to that goal.

The team event wasn't going to net her what she wanted, but it was a warm-up.

"Tia looks so good," Rory said, drawing her out of her own thoughts and back onto the ice, where Tia's program had started.

Rory was right. Tia skated with a great confidence. She slightly bobbled her triple lutz, but she didn't fall. That flub wouldn't be enough to lose a massive amount of points. The rest of her program went well.

"She did great," Amber said when Tia finished.

"She did." Rory smiled.

At twenty-one, Rory was four years older than seventeen-year-old Tia. But Tia would turn eighteen next month, so it wasn't outside the realm of possibility that the two of them would match up. Judging by the way Rory had watched Tia skate, and the way the two of them had bounced off each other when they'd sat together, Amber got the idea there was an attraction. She made a mental note to ask Tia how she felt about Rory.

Tia's score was good. Really good. It didn't surprise Amber since Tia had beautiful lines and solid jumps.

When Amber took to the ice, the US team was in first place in points.

She intended to keep it that way.

When her music queued up, she glided across the ice, confident in every movement, assured of her choreography, which she'd practiced over and over again. Her team was counting on her to give them her best, and by the time she finished her long program, she felt as if she had.

The crowd roared their approval. She soaked it in, not like she deserved it, but hoping she'd done her best to help win a gold medal for the team.

When she took to the seats to await her scores, the entire team crowded around her, since she'd skated last. Her scores would determine whether the US would win the team event.

Now she felt pressure. She didn't want to let her team down.

"You rocked it, honey," Telisa said, putting her arm around her.

"You were so good," Tia said.

She blew out a breath. "I hope I did enough."

Brandon rubbed her back. "It was flawless. If it isn't enough, then it's on the judges, not you."

The Canadian team had also skated nearly perfectly. They were in second place. It was going to be close.

When the scores came up, Amber scanned them quickly.

She had done enough. They'd won the team gold medal. The entire team erupted in cheers.

Her entire skating career had been a solitary endeavor. But now she hugged her teammates.

"You did it," Tia said.

Amber squeezed her. "No, *we* did it. We all did."

They posed for photos and interviews. Amber had never been more excited about anything in her entire life. It was her first gold medal, and while it wasn't an individual medal, she'd happily share this with her teammates.

They stood on the podium as a team. Russia had taken the bronze and Canada the silver. When they hung the gold medal around her neck, Amber felt a tremor zing through her body.

"I'm so excited I can barely breathe," Tia said, grinning.

"Ditto," Amber said.

She even teared up during the national anthem.

It was the best night so far in her career.

And that was saying a lot, because she had so many wonderful memories. But this one she'd shared with all her teammates.

With her friends.

"We have to go celebrate," Rory said.

"How about we head down the mountain to Vancouver?" Brandon asked.

Tia grinned. "That's a great idea."

"You have to run that by your coach first," Amber said. "Since you're underage and aren't supposed to leave the village."

Tia made a face. "Fine. Will you be my chaperone tonight, Amber?"

"Sure." Though she really wanted to see Will. Maybe he'd go with them.

"Thank you. I'll go check with my coach."

"Can I invite Sergei?" Brandon asked.

"I imagine we can invite whomever," Telisa said. "I'd like to invite Darren and Christina. They skated their hearts out."

Amber went to grab her bag. She pulled her phone out to text Will. There was already a message from him.

You were amazing. Not surprised at all. Congrats!

She smiled and texted him. Thanks! We're all headed down the mountain for dinner. You in?

It took him a few minutes, but he replied with, Hell yeah.

Why was it that everything about him made her happy, including a two-word text reply?

They were all going to change and meet up in the main lobby in an hour. She texted Will and let him know she'd meet him there.

She had a brief conversation with Yegor, who praised her for her performance and told her to get some rest, because she'd be back on the ice for practice tomorrow. Then she headed over to her apartment to change and tuck her gold medal into the safe.

She had a gold medal. It wasn't the one she'd come here for, but it sure felt amazing.

She took a shower and changed, then went into the bathroom and brushed her teeth, fixed her makeup and brushed her hair. She decided on a pair of leggings and a coral long-sleeved top, slid into her boots and was about to grab her coat when her phone buzzed on the kitchen counter.

It was probably Will so she dashed to grab it.

It was her mom. She thought about ignoring it, but that probably wasn't a good idea. She punched the button.

"Hi, Mom."

"You won a gold medal."

She smiled. "The team did, yes. Did you watch it on television?"

"No, honey. I'm here. In Vancouver."

Her stomach felt like it had dropped to her feet. "You're here? Already?"

"Of course. You didn't think I'd miss even one of your performances, did you? I can't wait to see you. I have a lovely hotel just outside of the venue. Come meet me and we'll have dinner tonight."

Amber squeezed her eyes shut, panic zinging her like electric strikes. "I . . . I have plans with friends tonight."

Her mother paused, the silence on the other end of the line feeling like judgement. "Change them."

It was amazing how quickly her mother's tone could go from excited to stern. Normally, Amber would toe the line, do whatever her mother told her to.

But she wouldn't, couldn't change her plans. "I can't, Mom. How about we meet tomorrow? I'm sure you're exhausted from your flight. Have a nice dinner at the hotel and I'll text you after practice tomorrow?"

"Excuse me?"

"I . . . I have to go now. I'll talk to you in the morning. Love you, Mom. Bye."

She ended the call and stared down at her phone, knowing she'd get a huge lecture tomorrow from her mother. In fact, her mother would likely call her back right away.

She waited for a full minute, but the call didn't come.

Huh. Maybe standing up for herself wouldn't be so hard after all. Maybe her mother would come around.

She laughed. Yeah, right. And tomorrow pigs would sprout wings.

She tucked her phone in her bag, grabbed her coat and walked out the door.

EIGHTEEN

AMBER HADN'T EXPECTED SUCH A BIG GROUP WHEN she gathered with everyone at the main lobby. Then again, she'd never won a gold medal before. It was a big damn deal and they had a right to celebrate.

It was more than the US skating team joining them. Obviously word had gotten out and there were Canadians, Russians, some French and Italians, as well as US athletes from other disciplines. Rory told her they had to rent a bus to take them down the mountain.

She looked around, searching their group for Will. So far, she hadn't spotted him.

"Looking for your boyfriend?" Tia asked.

Her lips tipped into a smile. "Girl, you are way too observant. And I was looking for Brandon."

Tia smiled. "Who is standing two feet away from you."

Dammit. "Okay, so I was looking for—"

"Me?"

She flipped around to see Will standing behind her.

"Oh. Hey, Will."

"Thought so," Tia said, giving her a knowing smile.

Amber cast a grin at Tia. "Stop being so smart. And so . . . I don't know . . . smart."

Tia laughed, then went over to talk to Rory, who'd just walked up to join the group.

"What was that all about?"

"It was about teenagers who see everything."

"I see. Maybe."

They all piled into the bus. They ended up at the Village Taphouse in west Vancouver. It was already crowded, but they were probably prepared for some of the athletes to descend on them, because they were more than gracious about setting up a table for the party of twenty.

Amber had told Tia if she was coming with them, she'd have to stick by Amber's side for the night.

"This is so exciting," Tia said. "I thought I'd be stuck in the village the entire time."

"It is fun to get out of there," Amber said.

She noticed when they were seated that Rory made sure to grab a seat on Tia's other side, which was fine with Amber as long as they didn't disappear. Then again, Tia was entitled to have a little fun, and since she was close enough to eighteen, as long as they didn't hop into a hotel room, what did it matter?

She was still going to keep an eye on the two of them, though.

"Chaperoning?" Will asked as he bent to whisper in her ear.

"Yes. And taking my duties very seriously."

He smiled. "I don't think they can get into too much trouble in here."

"Really. And did you get into any kind of trouble when you were seventeen?"

He gave her a hot smile. "Define trouble."

She shook her head. "Exactly. So I'll be keeping an eye on her."

The restaurant was a great place with incredible ambiance. Music was playing, and there were many TV screens and pool tables. They settled into their table—or tables, really—and everyone ordered drinks. Amber and Will both selected beers. Tia decided on a sparkling water. They looked over the menu.

Amber chose the Kung Pao Noodle Bowl and Will ordered the Backyard Bacon and Cheese Burger. She'd also thought about having that, but the noodle bowl had caught her eye almost immediately, and she couldn't waver.

"I might have to take a taste of your burger," she said to Will.

His eyes gleamed. "You can definitely put your mouth on anything that is mine."

She shook her head. "Such a man."

"Why, thanks, babe."

She looked over at Tia, who was engaged—deeply engaged—in conversation with Rory. But since everyone's hands were on the table, it was all good. Talking wouldn't get anyone in trouble.

"How did it feel, standing on that podium tonight?"

She looked up at Will. "You've been on the podium before. You know what it feels like."

"I've been on the podium for silver. You stood center and got gold draped over you. That had to feel special."

"It did. Even more so because the team won the medal. That was a first for me. It was incredible standing up there with my teammates. And you definitely know how that feels."

"True. It's pretty amazing."

"A once in a lifetime feeling," Brandon said, chiming in from across the table. "As individual skaters, we spend so much time chasing personal glory. I feel so privileged to have been involved in this as a team."

Sergei sat next to him and nodded. "We don't often have the chance to perform with our countrymen. It was exciting and humbling. And we won a medal. Russia will be proud."

Brandon beamed a smile. "You skated beautifully."

"So did you," Sergei said.

Amber slanted her gaze toward Will, who smiled knowingly at her. It was obvious that Sergei and Brandon were into each other. They were the same age, both incredibly good-looking, as well as talented. Since both of them were individual figure skaters, they had a lot in common. She was glad Sergei was able to come out with them tonight. She'd known Brandon for a lot of years, since they often competed at the same events. Though this was the first time she'd been able to spend time with him and really get to know him. He was personable and friendly and always eager to give advice to fellow skaters.

Of course, with very few exceptions, she could say that about almost all of her fellow skaters.

She'd missed out on so much by isolating herself all these years.

Their dinner arrived and they all ate while listening to Telisa and Robbie tell them about how they met and fell in love.

"I was paired with another skater when I first started out skating competitively," Telisa said. "The problem was, I couldn't stand him. He was arrogant, always out for his own glory, and we fought all the time. It showed in our performance. You can't be graded high when you're glaring hate at each other for four minutes."

Will grinned. "I dunno. It works for me."

Telisa laughed. "That helps you score points. For figure skating pairs? Not so much."

"So what did you do?" Tia asked. "It's not like you can abruptly change your partner when you're in the middle of performance season."

"I couldn't. I had to suck it up through the entire season. But at the end of the season I told my parents—I was your age at the time, Tia—that either we changed partners, or I was finished skating."

"It was that bad?" Sergei asked.

"It was awful. I was losing weight, crying all the time. It had been my dream to skate, and finding the right partner is everything when you're a pairs skater."

"It really is," Amaryllis said, looking over adoringly at her partner, Andrew. "We were so lucky to find each other."

Amber couldn't imagine how awful that must have been. She sent up a mental thank-you to the heavens that she'd never had to deal with that level of mental anguish.

"So what did you do?" Rory asked.

"My parents agreed."

Robbie put his arm around her. "And then I came into her life."

Telisa looked over at Robbie and smiled. "Yes, you did."

"And it was love at first sight?"

Robbie laughed. "Not exactly. She was so burned by her first partner that trust was a big issue for her. Let's just say she put me through my paces in the beginning."

"I really did," Telisa said. "I was mean to him. I didn't trust him and I was certain he was going to be as bad as my previous partner."

"Really?" Brandon asked.

"Really." Telisa shrugged. "I had issues and some serious baggage. But Robbie refused to put up with my shit. He told me he was a damn good partner, and after six months together he said if I didn't start putting all my trust in him, he was gone."

Amber blinked. "Wow."

"Yeah, I was harsh on her," Robbie said. "She'll be the first to admit she needed the wake-up call."

"I did," Telisa said. "Our first skate after that went really well. It went so well, in fact, that Robbie kissed me when it was over."

Robbie slanted the group a triumphant smile. "It was one hell of a kiss. I intended for it to be an 'I told you so' kind of kiss. But it ended up a 'Whoa, where did all these feelings come from?' kind of kiss."

Telisa nodded. "After that, our skating had so much emotion, so much passion. All I'd been looking for was a great skating partner. I found so much more. Robbie was the best thing that ever happened to me. Not only in my skating life, but in my personal life as well. I don't know what I'd do without him."

Robbie leaned over and brushed his lips across hers. "I love you."

"I love you, too," Telisa said.

Robbie smiled at her, then looked at everyone else. "And we got married last year."

Tia pressed her hand to her heart. "That's so incredibly romantic."

"It truly is," Amber said. "I'm so happy for both of you."

"Thank you," Telisa said.

"Okay, enough of this love stuff," Sergei said. "Now we kick your asses in pool."

Will laughed. "I'm up for that. How about you, Amber?"

"You may not know this, but I happen to be exceptionally good at pool."

Will leaned back and searched her face. "I think you're lying."

She shrugged and looked down to inspect her manicure. "I guess you could team up with someone else. But I wouldn't advise it."

She waited while he thought about it.

"Okay, you're with me."

She smiled up at him. "Good choice."

AMBER HAD LIED TO HIM. SHE DIDN'T KNOW SHIT ABOUT pool. Fortunately, Will was a patient teacher, and Amber learned fast.

Which didn't mean they were winning, because they were getting their asses kicked by Sergei and Brandon.

Not that he minded all that much. After all, he got to lean against Amber and rub his body against her every time he helped her line up a shot. It wasn't too much of a hardship to lose a couple rounds of pool as long as he got to put his hands on a beautiful woman.

Right now she was stretched across the table, trying to line up a shot in the corner pocket.

"Put your hands like this," he said, aligning his body next to hers and showing her how to handle the stick. Though frankly, she had it handled. She'd sunk the last three balls and she grew more confident with every ball she sank in the pocket.

"I think I've got it," she said.

Yeah, she had it all right. Her black leggings stretched tight across her very sweet ass, and he stepped back to enjoy the view as she took her shot.

"Damn," she said as she missed the shot. She straightened and moved over to stand beside Will, letting Sergei take his turn. "Sorry."

Will shrugged. "Don't be. For a beginner, you're doing great."

"Am I?"

"Yeah, you've got a natural feel for the stick."

She arched a brow. "Is that some sexual innuendo?"

He leaned down to whisper in her ear. "It can be if you'd like."

He felt the tremble in her body.

"I'd like anything you do to me, Will."

Now he felt the quiver, this time in his balls. Not a good place for his cock to decide to harden, so he focused instead on the game.

After about an hour, everyone decided to head on back up the mountain.

He pulled Amber aside. "How would you feel about hanging out with me here for the night?"

"In the bar?"

He cocked a half smile. "No, I've got another idea."

"I'm listening."

"I have a friend who rented a house down here. It's got plenty of bedrooms . . ."

Will had let the sentence trail off, obviously leaving it up to Amber to make the decision.

"Hmm. Lisa could have the apartment to herself. She'd like that."

"I'm sure she would." He liked how the first thing she thought about was her friend and roommate. It spoke to her generous nature, how she thought about someone else before she thought about herself. Yet another reason why he liked her.

"Plus, you and I would get some alone time," he added.

"Yes, I like that part."

"Me, too."

"Except there's one problem."

"What's that?"

"How will we get back up the mountain tomorrow? I have to be on the ice by nine."

"Dave will drive us up."

"Dave being your friend who rented the house?"

"Yes."

"Are you sure he wouldn't mind?"

"He won't mind. He's got a complete pass for all the games, and he never misses a single event. He'll want to be up there early before anything starts."

"Oh. Great. Then I guess . . . yes, if you're sure we're not imposing."

"We're not imposing. He's a friend from Chicago. I've known him my whole life. He brought his wife, and his brother is staying as well. His whole family has been coming to the bar for as long as I can remember."

"Oh, that's nice."

"Yeah. Anyway, he invited me to stay at the house anytime I wanted to."

"That's . . . convenient."

Will gave Amber a heated smile. "Isn't it?"

"Let's go."

"Sure." She started to get up, then sat back down. "Oh, wait. I can't stay. I'm Tia's chaperone."

"It's a drive up the mountain."

"But I'm still responsible for seeing her back to the village."

"Okay." He wouldn't do anything to compromise Amber's sense of responsibility.

She was thinking, so he let her do that. If they had to go back, he'd understand.

"Hang on a second." She got up and went over to talk to Telisa for a few minutes, then motioned for Tia, who came over and sat with them. Then more talking. When Amber came back and sat next to him, she looked more relaxed.

"Everything okay?"

"It is now. Telisa and Robbie are going to make sure Tia gets back to her room."

"Oh, good."

"Yes, I trust they won't let her make any detours."

"You mean, like detouring to Rory's room?"

Amber smiled. "Yes. Not that I think she'd do that."

"Why don't you think she'd do that? She's a healthy teenager who's got the hots for a guy. Just because you didn't doesn't mean she wouldn't."

"You have a point. I'm glad I'm not in charge of her all the time."

Will laughed. "Yeah, I wouldn't want to monitor a teenager here. Actually, I wouldn't want to monitor anyone's behavior here. Except my own."

She leaned into him. "Why, are you out of control?"

He gave her a look that told her just how much he wanted her. "I can be. Just wait 'til we get to Dave's."

"And just how far away does Dave live from here?"

"No clue. Hopefully not far."

"Then let's get going."

He stood and took her hand. "Yeah, let's do that."

They said their good-byes to everyone, then Will ordered a car that fortunately didn't take long to show up. The ride to Dave's house only took ten minutes.

Dave's rented house was a nice Victorian style, and much bigger than Amber imagined it would be. She wished it was light outside so she could check out the outside, but she could still see the gables, and the wraparound front porch was amazing. She couldn't wait to view it in the light of day.

Will entered a code at the garage door, and the door lifted.

"Shouldn't we knock at the front door?" she asked.

"They're all out," Will said as he led her through the garage and opened the door leading to the house. He punched the button to put the garage door down.

He took her hand and led her down the hall toward the kitchen.

"Let me find the light switch," he said. When he did, the kitchen was bathed in bright light. It was beautiful and modern, with gray cabinets and a dark granite island. The floors were gray wood plank that led all the way into the spacious living room, which was centered by a huge stone fireplace.

"It's beautiful here."

"Yeah, it is." He walked over to the refrigerator and opened the door, then craned his neck around. "Beer or wine?"

"That's not ours."

He laughed. "No, it's Dave's, and he said we could help ourselves. So do you want beer or wine?"

"I think I'm fine with a glass of water."

Will pulled out a beer from the fridge while Amber found a glass in the cabinet and made herself some ice water.

"Let's go check out the house," Will said.

"Sure."

She slipped off her boots. Will looked down at her feet.

"What are you doing?" he asked.

"It's not our house. I think we should respect that."

"It's not like I'm wearing high heels, Amber."

She gave him a look. "I know that, but still, we've been trudging around in the snow. Maybe the owners don't want melting snow all over their wood floors."

"My guess is they have someone in to clean before the owners come back. But I'm happy to wander around in my socks." He toed off his boots and left them next to hers, then led the way past the kitchen and living room through open French doors into an expansive library that also had a fireplace.

Amber wandered the built-in bookshelves and ran her fingers over the owners' books.

"Wow. There are some old books here. Some classics." She pulled one out, gently turned over the pages, then looked up at Will. "This is a first edition *Alice's Adventures in Wonderland*."

"Is that a big deal?"

"It's . . . rare. And yes, it's a big deal."

Will watched as she closed the book and slid it gingerly back on the shelf, then backed away.

"I don't think they bite," he said.

"I don't think we should be in here."

"Okay." He started to walk out, but he noticed Amber gazing longingly at the bookshelves.

"Something calling to you back there?"

"I love books. There's something about rare editions that I find so mesmerizing."

He came over to her and laid his hand on the small of her back to urge her back toward the room. "Well, come on."

She half turned to look at him. "Seriously? You don't mind?"

"I don't mind."

"I wonder if the homeowners would mind."

"I'll bet if the homeowners didn't want anyone in their library, they'd have put a sign up or locked the room."

She chewed on her lower lip. "You might be right."

"Okay, then, Belle, let's go explore the library."

Her lips tipped up. "Did I ever tell you that if I ever have a daughter I want to name her Annabelle?"

"No."

"One, because I'm crazy about the name Belle from *Beauty and the Beast*, and two, I fell in love with the name Annabelle the first time I read Poe's 'Annabel Lee.'"

He cocked his head to the side. "Those are total opposite ends of the Belle spectrum."

She laughed. "I know. But I still love them."

He took a seat in one of the comfortable wingback chairs in the library. "You're just full of interesting tidbits, Amber Sloane."

"Why, thank you, Will Madigan."

He sat back, sipped his beer and watched as she wandered the bookshelves. She occasionally exclaimed or murmured when she found some rare or first edition.

"Oh. *The Great Gatsby*. Wow, Faulkner. Oh, my God a signed Virginia Woolf. I might faint."

"Let me know if I need to catch you."

"Shut up," she said. "There are some magnificent works here. Who are these people?"

He shrugged. "People who love books would be my guess."

She swiveled to face him. "You don't like books?"

"I love to read. On my phone."

"I do that, too, but there's nothing like the smell of a book. Especially an old book. The pages have all that history in them."

"Yeah. Musty history and coffee stains and folded pages that sometimes fall out. I'll take a good book on my phone any day."

She wrinkled her nose. "Technology nerd."

"Thank you."

She had a book in her hand and sat in the wingback chair across from him. "What does it take to insult you?"

"Tell me I suck at playing hockey."

She laughed. "Can't do that, since you seem to excel in that particular area."

Of course he did. "Then I can't be insulted. Unless you tell me I'm bad at sex."

"Oh. Well, so far you're pretty good at that, too."

He arched a brow. "*Pretty* good?"

She lifted a shoulder while paging through the book in her hand. "I might need to be reminded."

He got up and took the book from her hand and carefully laid it back on its rightful spot on the shelf before coming back to Amber. He swept his hand over her face, cupped her neck and drew her close. He kissed her thoroughly, following the trail of satiny skin. Hell, her entire body was satiny skin. He kissed her jaw, nibbled on her earlobe, then trailed his tongue along the column of her neck, feeling the slight tremble in her body.

When he ran into clothes, he reached down to lift her sweater, sliding his hands underneath to palm her back.

"Mmm," she said. "I like your hands on me. Put your mouth on me."

He tilted her head back to search her face. "Where?"

Her eyes were pools of arousal. "Anywhere."

She lifted her sweater off, then released the clasp on her bra.

He liked that she was so open with what she needed. He cupped one breast, then fit his mouth around one pink nipple. It puckered like a soft flower against his tongue as he sucked. She moaned and tangled her fingers in his hair, letting him know she liked what he was giving her.

He wanted to give her everything, to make her moan and writhe with every flick of his tongue over her body.

He drew her pants and underwear down, then spread her legs. When he tilted his head back, she was watching him with an intent, sensual gaze.

He cupped his hands around her buttocks. "Tell me what you want, Amber."

She shuddered out a breath. "Lick me."

There she was, standing above him, legs spread, tempting him with her wicked words. His cock throbbed against the zipper of his jeans as he leaned in to swipe his tongue against the softness of her pussy.

She tasted like tart honey, her scent enveloping him in a haze of need. He'd wanted to be the one to mesmerize her, but he was the one who felt spellbound.

And the way Amber moved, undulating her sex against his face, made him want to take her right over the edge. He slid a finger inside of her, pumping faster as he sucked her clit.

"Oh, oh, I'm coming," she said, her body shuddering as she came.

Damn, it was good to feel her contract against his finger, to feel her shudder as he held onto her. When her legs quivered, he withdrew and pulled her down onto the floor, resting her head in the crook of his arm. He brushed his lips across hers.

She licked her lips. "You taste like my pussy."

Now it was his balls that quivered. "Do you always say what you're thinking?"

"Not always. Why? Shouldn't I?"

"You definitely should when we're naked together."

She raked a fingernail over his shirt. "I'm the only one naked here. And I was so lost in what you were doing that I wasn't even thinking that your friends might come home."

He hadn't been thinking about it, either. His only thought had been making her come. "You're right. Let's go upstairs."

She gathered her clothes and he grabbed his boots. He dumped his beer in the trash and they headed upstairs. Dave had told him his room would be the last one on the right. Amber, clothes piled up in her arms and seeming to not care at all that she was naked, stayed right next to him as he opened the door to the bedroom.

He flipped on the light.

"Oh, the room has a bathroom," she said, laying her clothes on the nearby chair and making her way into the bathroom. "And it has a huge tub, too."

He smiled and followed her into the bathroom, leaning against the doorway as she turned to face him.

It was a big bathroom for a guest room, with a nice-sized shower, a tub and a double vanity.

"This tub is spectacular. Want to take a bath?" she asked.

"What is it with women and bathtubs?"

She frowned. "I don't know what 'women' you're referring to, but the apartment in the village doesn't have a tub, and I love a nice warm bath."

"Then by all means, you should take a bath while we're here."

"So you don't want a bath?"

"I don't take baths. But you should go ahead."

She seemed to consider whether or not it was something she should do, but then she finally shrugged.

"I think I will." She wound her hair up in some kind of knot on top of her head, which by some miracle of gravity or geometry or something stayed put. Then she leaned over to turn on the water, giving him one nice view of her very sweet ass, which made his dick harden again.

He pulled off his shirt and undid the button and zipper of his jeans, letting them fall to the bathroom floor. His boxer briefs followed, and then his socks, until he was naked.

By then, Amber was in the tub, watching him. "What are you doing?"

He climbed into the bathtub, situating himself across from her. "Taking a bath."

"I thought you didn't take baths."

"Yeah, but then I saw your ass, and I changed my mind."

Her lips curved. "I see. Think you're going to get lucky in here?"

"I'm already lucky. I'm in the tub with you."

She raised her foot and pressed it against his chest, wriggling her toes against his pecs.

"I should get a tattoo," she said, her gaze roaming over his chest and shoulders.

"Yeah?" He picked up her foot, using his thumbs to gently massage the arch. She moaned. "And what tattoo would you get?"

"I don't know. Skates, probably."

"Good idea. Where?"

"On my foot." She sat up. "Could we do that here?"

"In the tub? Doubtful."

She tilted her head to the side. "Funny. You know what I mean."

"You can get tattoos almost anywhere."

"Would you go with me?"

"Sure. You should think about it, though. Tattoos are forever. I mean, sure, you can have them removed, but it's a long, painful process."

"Why would I want to have it removed?"

"You should still think about it. It also needs healing time, so don't do it while you have to tightly lace up your skates."

"Point taken. After I win gold, I'll have skates tattooed on my foot."

He could already picture that tat. "You do that. Plus, you know, it's a good goal."

"Besides winning a gold medal, you mean."

"Yeah, besides that." She swirled her foot around his chest, then lower, down his abs. When she reached his cock, she raked her toes over the shaft. He was already hard. Hell, he'd been hard ever since he'd put his mouth on her. Nothing had changed. Just looking at her gave him an erection. She looked like a water nymph leaning back in the tub, the water lapping over her breasts and nipples, reminding him what it was like to taste her.

Now he just had to bide his time until she was done tubbing, so he could slide inside of her and feel her gripping him.

Instead, she continued to rub her foot over his cock.

"I could fuck you right now," he said, leaning forward to pull her onto his lap. "But I can't put a condom on in the tub."

She reached for his cock, stroking him in a deliberately slow, torturous way. "I might still be a novice at this, but I've heard there are other ways to get off."

"Oh, you've heard, huh?"

"Yes. Like with my hand or with my mouth. Or I could even slide against you and get us both off."

Christ, she was a tease. And damn good at it, too. "Do it."

She pushed him backward and slid along his shaft, her pussy hot against his flesh as she moved back and forth over his straining flesh. She dug her nails into his chest, her gaze pinned to his, her expression one of utter pleasure.

"Oh, that feels so good," she said.

He gripped her hips as she rode his cock. The pressure of her body pressing his shaft against his stomach and the way she felt against him was all he needed. He was ready to burst.

So was Amber, because she leaned forward, let out a low moan, then rocked back and forth against him, crying out with her climax. Watching her come was a beautiful thing. He let go, spurts of come jettisoning from his cock as he shuddered through his orgasm. When Amber leaned against him, he wrapped his arms around her and smoothed his hand down her back, feeling her body tremble with the aftereffects.

Will felt Amber's heart beating against his chest. Yeah, his was rocking the beat pretty hard, too. How could it not, watching her ride him like that?

She finally sat up and smiled at him. "Well, that was fun. Now there's come in the water and I'm all sweaty."

He laughed. "Wanna take a shower?"

"Yes, let's do that."

He helped her stand, then they got out of the tub and let the water out. Will turned on the shower and they got in to do a fast wash. Will grabbed towels for them and wrapped one around Amber.

She yawned.

"Tired?"

She nodded.

"Come on." He tossed the towel on the counter, took her hand and led her to bed.

She climbed in and he wrapped himself around her. She rubbed her fingers over the "love" tattoo on his wrist.

"I like this."

"Like what?"

"This tattoo. It takes a man confident in himself to have 'love' tattooed on his body."

"I told you I believe in love, that I was surrounded by a prime example in my parents."

Amber felt the gut punch of sweet emotion. Not only had Will been nothing but nice to her since she'd met him, but he held a firm belief in love, even to go so far as to get the tattoo. She'd never known love like that, didn't have an example set before her.

"Like Telisa and Robbie," she said. "And their love story they told earlier."

Obviously, that kind of love existed.

Will tightened his hold on her. "Sweet, huh?"

She turned around to look at him. "Yes, it is. Is it like that with your parents?"

"Yeah, they're disgustingly in love, even now after all these years."

"Disgustingly?"

He laughed. "I was teasing. But yes, they kiss at the bar all the time. There isn't a day where my dad doesn't stop what he's doing to put his arm around my mom. There's never been a lack of affection. They don't hold anything back." He looked down at his wrist, where the "love" tattoo stood out. "That's why I got this. It's real and it's out there."

She sighed. "That must have been so nice, to be surrounded by all that love and affection."

"It was."

She realized how much she'd missed out on. It was hard not to feel resentful, but she couldn't blame her parents. They had to have loved each other at some point. They got married. They'd had Amber. They had stayed together. Not that being in love was necessary to continue a marriage, she supposed. Their relationship was just . . . different. Maybe her parents did love each other. They just had never shown it in a demonstrative way.

Still, how was she supposed to learn how to love romantically if it was never shown to her?

She shoved the thought aside. This wasn't the time or place to dwell on it.

Will swept his hand down her back. "What are you thinking about?"

"My parents. How they never show affection to each other."

"Maybe they just don't show it in front of you. Some people aren't comfortable with public displays of affection, even in front of their kids, so they save it for when they're alone."

"Maybe." But she knew her parents better than she knew anyone else. She just didn't think it was a "behind closed doors only" kind of relationship.

"So what's bothering you?" he asked.

"I don't know. Maybe hearing Telisa and Robbie talk about their love story, and you telling me about your parents, makes me feel that I might never know what real love is like because I never had a good example of it at home."

He played with the ends of her hair, and she realized how tactile he was. "Oh, I disagree. Despite your upbringing, and I have to admit to not knowing much about that, I think you're a woman capable of passion and a great depth of emotion."

"Really. And how would you know that?"

"Well, we've been intimate, so I know how passionate you are."

"That's just sex."

He grinned. "I've been in bed with women who aren't half as expressive as you are, Amber. You either have a loving, passionate nature or you don't. There are plenty of people out there who feel intensely, and some who don't possess the capacity for deep emotion."

She considered that. Maybe her parents were the latter. "Okay, I understand. So what you're saying is that maybe my parents just aren't the kind of people who demonstrate love in that way."

"Right. Which doesn't mean they don't feel love. You, on the other hand, are incredibly sensual and tactile and emotional. When you fall in love, Amber, it's gonna be epic."

She smiled. "Or it'll be a total hot mess since I'll have no idea what I'm doing."

"Most people who fall in love don't know what they're doing. There's no road map for it. You just . . . do it."

She studied him. "Have you ever been in love?"

He waited before answering. "Yeah. Once. Several years ago."

"And how did that go?"

His lips curved. "In the beginning, it was amazing. All these emotions boiling to the surface. Lots of passion. We couldn't get enough of each other, and not just the sex, ya know? We'd spend hours talking. We had a lot in common. We grew up in the same area; we knew a lot of the same people. We just clicked. I thought she was it for me."

"So what happened?"

He reached out to take her hand, entwining his fingers with hers. "My career was taking off. I got called up by St. Louis and had to move there. She was firmly planted in Chicago and building her career. She was a lawyer, working her way up at a prestigious law firm. We tried the long distance thing for a while, but after a year or so it became clear it wasn't going to work out. I wanted her in St. Louis with me, she wanted me in Chicago, and neither one of us would give, career-wise."

"She couldn't find an equally awesome job in St. Louis?"

Will shook her head. "It wouldn't be fair for me to ask her to give up her job. She was on the partner track, and she was bringing in clients worth serious money to her firm. To ask her to start over in a city where she didn't know anyone would mean taking a pay cut. Not that I couldn't afford to support both of us, but she had a pretty kick-ass job."

"And so did you."

He nodded. "Yeah. So our personal relationship suffered. In the end, we both decided it was in our best interests to cut the relationship cord."

She couldn't imagine how awful that must have been—for both of them. "That was probably really hard."

"It was. She was an amazing woman. Ending it wasn't easy on either of us, but we both felt like we were spinning our wheels."

She nodded. "That is sad. I'm sure you missed her."

"For a while, I did. I moped for a long time, until a teammate told me I needed to get off my ass and get out there again, because that relationship was over."

"Ouch. Harsh."

"But true. So I started dating my ass off. I heard from friends in Chicago she had done the same thing. It was like we had been holding on to something that wasn't there anymore just because we thought it was the right thing to do, when in reality we'd been over for a long time."

"Huh."

"Yeah. It was great when we were in love. But once we realized we weren't meant to be together, it was over. To be honest, we probably lingered too long because neither of us wanted to be the one to end it."

She flipped over onto her back and stared up at the ceiling. "Well now I'm confused."

"About what?"

"About how you know when you've found the one? How will I ever know? You thought you knew, and look what happened."

He teased his fingers over her stomach, unable to get enough of touching her skin. "I don't know if anyone knows, babe. My guess is when you find that right person, it all clicks and falls into place, and then no matter what happens, you're confident it'll all work out okay."

"I guess so." She rolled over to face him. "I do know this. I'm having a great time with you. And I don't think I want to fall in love, ever."

He frowned. "Why not?"

"Too much risk."

He laughed. "I can't believe you of all people just said that."

"Why?"

"You take risks every time you skate out onto the ice. You're brave as hell, Amber."

"Thank you. But that's just skating. Win or lose, my heart will be intact."

"So you're saying your emotions aren't involved when you skate? That if you don't win a medal here, you won't be heart-broken?"

"No. Winning a medal is always a challenge. Since I was ten years old, skating was my business, not my heart, not my ever-lasting love."

Will found it fascinating hearing Amber's perspective, not only about love, but how she felt about figure skating. He had an entirely different feeling about being on the ice. "Huh. Okay."

"You feel differently."

"Hell, yeah. I love being on the ice. Winning is everything. And losing is awful."

She circled her finger around his nipple, making him suck in a breath. "When you lose, does it hurt your heart?"

"No, but it sucks."

"If you don't medal here, will your heart be broken?"

He had to think about that. "I guess not. But it'll suck."

"I think I've made my point."

He swept his hand upward, cupping her breast, teasing her nipple with his fingers until her breathing grew faster.

"And what was that point?"

She made a moaning sound. "I forget. I'm sure if you fuck me it'll jog my memory."

He rolled over to grab a condom. "My pleasure."

"Oh, no, Will. It'll definitely be my pleasure."

NINETEEN

AMBER BARELY MADE IT BACK TO THE VILLAGE THE next morning in time to change clothes and dash to the ice arena in time for practice.

"You are late," Yegor said, giving her his signature look of disapproval. Brows furrowed, arms crossed, head down. When she was twelve, it had been highly intimidating. Now, not so much.

"I know, I know, I'm sorry," she said, dashing to the bench to put on her skates.

"You need to stretch first," Valeria said. She also gave her a stern look.

"I don't have time. I'll go easy on the jumps."

"You'll get hurt without stretching."

"I won't, Valeria, I promise."

She started to move away, but Valeria grabbed her arm.

"Let me stretch you."

Amber shook her head. "There's no time. I have to be on the ice right now."

She heard Valeria's sigh as she made her way across the carpet to the ice.

It was much more important for her to get her practice time in rather than sacrifice that time to stretch. She took to the ice, did several laps around the rink, then went into a few easy jumps.

Her body felt good, and after a few more times around the arena she felt limber, so she signaled for her music for the short program so she could do a run-through. She got up to speed and did her first required element, a triple jump.

She felt the twinge in her hamstring almost immediately after coming out of the jump.

Shit. She continued on, hoping it was just a lack of warm-up that was causing her muscles to freeze up and nothing more. But as she went into the second jump, she felt that tightness again and, even worse, pain.

She didn't finish going through the rest of her program. Rather than risk an injury, she skated off the ice.

Valeria was right there, concern etched on her features. "I saw the way you came out of that triple axel. What's wrong?"

"I don't know. I felt a twinge in my right hamstring when I landed the jump."

"Come. Let's take a look at your leg."

She cast a look over at Yegor, who only shook his head and walked away.

A feeling of dread overcame her.

She unlaced her skates, casting them a look of longing, then followed Valeria into the locker room. She undressed, then hopped up on the table, wincing at the tightness in her hamstring.

She flipped over on her stomach and closed her eyes as Valeria put heat on her hamstring. She hoped she hadn't screwed this all up. Had she done something terrible? Had her refusal to adequately warm up done irreparable damage to her career? Had she thrown away her shot at winning gold?

"How does this feel?" Valeria asked as she removed the heating pad and began pressing in hard on the muscles of her hamstring.

It didn't hurt, so that might be positive. "It feels fine. Good, actually."

"No pain?"

"No pain."

"Good sign." Valeria worked her over for about half an hour, then told Amber to roll over. Valeria stretched her thoroughly. When she finished, Amber got dressed.

Yegor knocked on the door and ducked his head in.

"Got permission for you to skate again, if your leg is okay."

She did a few lunges, and felt no pain. "I can skate."

"Good. You will have time on the ice in fifteen minutes after Petrova has completed her skate. Stay warm."

She got dressed and grabbed her skates, then made her way out onto the carpet again, this time making sure she continued to stretch. When Petrova finished, she skated out there, feeling much more relaxed and limber than she had when she'd skated cold earlier.

The true test would be the jumps. She started her program, and when she did the triple axel, she held her breath, but landed the jump with no pain.

She exhaled a sigh of relief, went through the rest of her routine, feeling solid on all the required elements. When she finished, she skated off the ice toward a waiting Yegor and Valeria. Actually, she wanted to fling herself into Valeria's arms and sob with gratitude and relief, but she held it together.

"That looked much better," Valeria said.

Yegor nodded. "Stronger. You skated with confidence."

"I agree," Valeria said. "How was your pain level?"

She sat and unlaced her skates. "I felt much more relaxed. No tightness. No pain."

"Perfect," Valeria said. "No need to worry. You just had a twinge because you weren't warmed up."

"Which won't happen again, correct?" Yegor asked, slanting a stern look at her.

"It won't happen again."

She changed and left the arena, heading straight to her apartment.

"Lisa?"

Lisa didn't answer. She was either with Blake or out on the half-pipe doing her own practice.

She tossed her bag down inside the front door and went straight to the kitchen to grab a glass of juice. After she poured it, she sat at the counter.

How could she have been so careless, so stupid? She'd lost focus, had treated her skating career cavalierly, all in favor of some sexual fun and exploration. She'd even told Will last night that skating meant virtually nothing to her, that it was just a job.

It was so much more. When she'd felt that pull in her hamstring today, she'd panicked. It was only then she realized how much skating meant to her, what a blow it would be to not be able to compete.

Competition was everything to her. Nothing else mattered.

No one else mattered.

She had to get her focus back.

Her phone buzzed. She ignored it, figuring it was Will. She wasn't ready to talk to him. Not until she formulated a plan for their next conversation. Because things were going to change between them. They had to.

Her phone buzzed again.

"Dammit." She was just going to have to tell him that—

She looked at the phone. Oh, shit. Her mom. She'd forgotten all about her mom. She pressed the button. "Hi, Mom."

"Where have you been?"

"I'm at the apartment."

"I called you six times this morning between the hours of six and nine. You didn't answer."

She had her phone on silent in her bag, and because she'd been running late she hadn't bothered to look at it. "Sorry. I was running late this morning and I had short program practice. I just got back."

"Running late? You're never late. You're always early. What's going on, Amber?"

"Nothing's going on, Mom. So, how about lunch? Would you like to meet outside the village? There's a great bistro that I think you'd really like."

"Lunch would be fine. We need to get to the bottom of what you've been up to."

Amber rolled her eyes. "I miss you, too, Mom."

"Don't you get smart with me, Amber. We've worked way too hard on your skating career for you to throw it all away now."

"I'm not throwing anything away. I'm still working toward getting that medal."

"We'll see about that."

Amber made plans to meet her mother, then clicked off the phone, realizing as she did that her left hand had been clenched into a fist the entire time she'd been on the phone. She relaxed her hand and looked down at the deep grooves her nails had carved into her palm.

No tension there, huh, Amber?

Blowing out a breath, she got up, paced around the apartment and did some deep breathing in an effort to calm herself down. She changed clothes, making sure her hair was brushed and pulled back into a ponytail. She put on her leggings, boots and a sweater, then grabbed her jacket and gloves and left the apartment.

The restaurant was a few blocks outside the village. The cold air cleared her head, which she desperately needed. By the time she made it to the restaurant, she was ready to face her mother.

Her mom had texted her to tell her she was already there and had a table. Amber walked in, and it was hard to miss her mother's flaming red hair and bright patterned clothing. The one thing Amber knew about Denise Sloane was that she liked to stand out in a crowd.

No problem there. Mom stood and waved her hand, as if Amber would have any problem spotting her. She made her way around several tables and leaned over to kiss her mother on the cheek.

"Hi, Mom."

"You look tired. And are you gaining weight? You aren't eating junk food, are you?"

Amber drew in a deep breath, saved by their waitress who came over to take Amber's drink order. She asked for a glass of lemon water, then faced her mother. "I'm sleeping fine. My weight is perfect, and I'm eating right. How are you?"

"Concerned. Why were you late for practice this morning?"

She could tell her mother the truth, that she'd spent the night with Will last night, but that would only open up a hysterical fielding of questions Amber wasn't ready—or in the mood—to answer.

She waited until the waitress set her water glass in front of her, and then they ordered their lunch. Knowing how her mother watched every calorie she consumed, Amber chose a grilled chicken salad.

"I forgot to set the alarm on my phone. But I had plenty of time to run through my program, so it worked out fine. I'm sorry I missed your calls and worried you, though."

That seemed to settle her mother, because the barrage of questions and accusations ceased. "So you won a gold medal, finally."

Amber smiled. "Yes, it was a thrilling competition. We were all rooting for each other. The team was so excited to win the medal."

Her mother nodded. "Yes, but it is a team medal, so not as good as an individual one."

Gee, Mom, how about an "I'm so proud of you" or "You did great"? Instead, she got the typical "That's not quite good enough, Amber."

A biting retort sat on the tip of her tongue, just waiting to fall out of her mouth.

Amber swallowed it instead of spitting it out. The taste was bitter, as always. She washed it down with a sip of lemon water.

"How's Dad?" Amber asked.

"He's very busy, as usual. Right now he's in Boston meeting with one of his biggest clients. He said to tell you he'd try to be here by the time you skate your program."

Amber ignored the twinge of disappointment. "He'd try? But he's going to make it, right?"

Her mother shrugged. "He said he'd try. You know how busy your father is, Amber. But I'm here. I'm always here."

She reached across the table to squeeze her mother's hand. "Yes, you are. Thank you for that."

Her mother looked surprised by the gesture. "You're welcome. Now tell me what you've been up to."

"I'm roommates with Lisa Peterson again."

"Really? That's unusual."

"Not really. Lisa made arrangements for it to happen."

Her mother frowned. "I didn't know she had that kind of pull."

Amber laughed. "I don't know what kind of pull you need as far as putting roommates together, but I love Lisa, so I'm glad we're roomies."

"Hmm," her mother said.

Amber had no idea what that meant. "Anyway, we've been hanging out in groups. I've made friends with so many of my fellow figure skaters."

"Oh, Amber, you know I don't think that's a good idea."

She sighed. "Why, Mom? Why isn't that a good idea? How could me making friends with other skaters possibly hurt the way I skate?"

"It clouds your perspective, takes away your competitive edge."

"That's such a load of bullshit."

"Amber Sloane. You will not speak to me that way."

Her first instinct was to take it back, but she had to start acting like an adult, and it was high time her mother stop treating her like a child. "Come on, Mom. I've made friends with a seventeen-year-old who's my teammate. Tell me how me being friendly with her, or with pairs skaters and male individual skaters, could possibly affect my competitive edge?"

Their waitress brought their lunch, so her mother waited before she answered. She looked around the restaurant, as if there were someone here who could possibly be interested in what she had to say. Amber wanted to roll her eyes but she held back, figuring she'd already pushed her mother's buttons enough.

Her mom leaned forward and whispered. "First, because that level of friendliness relaxes you instead of you constantly being on your toes. Second, you could lose your focus. Instead of seeing these fellow skaters as competitors, you view them as your friends. And because they're your friends, you might not want to beat them on the ice. It reduces your edge."

Amber stared at her mother for a few seconds. "That's the most ridiculous thing I've ever heard. We all want to win a gold medal. How could you possibly think that hanging out with these people could affect my performance on the ice?"

Her mother bit into her sandwich, chewed then swallowed.

"Because I've seen it happen. Not in skating, but in dance. You have a group who go out together, get friendly, and all of a sudden they don't work as hard as they once did because they didn't hold themselves separate from their competition. Or maybe they heard so-and-so's sob story about how if they don't win it will affect their lives in a negative way, and subconsciously it causes them to alter their own performance."

Amber laid her fork down. "You mean someone from another country might be punished if they don't win gold, and that could affect my performance because I'm worried for their future?"

"Yes. That exactly."

"Mom. Come on. That's not going to happen. First off, no one has said anything like that to me, and second, even if they did, I have to skate for myself, not anyone else."

"I'm glad to hear you say that, but still, there's a good reason I never wanted you to get close to other skaters."

Amber pushed the lettuce around on her plate. "Yeah, you never wanted me to have any friends."

Her mother gave her a critical look. "Do you really think that was the reason?"

She lifted her gaze to her mother. "I was lonely. My entire life, I've been lonely, Mom. I'm tired of not having any friends. This competition, I have friends and I like it."

Her mother's hard stare continued. "And it's already affecting you. You were late for practice today."

She hated to admit her mom might have a point. She was late today, because she'd been out playing with Will last night. She *had* lost focus at a critical time in her performance schedule. But she'd never admit that to her mother.

She knew what she had to do, and she'd make sure to take care of the focus part.

It wouldn't stop her from having friends, though.

"I've got it under control, Mom."

"We'll see, Amber. Just don't expect your father and I to continue to support your career if you're not willing to give one hundred percent of your time to it."

And now it was time for threats. She was so tired of the threats. She'd heard them for years, knew it was another method her mother used to control her. She gave her a direct stare, refusing to be cowed into submission any longer. "I'll continue to give it everything I have, just like I've always done. You and Dad do what you have to do."

She got up and came around the table, kissing her mother on the cheek again. "Thanks for lunch. I'll see you again soon."

She put on her coat on the way out the door, slid on her beanie and her gloves and headed back toward the village.

She was halfway there when the trembling started.

What had she done? She was so fucked.

That had been a first. She'd never once stood up to her mother. Her mother had always been her confidant, the person she'd gone to in times of crisis. Family was all she had and she might have just screwed that up.

She wasn't brave. She was dependent on her parents, had no source of income and had just basically told her mother to go fuck herself.

Oh, God. That had been so incredibly stupid. Her breathing increased, then a wave of dizziness and nausea swept over her and she could barely feel her limbs. She was cold and hot at the same time.

Her heart rate skyrocketed. She wasn't going to be able to make it back to the village.

She stopped and sat on a nearby bench, realizing she was having a panic attack. She stared straight ahead, blocking out everything around her. She forced her breathing to slow, to draw deep, even breaths.

Okay, Amber, what to do, what to do.

She didn't know who to turn to.

Yes, she did.

She pulled her phone out of her pocket and found herself sending the text message, despite her better judgement, despite her resolve to focus, to steer clear.

It didn't matter. Not right now. She didn't care. She needed him.

The reply came instantly. When she could manage to breathe evenly again, she stood and started walking. When she arrived back at the village, Will was in the main lobby waiting for her.

He took her hand, concern etched on his face. "What's wrong? You're pale. Are you sick?"

She shook her head. "I had lunch with my mother."

"That must have been some lunch. Wanna talk about it?"

She shook her head. "No. I just need . . ."

The sentence trailed off. She didn't know what she needed. Other than comfort and strong arms around her.

"Come on."

She felt a strong solid arm encircling her waist. He tugged her along to his building, and hit the elevator button. She gripped the hand holding onto her and held on.

She felt like she was having a weird out-of-body experience, like she was floating above the clouds. She still felt weak, like she wanted to slide down the wall of the elevator and pass out.

Until the squeeze of Will's hand on hers brought her back to reality.

"Almost there," he said.

She barely registered his words as he led her from the elevator down the hall to his room. He slid the key card in and opened the door, then pulled her inside. She went inside, followed him to his room. He undid her parka, took off her beanie and gloves, then laid her on the bed.

He followed her there and pulled her into his arms.

She listened to the sound of Will's heartbeat. Strong and steady. That's what she needed. That and the way he smoothed his hand down her arms.

"It's okay," he said. "You're gonna be okay."

She wanted to believe that. She closed her eyes, willing everything to be okay.

She must have drifted off, because she woke up to the feel of strong hands stroking down her back. Not an unpleasant feeling at all. In fact, she felt much more relaxed than she had when Will had taken her to his apartment. She nestled into his chest, breathing in his male scent. There was something comforting and strong about the smell of a man, so potent and powerful, and one hell of a turn-on, too.

She lifted her head and looked up at him. "Thank you."

"You know, it's not a hardship to have a beautiful woman asleep in my bed."

Her lips curved. "A hot mess of a woman who fell apart and then passed out in your bed."

He shrugged, then sifted her hair through his fingers. "You had a bad day. Everyone's entitled to a bad day."

"That's an understatement. I totally wigged out about my mother."

"Feel better now?"

"I do. Thank you. I just needed to fall apart somewhere, I guess."

"Thanks for choosing me."

She rolled over onto her stomach. "Funny thing about that. I had another incident earlier today."

"You have had a bad day. Tell me about it."

"I was late for practice, so I didn't warm up. And then when I did my first jump, I felt a twinge in my hamstring. I couldn't even finish practice."

He sat up and frowned as he looked down at her. "No shit? Are you okay?"

She sat up as well, crossing her legs over each other. "I'm fine. My trainer massaged my leg after I got off the ice, and then I was allowed to run through my program. My leg is fine."

He swept his fingers over her hair. "Jesus, babe. I'm so sorry. I should have never suggested we spend the night down the mountain when you had an early practice. That's on me."

She felt better hearing him take responsibility, and hearing his concern was like a balm to her tortured senses. "Thank you. But I'm really okay. At least now I am. I totally freaked when I thought I wouldn't be able to perform. I actually—well, let's just say your name entered my mind, and I had all these thoughts about how I shouldn't be having fun—or sex—when competition is looming so close. I blamed myself and I blamed you. It wasn't a pretty thought process."

"I see. And then you had lunch with your mother, which just made things worse."

"Yes. She was upset, because I was late for practice. Oh, and that I have friends I've been hanging out with."

He frowned. "Having friends is bad?"

"To her it is. She told me I'll lose my edge." She looked down at her fingers, then back at him. "I didn't tell her about you."

"I don't think you have to tell your mother everything. But that's up to you, Amber."

She was glad he understood. "I didn't want you to think I was trying to hide anything, or that I was ashamed of what you and I have going on."

He leaned over and brushed his lips across hers. "You wanna know what I think?"

"Sure."

"I think you can choose to say or do whatever makes you happy. Being here and competing comes with enough stress. I'm not here to add to that."

Relief washed over her. "You know what?"

"What?"

"Despite my freak-out earlier, which was totally unwarranted, you are the person who is least likely to add to my stress level. Obviously the fact that you were the first person I texted when I was having a meltdown means that you're the one person here I know I can count on." She reached for his hand. "Which I hope doesn't cause you to have a meltdown, because I don't mean that in a 'Let's get married and have ten babies' kind of way."

He laughed. "I didn't take it that way. I'm glad you texted me."

She climbed onto his lap and wrapped her legs around his hips. "I feel the need to properly thank you."

He rubbed his hands over her thighs. "Totally unnecessary, but I feel I should tell you that I know many different ways to reduce stress."

"Is that right? Do tell."

"I'd rather show."

He cupped her face in his hands and kissed her. It was a gentle kiss, and she knew he was going easy on her because she'd utterly fallen apart on him earlier. But she wasn't fragile and she needed him to know that, so she was the one to deepen the kiss, to slide her tongue between his teeth to search out his.

He groaned and wrapped his arms around her back, bringing her body more closely aligned with his. The contact of their bodies touching was electrifying, igniting a fire inside of her.

His lips burned a path down her neck and across her collarbone. She tilted her head back, wanting more. He gave her more by raising her shirt, his fingers blazing a hot trail along her back.

There was something about Will's touch on her skin that sent her libido into overdrive. Even the barest slide of his fingertip along her skin was like a lightning rod on her nerve endings.

He leaned back. "What do you do to your skin to make it feel like this?"

"Like what?"

"I don't know. Like sliding my hands through soft water, or melted butter."

She shuddered as he moved his hands upward, teasing her back with the barest strokes of his fingertips. It was warm in the room, but chill bumps broke out on her skin.

It wasn't like she'd never been touched before. She might have been a virgin before she'd had sex with Will, but she'd made out with guys. She'd never felt this undeniable zing of attraction like she did with Will. All he had to do was look at her and she felt his gaze like a caress all over her body.

Like now, when he raised her shirt over her head, then raked his gaze over her body. It wasn't like he was ogling her boobs or anything. He looked at her neck, leaning in to press a kiss at the hollow of her throat. She felt her blood pulsing against his lips, her heart pumping a fast beat so incongruent to the gentle licks he laid across her skin.

He drew her bra strap down, raking his teeth across her shoulder. He held her, sliding her off his lap and rolling her back onto the mattress, following her so he was above her. Then he moved down and kissed the swell of her breast before pulling the cup of her bra away to capture one of her nipples in his mouth.

Everything seemed to happen in slow motion, as if he had all the time in the world to explore her body. He sucked and licked her nipple until she felt each pull all the way to her pussy. She was panting, needy and ready to feel the length of him inside of her.

But Will seemed to have other ideas, because he left her like that and glided smoothly down her body, removing her pants and underwear.

"Which leg?" he asked.

She lifted her head. "What?"

"Which one did you hurt today?"

"Oh. The right one."

He lifted her leg and slowly massaged her foot, then made his way to her calf, taking his time to gently work each muscle. He laid her leg over his shoulder and started massaging her hamstring as if he knew what the hell he was doing. Not too hard, not too gently, but with authority.

It was kind of like nirvana, because while it was like getting an actual massage, she was naked, Will was a man she was having sex with, and it felt great to have that twingy muscle massaged, but it was also incredibly sensual.

"You don't have to do that."

His lips curved in a way that made her want to jump on his cock and rock against him until she stopped aching, until she came— hard.

"Relax, babe," he said. "Let me do this for you."

She lay back on the bed and closed her eyes, giving herself up to the magical sensations his touch evoked. She'd never realized how erogenous her hamstrings were.

In truth, her hamstrings were not erogenous zones at all. It was just that Will was touching her and he could probably massage her elbows and she'd want to have an orgasm.

She let her body go lax, every muscle completely relaxed. Until he moved from her hamstring to her inner thigh, using the same gentle motions. And as he inched closer to her pussy, she tensed, needing him to use his talented fingers to get her off.

She desperately wanted an orgasm.

"Relax," he said, rubbing her inner thigh with his fingers. "I'll get you there."

Then he cupped her and used the heel of his hand to glide over her sex. She lifted, driving her pussy against his ever-moving fingers.

She was already so close, so charged up, and Will had found her clit with his thumb. It didn't take her long to hit her climax. She let out a moan as she released, shuddering against his hand.

He got up on his knees and took off his shirt, then sat and wriggled out of his jeans. He rolled over and pulled a condom from the nightstand, put the condom on and came back to her, lifting her leg as he slid inside of her.

She gasped, still shuddering from the aftereffects of that amazing orgasm. Now he filled her, sliding in and out of her with slow, easy thrusts that made her quiver, made her body clench around him in a fierce show of possession.

"Oh, fuck, yeah," he said, surging against her.

"I feel that, Will. When you grind against me like that? Oh, God, it's so good."

He lifted up on his hands, looking down at her. "You're so tight, so hot, squeezing my cock and making me want to come. I love fucking you, Amber. Being inside of you is like nothing I've ever felt before."

His words sent her reeling, and when he took her mouth in a searing kiss, it made her senses go haywire. She was wrapped up by him—in him—every part of her under sensual assault. Sweat beaded down his chest. She snaked her fingertips along that sweat line and over his abs, watching them clench in response.

The scent of sex filled the air, an aphrodisiac sweeter than any cologne she'd ever worn. She breathed in its perfume, letting it fuel her senses. His body moving against hers was an agonizingly sweet sensation, leading her ever closer to the orgasm she needed.

"I'm gonna make you come, Amber," he said, using his fingers to brush across her nipples. "And then I'm gonna come hard inside of you."

Every word that spilled from his delicious lips was a tantalizing tease, a promise of how good this was going to be when she came.

She felt as if she was riding a rollercoaster, taking that first exciting climb upward, and then hovering at the top, suspended, just waiting for that moment when she took that thrilling, death-defying fall.

Will's face loomed above her—his features tight, fueled by passion, urging her to continue the climb.

Almost there. So . . . close.

She was on the precipice. Right at the top, ever so close to the drop.

And then she fell. She gripped Will's arms and arched against him, crying out in unintelligible words as she came. She rocked hard against him, shuddering and trembling as her orgasm rocked her world in one brain-blasting wild ride.

Will went with her, gripping her buttocks in a tight hold, shuddering against her as they both went on the ride together.

She felt like she was spinning out of control, her climax continuing as he thrust over and over inside of her until she barely remembered her own name.

She finally caught her breath, swept her fingers over Will's sweat-laden back and reveled in the languor. She slid her foot over his calf, certain she'd never be able to move again.

Holy shit that had been amazing.

"Yum," she said.

"Good?" he asked.

"So good I think my limbs have liquefied. You're like magic."

He let out a soft laugh, then rolled over onto his back. "I think you bring out the best in me. And for the record, I might not be able to move for the next hour."

She shifted onto her side to face him. "I don't have anywhere I have to be until tomorrow."

"Neither do I." He turned to look at her. "Though I'm getting hungry."

"We'll have to do something about that. We need to replenish your reserves."

"Yeah? Planning to use me again?"

"Oh, definitely. I might get stressed again, and I skate tomorrow."

He rolled over to look at her, circling her hip with his finger. "Then we'll need you relaxed."

"Very relaxed."

"Did I mention I can help with that?"

She grinned.

TWENTY

SWEAT POURED DOWN WILL'S FACE. HE SHUFFLED HIS stick back and forth from one hand to the other, ready for the face-off.

They were deep in the third period, tied two to two against Russia. After beating Switzerland two days ago and Sweden yesterday, they only had to win against Russia and they'd make it to the quarterfinals.

This team was on fire. There was no way they were going to lose. Their face-off was near the Russian goal. Will was determined they'd stay down there. The clock was ticking down and the last thing he wanted was to go into overtime.

Oster got the puck and Will skated to the goal. Hogan was there to accept the pass.

He took a shot, and the goalie blocked it, sending it back around behind the goal.

Will chased it, along with Ivan Petrov. Petrov was his teammate on the Ice, but during this game they were opponents. Weird as fuck, but they both knew going into this they'd be battling each other. They wrestled for it against the boards and Will came up with the puck, sending it sliding along the side toward a waiting Drew.

Drew passed it off to Oster, who shot it to Will. Will hustled with Ivan behind the goal. Petrov slammed him into the boards, hard. Their sticks battled and so did their bodies. Ivan jabbed his elbow into Will's ribs, causing him to suck in a hard breath. That would hurt later, but for now, he wanted that fucking puck.

He won the battle, hearing Ivan's curse. It was in Russian, but it wasn't the first time he'd heard it. Adrenaline pumping, he knew he'd only have a matter of seconds to hustle that puck to the goal. He skated those few feet as fast as he could, seeing Hogan right in position. He shot the puck to him, and Hogan slapped it with his stick.

The only thing Drew saw was the lamp light above the net. He raised his stick and yelled as loud as he could. The crowd erupted with cheers—and some groans, too.

Drew made his way over to Will.

"Hell of a pass, man," Drew said.

"And you were right there." Will patted Drew on the helmet, then glanced at the clock. A little over a minute left.

At the face-off, the US took the puck down to Russia's end. Will took a hard shot at the goal, but Russia's goalie defended. Russia moved it forward, but the US defenders and their goalie held solid until the buzzer.

They'd won. It was a tough damn battle, but they were moving into the quarterfinals.

Will was exhausted, sweating and damn satisfied. He was as excited as he'd ever been, but he tried to button that up. They had a couple more games to win yet.

They lined up to shake hands with the Russian team. When Will got to Ivan, he brought him close, touching his head to Ivan's.

"Great game, Ivan."

Ivan hugged him. "Fuck off, Madigan."

But Ivan slanted a grudging smile at him. Will grinned back.

Ivan would be okay. He was mad as hell, but he'd be fine. If Will had lost, he'd be pissed off, too. He understood.

They hit the locker room and everyone cleaned up while chatting each other up about the victory.

"Two more and then we're in the medals," Drew said, grabbing his towel after he turned the shower off. He stepped out of the shower and wrapped a towel around his waist, standing in front of Will, who was just finishing up his shower. "I gotta call Carolina. She's probably freaking out."

"Yeah, my parents are likely going crazy right now, along with everyone at the bar." It would be good for the bar's business, and Will was happy about that. He made a mental note to call his parents.

After he got dressed, he pulled his phone out of his bag. There were text messages from his brother and his dad. And one from Amber, who told him she was at the arena along with Lisa and Blake and that everyone around them had gone crazy after that last goal. She said they all wanted to go out for lunch to celebrate his win. He sent Amber a quick message.

Gotta call my parents. Tell me where to meet you.

He pushed the button for his mom's cell phone number, since she always answered, whereas his dad would often ignore his cell if he was busy. His mom picked up on the first ring.

"Will. You were amazing. We all watched here at the bar."

Even though the game had taken place in the morning Vancouver time, he knew his parents had opened the bar early, his mom most likely providing nonalcoholic drinks for the typical bar crowd.

"Thanks, Mom. It was an exciting game."

"We're all so proud of you. We even let Ethan leave school early to watch your game. He's off at hockey practice now, no doubt celebrating with all his teammates. He said he'd call you later."

Will grinned, imagining how excited his brother must be about the games. "Okay, I'll look forward to his call. Where's Dad?"

"Entertaining everyone who crowded in to watch your game this morning. I made muffins and we served juice and coffee and tea and sodas."

He grinned. He'd called that one. "That's great, Mom. I gotta run. Tell Dad I'll talk to him later."

"Okay. Love you."

"Love you, too, Mom."

He hung up and realized how much he missed his family. He saw them a lot during the off-season, but during hockey season he was often playing home games or traveling. Whenever the Ice played Chicago, it was great because he could visit home.

It didn't matter where he lived or where he'd ultimately end up. Chicago would always be home to him. As long as his family lived there, that's where home was.

He got dressed and headed over to the main building where Amber told him she'd meet him. He found her, along with Lisa and Blake, in the games room, which had everything from pool tables to big-screen TVs, to table tennis to air hockey to video game machines. There was also plenty of seating to just sit back and chill with friends. It was like the arcade of Will's dreams, and much more.

He made his way to the table where they were sitting and slid into the chair next to Amber.

When she saw him, she smiled.

"Will." She put her hand behind his neck and pulled him close for a kiss. "Great game today."

"Yeah, we really enjoyed it," Lisa said. "Thanks for not sucking."

"Good game, buddy," Blake said.

"Thanks. It was tight. Russia was a good opponent, but we hung in there."

Lisa sat back in her chair. "They were okay. You haven't played Canada yet. We're formidable."

Will grinned at her. "We'll see."

"So now what?" Blake asked. "You move to the next round?"

Will nodded. "We're in the quarterfinals. We wait for the qualification round, where the teams that have lost play each other again. That'll happen tomorrow. Then we play one of those teams and once we beat them, we'll move on to the semifinals."

Amber rubbed her hand over his arm. "I like that confidence."

"Gotta be confident that we'll win."

"Canada's in the same position," Lisa said. "Maybe you'll meet up with them in the semis."

"Or the finals," Will said.

Lisa put her hand to her chest. "Oh, God, I don't know if my heart could handle that."

"Mine, either," Amber said. "But it would be the best thing, wouldn't it? Your country and ours, in the hockey finals?"

"It would be. Let's wish for that."

"Hey," Will said. "No wishing. Talent will get us there. Or at least it'll get the US team there. I don't know about your losers."

Lisa laughed. "Some of my 'losers,' as you call them, are your teammates."

"True. Like I said . . . losers."

"I'm telling McCaffery you said that," Lisa said.

"Go ahead."

Amber looked over at Lisa. "Boys."

"Right?"

"When do you compete, Lisa?" Will asked.

"Tomorrow."

"I'll be there, for sure."

"Me, too," Amber said. "I can't wait to watch you."

"We should meet up so we can all sit together," Blake said.

Lisa told them what time she was slotted to compete, so they made plans to get together an hour before.

"I don't know about the rest of you," Will said, "but skating my ass off works up an appetite. Let's grab some food."

Blake was skiing later, which meant they needed to stay close to the slopes, so they headed into the dining room to eat.

Will was craving something substantial, and even though it was still early, he ordered a sirloin with potatoes and asparagus, along with apple pie and ice cream.

When he met everyone back at their table, Lisa looked over at his plate. "Burn some calories today?"

"By the end of the game it felt like a million calories. I was out of juice."

"It never showed," Blake said, as he sliced into his chicken breast. "You carved it up like a beast out there."

"Or a mad dog." Amber gave him a knowing smile.

Will shot her a grin as he was chewing. After he swallowed, he said, "Now you're getting it."

"Hey, you gotta give it your all when you're competing," Blake said. "You leave nothing at the end. If you do, you'll live with regrets."

Will took a sip of his iced tea and nodded at Blake. "Exactly. I play every game as if it's our last one. We have to push hard to make it to the next game. Otherwise, how will we make it to the last one?"

"I've never pushed as hard in my life as I've done here," Blake said. "Knowing how good my competition is, I know I have to give it more than I ever have before. You train and train for this for years, and then you stand there and wait for your turn and you watch your competitors, and goddamn, they're good. Like, really fucking good."

Lisa wrapped her fingers around Blake's upper arm. "You're just as good, better in fact. You have to believe that."

"Yeah." Blake nodded, then looked down at his plate and continued to eat.

Will knew it was competition jitters talking, that Blake had that mindset they all sometimes got before a game or a competition, especially when you knew you were facing an uphill battle against a competitor who might be better than you.

There wasn't anything Will or any of them could say to Blake to pump him up. That fire to win had to come from within. You either had it or you didn't.

Will didn't know Blake well enough to know if he had it within himself. He hoped so. He liked the guy. He really liked Lisa, and Lisa was a strong competitor. He knew she'd give it her all. He hoped she'd found someone who had that same fire.

Because the one thing he did know was you couldn't make a relationship work with someone who didn't understand that constant edge you lived on, where competition was fierce and some days you were so tight with nerves that even the slightest nudge could send you over. Someone who competed at that same high level would know to leave you the hell alone because you needed time to think, to get yourself mentally prepared for a game.

Amber was one of those people who understood. They'd been together last night, but she'd left his room early, kissed him and told him he had a game today, that he needed his sleep, and he needed prep time this morning to get game ready. He'd actually been the one to argue with her. He'd wanted to keep her in his bed last night.

She'd been the one to know better.

She'd been right. As soon as she'd left he'd conked out and slept well.

After Blake finished eating, he had to leave to get ready.

"Good luck, man," Will said.

"We'll be there to cheer you on," Amber said.

"Thanks."

"I'll be right back," Lisa said. She got up and walked out with Blake.

"He's nervous," Amber said.

"Yeah. A little bit of healthy anxiety isn't a bad thing, as long as it doesn't affect his ability to get the job done as he heads down the slopes."

AMBER FINISHED THE LAST OF HER SALAD, THEN LAID her plate on top of everyone else's. "I worry he's fixated more on his competitors."

"I thought about that, too. Let's just hope he's got his eye on them, knowing they're the ones to beat, rather than being intimidated by them."

Amber couldn't agree more.

Lisa rejoined them and took a sip of her water.

"Is he okay?" Amber asked.

Lisa nodded. "He's going to be fine. He's nervous. The giant slalom is going to be tough for him. He said he's the least confident in this event. He's never placed well in it before, but I know he can handle it. He's practiced hard and he's done very well the past year in competitions. The thing is, there are two Austrians who are just killer at it, along with one of his friends from Norway who won the gold last time."

"Then we'll just have to make sure to cheer extra loud for him," Amber said.

"All he can do is his best out there," Will said. "If he does that, he should be satisfied."

Lisa nodded, then leaned back in the chair. "I just want him to do well. And, like you said, I want him to be satisfied with his standing at the end."

Will squeezed her hand. "Honey, he won't be satisfied unless he's standing at the podium with a gold medal. You're a competitive athlete. You know how it is."

She sighed. "I know. We're either in first or we suck."

Amber laughed. "This is true. Though I've learned to love my bronze and silver medals."

"Hey, I have a few of those myself," Lisa said. "But there's nothing like gold."

Will lifted his glass of water. "To gold."

They both lifted their glasses and clinked with his. "To gold."

TWENTY-ONE

AMBER FINISHED HER PRACTICE FEELING SOLID ABOUT her performance tonight. She wasn't nervous, she knew her short program routine was solid. She lingered long enough to watch Tia go through her practice.

Tia's jumps were on the mark. She would do well as long as she kept her nervousness in check.

Amber checked her phone. She had just enough time to change and head over to the other ice arena for Will's game.

It had been nonstop competitions the past few days, and she'd loved every minute of it. After Blake had won bronze in the slalom, surprising even himself, they'd celebrated late into the night. Fortunately, her practice hadn't been until ten the next morning, because she'd been exhausted. Blake had been so shocked to medal he'd cried, then Lisa had cried. Then Amber had teared up, and Will had laughed at them. But she knew Will had been stoked for

Blake, because he'd fist pumped and shouted as loud as anyone when Blake's time had come up on the boards.

The next day, Lisa competed in the slopestyle event. She'd won the bronze and one of her Canadian teammates had won the gold. It had been another crazy celebration, but at least Lisa had competed in the afternoon. It had been a bright sunny day and they'd thrown snowballs at each other outside.

It had been a fun couple of days, and Amber was having the time of her life.

Now she hurried over to the other ice arena. She was meeting Lisa there, along with Sergei, Brandon, Telisa and Robbie, who had also finished their skating practices.

She got a text from Telisa, who told her they'd already gotten seats at the arena and where they were located. She sent a quick text back to let Telisa know she was on her way.

Her phone buzzed. It was her mother. As she walked, she punched the button.

"Hi, Mom."

"Amber, how are you feeling about your performance tonight?"

"I'm feeling great."

"Are you resting? Where are you right now? We should have lunch together."

"I'm sorry, Mom, but I'm headed to a hockey game. Maybe later?"

The silence on the other end of the line meant her mother wasn't happy with her answer. She should have told her she was napping.

"Now would be better, and why would you go to a hockey game when you have a competition tonight?"

"Because the hot guy I'm having sex with is playing" probably wasn't the answer her mother wanted to hear. "I like hockey."

"Since when?"

She'd always loved hockey. It was unfortunate her mother didn't know anything about her interests other than figure skating. "I have to go, Mom. How about I call you after the game?"

"I'm at the event center. I can meet you at the game."

"I'm . . . I'm with friends, Mom."

Another pregnant pause. "Great. I'll meet your friends. Text me your location and I'll meet you there."

With a sigh, she said, "Fine. I'll text you the details and see you soon."

She hung up. This wasn't going to go well.

When she got to the arena, she found the seats. Fortunately, there was an extra one available where they were sitting.

"You all, my mom is here and she wants to come to the game."

"Great," Lisa said. "We've got an extra seat. Did you text her our location?"

"Not yet. Are you sure you're okay with this?"

"Why wouldn't we be?" Telisa asked. "It's great that your mom is here. And the game hasn't started yet. They're cleaning the ice now."

Amber sighed. "Okay." She texted her mom the seat location, wishing her mother had . . . gone shopping or something.

She instantly felt like the worst daughter ever, that knot of guilt forming in her stomach. Her mother had come here for her. She should be spending time with her.

So why did half of her feel resentful, and the other half of her feel guilty?

"What's wrong?" Brandon asked, laying his hand over hers.

"My mother is coming to the game to sit with us." Amber shot him a helpless look.

Brandon nodded. "Say no more. She probably expects you to be taking a nap or something. My mother has already called me three times today, asking me what I ate for breakfast and what time I went to bed last night, and has double-checked with me four times about the time of my performance so *I* don't forget what time I go on."

That actually made Amber feel better. "Oh, so we have the same mother."

Brandon laughed. "Apparently."

Sergei leaned forward. "I have the same mother. She sends me e-mails with lists of things I'm supposed to do before a performance. One: Get sleep. Two: Eat big breakfast. Three: No boyfriends. Four: No boyfriends. Five: Shoulders back, chin up. As if I forget how to skate."

"You duplicated three and four," Brandon said.

"No. She thinks boyfriends are distracting, so she makes sure to put it twice so I don't forget."

Amber sent a warm smile to Sergei. "Well, boyfriends *can* be distracting."

Sergei leaned into Brandon. "Also good motivation to skate well so your boyfriend thinks you're hot."

"This guy already thinks you're hot," Brandon said.

"I will still skate well and win a gold medal."

"You do realize we're competing against each other," Brandon said.

"Yes. That's hot, too. You're very good. I will still win a gold medal."

Brandon grinned and looked over at Amber. "I'm going to kick his ass on the ice. He's good, but he'll win silver."

"You keep thinking that, but you will be mesmerized by my amazing eyes and will forget to do a double axel. Big shame for you."

Amber laughed. "I love you two together."

Brandon laid a sweet smile on Sergei. "So do we."

Amber turned her attention to the ice, where the US team had come out to warm up. She zeroed in on Will's number-seventeen jersey.

He skated with such ease, his skates an extension of the ice.

"He's so fast," she said to Lisa, watching him go after a puck one of his teammates shot. "He's like a rabid dog chasing a rabbit."

"Hence the moniker," she said.

Amber grinned. "It definitely fits him."

"Fits who?"

Amber's head shot up at the sound of her mother's voice. She stood. "Oh, hi, Mom."

"Who are you talking about?"

"We're talking about how great the US hockey team is. Mom, let me introduce you to all my friends."

She made introductions, then got her mother situated.

"Game hasn't started yet."

Her mother looked her over. "You seem nervous."

Amber tucked her hair behind her ears. "I'm not."

"See, I told you that you should be resting. Instead, you're at this hockey game, and these games are all hyped up and adrenaline fueled, which will only amp up your anxiety level. This is not a good idea."

"I'm fine, Mom."

"You should be napping."

"Napping would be inappropriate at the hockey arena."

Her mother leaned back and gave her a look that Amber was oh so familiar with. "Are you sassing me?"

She absolutely was. "No ma'am."

Fortunately, the announcer came on and the game was about to start, so the back-and-forth with her mother was called to a halt.

Amber snuck a glance at Brandon, who smothered a smile.

Yeah, laugh it up, funny boy. Just wait until I meet your mother.

From the start of the game against Finland, it was nonstop

action. Amber leaned forward in her seat, trying to keep her eye on both the puck and Will.

The game went scoreless through the first period. In the second, the action heated up. When the US went up one player on a power play after a high-sticking penalty, Amber felt really good about the US's chance to score.

Eddie passed the puck to Will and he strung it along the ice, then passed it to Drew. Drew and the Finland defender fought for it. In the meantime, Will had made his way toward the goal.

It happened lightning quick. Drew moved forward, shot the puck across the ice to a waiting Will, who delivered it into the goal before Amber even blinked.

She jumped out of her seat, her arms raised above her hands.

"Yes! Yes! Yes!" she screamed, then high-fived Brandon and Sergei before turning to look down on the ice. "That was an incredible goal, Will."

"You know this Will?" her mother asked.

Amber was grinning when she turned to her mother. "Yes, I do."

"I see. And how exactly do you know him?"

She waved her hand in dismissal. "Not now, Mom."

She was engrossed in the game, in the nonstop action as Finland took the puck and raced down to the US goal. She grabbed Brandon's arm and held tight as the US defenders fought off the attack, slicing at the puck and sending it toward their teammates, who brought it to the Finland side. Will grabbed it and skated, fast, toward the Finland goal. He passed it toward Drew who sent a shot to the goal.

Missed.

"Dammit," she said.

Finland had the puck and raced toward the other end. It went back and forth like that until the end of the second period.

Amber finally exhaled.

"We're going to need more goals," she said to Brandon, who nodded.

"That was intense," Telisa said.

"My heart is racing," Lisa said. "And Canada plays later. I don't know how I'm going to survive this."

Amber looked over at her mother, hoping she was dialed into the action. She sat, ramrod straight, staring at the game. But Amber knew she wasn't really watching. Her mother often had that look when she was deep in thought, typically making lists of Amber's infractions.

There'd be a lecture coming.

She shrugged it off, concentrating on the game when the third period started. She refused to worry about her mother right now, not when Will had the puck and was fighting off one of the defenders. The defender pushed him up against the wall and Will shoved a forearm into him, then raced away with the puck, passing it off toward Drew.

"We need another goal," Brandon said.

Amber nodded, clutching Brandon's arm as Adrian Parker passed the puck off to Will, who lined it out to a waiting Drew.

Drew shot it into the goal and the lamp lit up. It was another goal, one they really needed.

They all screamed. Amber looked at her mother, who smiled politely.

Really? What did it take to get her mom excited? How could she not be caught up in the thrill of this game?

By the third period, Finland had scored a goal, but the US had also scored again. And with the last seconds on the clock ticking down, Amber and the rest of them were holding their breath.

The game ended at three to one. They all erupted in cheers, high-fiving each other.

"That was one hell of a game," Amber said. She turned to her mother. "Did you enjoy it?"

"It was very exciting."

She resisted rolling her eyes at her mom's lack of enthusiasm. Instead, she pulled out her phone to send a congratulatory text message to Will. Since she wouldn't be able to linger to see him, she let him know how well he'd played. Hopefully, she'd see him later.

"I've gotta run," she said to her friends.

"We'll be there cheering you on tonight," Brandon said.

"Thank you."

"I have to go, Mom," she said.

Her mother gave her a polite nod, then smiled at her friends. "It was nice meeting all of you."

They all said their good-byes.

"I'll walk out with you," her mother said.

"Sure."

They headed down the steps, walking with the crowd.

"Did you enjoy the game, Mom?"

"It was good. A lot of action."

"That it was."

When they got to the bottom of the stairs and cleared the crowd, her mom stopped and turned to face her. "So who's this Will guy?"

"He's a friend. Just like all those people we sat with were my friends. And Drew, the other forward on the team, is my friend. His wife is a New York fashion designer."

Her mother didn't respond, just gave her a look like she didn't believe what she'd told her, then started walking again.

This would generally be the part where Amber would have to try and explain her relationship with Will, but she wasn't going to do that. So she kept in step with her mom.

"I assume you're heading to the village to change, and then right over to the ice arena to prep for your performance."

"Yes, that's exactly what I'm doing."

"Without any time to rest."

She stopped and turned to face her mother. "Mom, I'm not five. I don't need naptime. I'm prepared for this program tonight. And actually, going to the hockey game today took my mind off my own performance. So it's likely I'll be a lot less nervous than I would have been if I'd been pacing the apartment where I would have been not napping."

Her mother stared at her. "I see. Well, I suppose at the ripe old age of twenty-four, you know what's best for your career."

"I don't know that I do. But before you and I started arguing, I was pretty relaxed. Now I'm tense."

"So you're saying I'm causing you tension?"

"At the moment? Yes."

"I'll leave, then."

She sighed. "Mom, I don't want to argue with you or hurt your feelings. I'm just trying to get you to understand my point of view."

"I am trying. Only I . . . don't understand why everything we've worked for all these years is being jeopardized over your desire to have fun."

"Fun? So now I'm not allowed to have fun?" This was getting her nowhere except on the express train to stressland. "I've gotta go, Mom. I'll see you after the performance."

She pulled her mother into a hug, even though her mom was stiff and unyielding. But Amber had done her part. She dashed off, refusing to let her mom hold her back, or stress her out.

Or alter the way she was living her life now.

Because she was having a great time, and she didn't intend for that to change.

TWENTY-TWO

AMBER WAS MORE THAN READY FOR TONIGHT'S SHORT program. She had stretched, she felt limber and, despite her altercation with her mother earlier, she was relaxed. She just had to patiently wait for her turn. Since she was second to last, that meant she'd have to be extremely patient.

She waited with her teammates and watched the other skaters perform.

Tia would be up second, which was both good and bad. For a first-time performer like Tia, it was a good thing to skate early. Once Tia skated, she'd have that first performance out of the way and she could relax.

As Gretchen Bader performed, Tia stretched and got her skates on. Amber didn't bother her or try to give her any pep talks. Amber knew Tia was in her own head, likely mentally playing through her performance.

Tia did glance her way and Amber smiled and nodded, hoping she was giving Tia the confidence she needed.

This was the compulsory round. There were specific elements the international skating organization required of the skaters. Not only did they have to skate beautifully, but they had to meet required jump and technique elements. If you didn't score high enough in this round, you didn't have a chance in the long program.

The German skater had skated decently and received a fair score. She wasn't in contention, though. Tia was up next and she took to the ice with a bright smile and lots of applause. Hopefully that would bolster her confidence.

She took her position and began her program, going through her required elements, starting with a triple axel. Most skaters, Amber included, began with the hardest jumps first, so they could get them out of the way while their legs were still fresh.

Amber held her breath when Tia did the jump. She landed it without a bobble. She skated through and moved on to the next jump, a triple jump with connecting steps. She landed it, her form perfect.

Amber exhaled. Hardest part was over. Now she had to go through the rest of the compulsory steps.

Tia looked beautiful and confident. Her program wasn't the hardest, and she definitely lacked experience, but she should score well enough.

When she finished her performance, Amber clapped wildly for her. She saw the look of utter relief on Tia's face as she came off the ice and knew exactly how she felt. She'd gotten through it, and Amber remembered her own first performance at the international games. It had been a huge deal just to make it through the short program.

All the female skaters came over to hug her, including Amber.

"You were perfect," Amber whispered in her ear. "Well done."

Tia hugged her back. "Thank you."

She sat with her coaches in the scoring area to wait, another nerve-wracking few minutes. When her scores came up, they all cheered again. For a first-timer, they were great scores. Tia was currently in first place. She was certain Tia would enjoy those moments.

They watched a barrage of skaters, some very good, some not so good. Olena Brutka of Ukraine skated a very strong, clean program. She was always technically proficient, but Amber thought her program lacked style and beauty. Nevertheless, she scored very high.

Hua Ping of China had just finished skating and Amber watched her scores go up. Hua was also technically superior, but unlike Brutka, she had some beauty to her skating. Her scores were extremely close to Brutka's, but just above them.

Lacey Davidson from Canada was up next, and then it would be Amber's turn, so she went to limber up again. Lacey was young like Tia, so she kept an eye on her skate while she stretched.

She was very good. She and Tia would be the next generation of amazing skaters to dazzle the figure skating world.

Yegor came up to her and put his hands on her shoulders. "You will do well."

She looked back at him and smiled. "Yes, I will."

She felt calm, centered and confident. She'd worked so damn hard for this the past four years.

She laced up her skates and took several calming breaths.

She was ready.

When they announced her name, she felt that energizing jolt, the one she always felt when it was performance time. She skated to the center of the ice, got into position and waited for her music. When her music started, she felt the adrenaline rush, the thrill and excitement that it was finally time to showcase her new routine.

She started around the ice, gathering momentum, then launched into her first jump, a triple axel and triple flip.

When she stuck the landing and heard the applause, she used that as momentum to push her forward to the next jump.

The music and the crowd became part of her. This was a short program, only two minutes and forty seconds, so it would go by quickly. Before she knew it, she had completed all of her required elements and was winding into her spin and hearing the end of her music.

She finished with her arms up, her gaze turned toward the top of the arena, a huge smile on her face.

The crowd erupted into cheers and applause. She paused for a few seconds, then bowed to the audience.

That had felt so good. She had done her best, and she thought her best had been pretty perfect.

As she skated off the ice, she could only hope her best was good enough for the judges.

Her teammates surrounded her.

"You were amazing," Tia told her as she hugged her.

"Thank you."

"Your jumps were so high. And your landings were spot on. I think your scores will reflect that."

"We'll see."

As she made her way to the results area, her stomach knotted. Yegor met her there.

"You skated well," he said. "Very well."

She nodded and smiled as they waited. She was never nervous on the ice. But here, waiting for scores? The tension was nearly unbearable. If she didn't score well here, she was done.

When the scores came up, she breathed a sigh of relief. Her scores were damn good. And she was currently in first place, with only Sasha Petrova of Russia left to skate. Which meant the worst she could do after the short program would be to finish in second place.

Sasha was already on the ice warming up. And as her biggest competition, she was the one to watch.

Amber gave a short interview for television, saying she was happy with her performance and looked forward to the long program. Otherwise, her coach moved her along. Fortunately, the media didn't have a lot of access to the athletes until after they had completed their skate.

She tuned out everything except to watch Sasha's performance.

Sasha started out in an elegant pose, her arms elongated above her head. She moved like a snake, slowly slithering across the ice. As always, she was elegant and mesmerizing, falling into her jumps in a way that made the crowd gasp. Even in her short program, she enraptured the audience, and every jump was perfectly executed. Amber looked for even the tiniest flaw either in the entry or exit of her jumps, but didn't find a thing.

Damn, she was amazing.

Sasha had started strong and she finished strong. She'd done every compulsory item, plus performed an intricate dance on her skates that no doubt the judges would love.

She'd score very high on that performance.

Amber sighed. Her own skate had been extremely good.

Sasha had been better.

Yegor stood behind her. "It's only short program. Your long program is exceptional."

It wasn't like Yegor to pump up her ego like this.

She turned to face him. "Yes, it is. But Sasha is formidable."

She watched as his normally implacable expression turned to a frown.

"And I have never known you to doubt that there is anyone on the ice that you cannot defeat. So don't doubt it now. You are better than Petrova. She has weaknesses."

"Really. And what might those be?"

"Skating with confidence is always an asset. Too much confidence means you don't know how to correct if you miss something on the ice. If she bobbles even a little, she'll crumple."

Amber switched her attention to the scoreboard, where Sasha's scores had just gone up. Just as she'd expected, Sasha had scored very well. But not as high as Amber had thought. Their scores were close.

Amber was now in second place, but not so far behind she couldn't catch Sasha in the long program.

"She will have expected higher scores than that," Yegor said. "It will get into her head, allowing her to potentially make a mistake in her long program. You, on the other hand, are always realistic. You have the advantage in the long program."

She hadn't considered that. "Thank you, Yegor. I'll keep that in mind and adjust accordingly."

Yegor gave her a short nod and walked away. For him, that had been a massive pep talk.

He had no idea how much she'd needed to hear it.

TWENTY-THREE

LISA WAS WITH BLAKE AT HIS PLACE—OR AT A BAR somewhere. Amber didn't know. All she knew was that she was pumped and jazzed and loaded with adrenaline after tonight.

She'd ended up doing several more media interviews, and had a phone conversation with her mother, who'd actually told her she did well. She was pretty happy about that. Then she'd hung out a bit with Tia, who felt down after landing in sixth place after the short program. She'd reminded Tia that sixth place was damn good, and that she had a very strong long program. Amber was convinced Tia would move up in the standings because some of the other skaters weren't as strong in the long program. After they'd eaten and had a long chat, Tia felt better.

She'd also texted back and forth with Will, and they made plans to hang out later.

She really wanted to see Will.

She'd gone back to the apartment and showered, changed into

shorts and a tank top and dried her hair. When she heard the knock at the door, she hurried to answer it. She peered through the peephole to see Will outside. She opened the door and he grinned at her.

"You're one hell of a figure skater."

"Thank you. And thanks for being there to watch." She stood aside so he could come in.

"Nowhere else I'd want to be."

She closed the door behind him. When she turned around, he pulled her into his arms. She went willingly, loving the feel of his well-muscled, hard body against hers.

He buried his face in her neck. "You smell good."

"Freshly showered. I work up a sweat on the ice."

He pulled back. "Huh. Me, too."

She laughed. "Your skating is a lot different than my skating. You're a madman on the ice."

"Excuse me, but that's 'Mad Dog.'"

"Yes, that, too." She wriggled against him.

He smoothed his hands down her body. "You're still fueled, aren't you?"

She stepped away. "Yes. I can't help it. It was a good night."

"I get it. You want to go out?"

"Honestly? No. I mean, I love all our friends. But tonight I just want to be with you. I just . . . I don't know. I have all this pent-up energy."

He looked at her for a few seconds, then nodded. "I've got an idea. Give me a few minutes. I need to make a phone call."

"Okay."

He pulled out his phone and walked into the bedroom. She had no idea what was going on. When he came back, he had a satisfied smile on his face. "Get dressed, we're going out."

"Will, I—"

"Not with other people. I have a surprise. Oh, and bring your skates."

She tilted her head, confused about what was going on. "My skates?"

"Yeah. I'll be right back."

Before she could question him any further, he'd left.

That was so weird. She needed to get dressed, and bring her skates?

Where were they going?

She pulled on leggings and a sweater, then her boots, and put her skates in her bag. Will returned with his own bag.

"Ready?"

She nodded, slid on her coat and followed him out the door.

When they got outside, he took her hand and they walked outside the village. And then kept walking.

"Care to tell me where we're going?" she asked.

He turned to her and smiled. "You'll see."

When they made their way toward the ice arena, she tugged on his hand. The arena was dark, the parking lot empty.

"You do realize it's closed."

He led her toward one of the back gates where he met up with an older guy in an official international games uniform.

The guy smiled at him. "Hey, Will."

"Hi, Emile. Thanks for doing this."

"No problem." The guy nodded to her in greeting before focusing his attention back to Will. "You got an hour at most, buddy. Then the cleanup crew will be here."

"Got it. Thanks a lot."

They went inside. The lights were already on, but just over the ice rink. Will took her down to the carpeted area.

"Ready to put your skates on?"

"So, we're skating?"

"Yeah. Thought maybe you could work off some of that adrenaline on the ice."

He shrugged out of his coat, sat next to her and laced up his skates, then went onto the ice, skating backward while she finished putting her skates on. She sailed out onto the ice and he skated toward her, pulling her into his arms.

"I'm used to being on the ice alone," she said.

His hands felt warm against her back. "Not tonight. Tonight, we're pairs skating."

He skated backward, taking her with him.

"I like this," she said. "Should we cue music and do a few double axels?"

"Sure. If you'd like to see me fall on my ass."

She pushed back and took his hands, leading him this time. "Oh, come on. You're a pro on ice."

"Skating? Yeah. That fancy shit you do? Not a chance."

"Come on. I'll teach you a few simple things."

He dug in his skates. "I don't think so."

She moved into him, rubbing her body against his. "Oh, come on, Will. You're tough. Give it a try."

He gave her a suspicious glare. "I think you just want to see me fall."

Her lips twitched. "I would never want to see that. Now where is my phone again?"

"Oh, I see how it is. It's on. Show me what you got."

Will knew he was being set up, but Amber had been so wound up he wanted to get her back out on the ice, so she could burn off some of that excess energy. He hadn't expected the skating challenge, but he was game.

She showed him some basic steps like the swizzle and the cross-over, both front and back, along with the three-turn.

"You could do a lot of these since you're used to skating front and back."

"Yeah, but you do it a lot prettier than I do."

He could handle them, though he didn't have the finesse Amber did. All he could do was follow along. He felt clumsy performing some of the things that made her look graceful. A lot of what she did she made look easy.

It wasn't easy at all. It took a level of skill he didn't have.

"How do you jump?"

She crooked a smile. "First, you don't have the right skates to do jumps. You don't have the toe pick at the front of your skate to push off the ice, and without that, you could hurt yourself. But I can show you a few moves you can do without the jumps."

"Gotcha."

"How about a lunge?" she asked, then skated forward, held her arms out to her sides and leaned down with her thighs.

He skated forward and tried, already feeling his thighs burning. It was also hard to balance. He raised up and rubbed his legs. "How the hell do you do that?"

"Years of practice. Plus dance and yoga."

"In other words, you work your ass off. And your legs. Which, by the way, are gorgeous and now I know why."

"Thank you. It does take a lot of practice to perfect even the most rudimentary position."

She pulled up some speed, then moved into a spin that made him feel dizzy.

"Damn, woman."

She came over to him and put her arms around him, breathing heavily but smiling widely. "It's all about practice. Same as what you do. I'm exhausted just watching how hard you work during a hockey game. I skate for four and a half minutes, max. You're at it for several hours. That takes so much stamina."

"Yeah, but all I'm doing is pushing a puck around. You're jumping, performing complicated tricks and dancing on the ice during those four and a half minutes. That's equally as hard."

She pressed her lips to his. "Thank you for saying that. Now show me what you do."

He held his hands out. "No stick. No puck."

"So, we'll pretend."

He liked that she was so eager to play at playing hockey. "Okay. You be the offense. I'll be the defense. Skate fast and I'll defend." He pointed to the other end of the ice. "The goal you're trying to get to is on that side."

Amber crouched down, a make-believe stick in her hands, visualizing where the puck would be. Her obstacle was the big hunk of sexy man in front of her.

She mentally planned her strategy, leaned right, then dug into the ice with her skate, pushed off, and shot left, moving around him and skating for all she was worth toward the other end of the ice.

She felt Will behind her, heard the whoosh of his skates and knew he'd catch up to her in an instant. It was likely he wasn't skating to his maximum speed in order to give her an advantage. She intended to take it. She pushed harder, but suddenly he was in front of her, blocking her way. She skated to the right, toward the edge of the arena.

Will was right there, grabbing her around the waist. But instead of slamming her into the boards, he eased her there, slowing both their speeds until he had her pinned between his body and the glass.

She took a moment to catch her breath, to enjoy the feel of

having Will on the ice with her. This was home for both of them. It was where they both worked.

But now she wanted to play. She splayed her hands across his chest. "Now that you have me pinned, what do you intend to do with me?"

His hands roamed down her sides and behind her, cupping her butt. "I have a few ideas."

"You do? Care to share them?"

The heated look he gave her promised something hot. The ice felt cool around them, but she was plenty warm, nestled up against Will.

"I thought I'd start out by making you come. You're all pent up and you need a release."

She looked around. They were all lit up, bright lights showcasing the ice. "Here?"

"We're alone, Amber. Emile is the only one who knows we're here, and he's got the keys. He's also outside. No one's coming in."

"How do you know he's not coming in?"

"I know Emile. He's from Chicago and now makes his home here in Vancouver. I trust him."

If Will trusted in Emile's discretion, then so would she. She relaxed against him. "Okay, then. Back to what you had in mind."

"I've got a lot of things in mind." He caressed the nape of her neck and moved in to kiss her.

His lips were soft as they brushed across hers—the kiss easy and gentle at first. And then he pressed in, sliding his tongue along hers, ramping up that adrenaline she'd barely been able to keep at bay. Will got closer, lifting her butt to tilt her against his erection.

She was damp and excited as she rubbed against him. She couldn't believe they were grinding against each other on the ice.

But when he slid his hand between them to cup her sex, she moaned, giving up any pretense of shock or dismay at their location. All she wanted now was an orgasm.

So when he slid his hand inside her leggings, and then her panties, his rough palm making contact with eager, throbbing flesh, she widened her stance. Will had a grip on her and she had hold of him. He rubbed her sex with expert precision, using the sweep of his hand in all the right ways to take her to the edge.

She hovered, taut and expectant, waiting to fall. And then Will shocked her by dropping to his knees and dragging her leggings down.

She barely had time to say a word when his mouth was on her, his tongue hot and wicked. She felt off balance, her world tilting sideways as he licked the length of her, then put his lips over her clit and sucked.

The ice was cold, but she felt steam rising all around her as she quivered with her impending orgasm.

"Ohh, yes." She screamed out with her climax, feeling as if she was drowning in a sea of epic sensation. He let her come down gradually from that orgasm, and when she could take it again, he brought her back up, taking her so high her legs trembled.

She came again, raising her arms high to grab onto the glass for support. She panted hard as pulses of delicious pleasure shot through her.

While she was recovering from back-to-back orgasms, Will backed up, shrugged his track pants down, and pulled out his cock.

Amber breathed deeply as he pulled a condom packet from his pocket.

"Ever prepared?" she asked.

"Hell, yeah." He skated forward and slipped his hand between her legs. "I have to be ready around you. You never know when opportunity could—pop up."

She reached for his cock, sliding her hand up and down the shaft. "You've definitely popped up."

"You make me hard every time I'm around you."

Hearing Will say that made her sex convulse. "I'm ready. Let's do this."

He pressed her up against the glass. Then he bent, grabbed her butt and slid into her.

She gasped and used the toe pick of her skate to plant herself on the ice as he thrust upward. She tilted her head back against the glass, letting her body feel . . . everything.

Everything was so, so good. Since she was still wearing her pants, it forced her legs together and squeezed Will's cock, his pelvis rubbing deliciously against her clit every time he drove into her.

The ice beneath them was cold while her entire body was drenched with the heat of friction, of desire, of the wanton need to feel every thrust from Will over and over again.

She grabbed onto his shoulders, arching against him, needing more of that heated contact.

She made eye contact with him. "Ever done this before?"

"Fucking?" He teased her with a half smile, then withdrew halfway, then slowly eased into her again, making her breath catch.

She lightly teased her nails along his jaw. "No. This. On the ice."

His gaze was dark, intense. "No. Never thought about it before. Until you."

"Everything with you is a first time for me. But this—Will, this."

"Yeah, I know."

He powered into her, increasing his pace, the friction he caused every time he rubbed against her a sweet torment.

"I'm going to come," she said.

"Yeah. Make me come inside of you, Amber. Squeeze my cock and make us both come."

She was so close, and watching Will's face, the way he looked at her as he moved within her, was going to take her right over. His fingers dug into the flesh of her butt and he ground against her, sending those fierce sparks of pleasure right to her clit.

Her body quaked with the force of the orgasm that slammed into her. Will gathered her close, took her mouth in a deep, forceful kiss, then shuddered against her with his orgasm. He rocked her hard against the wall. It was wild and amazing and made her orgasm go on and on until he stilled, pressing his lips against her collarbone, breathing heavily against her.

She was glad she was pinned between Will and the wall, because she could no longer feel her legs. Will kissed her neck, her jaw and her lips, then leaned back to search her face.

"You have one hell of a smile on your face," he said.

"You do realize I've now likely had sex where no one else has."

"I don't know if no one else has ever had sex on the ice. But you're probably one of a few."

She grinned. "And here I am, still a novice."

"Babe, I wouldn't call you a novice at this." He disengaged and she righted her clothing, her legs still feeling a little wobbly. While Will left the ice for a few seconds, she pushed off the wall and skated a few rounds, trying to get feeling back in her legs. By the time he returned, she'd skated over to the gate and off the ice.

She sat and unlaced her skates, occasionally glancing over at Will to give him a grin.

"You're pretty satisfied with yourself," he said.

She slipped her skates in her bag. "How could I not be? I came three times. On the ice. I don't know that I'll ever look at an ice arena in the same way again."

He leaned over and kissed her. "Good. I've always wanted to be memorable."

She braced her hands on either side of his face. "Will Madigan, you are definitely memorable."

It was possible she had feelings for Will that went beyond just fun sex. He was exceedingly charming and amazingly handsome, not to mention creative and sexy and sweet.

Was this love? She wasn't sure she could recognize it even if it was.

She had to talk to someone about love. But who?

TWENTY-FOUR

AMBER KNEW IT WAS THE WRONG TIME TO HAVE THIS conversation. Lisa was getting ready to run the half-pipe, and she was sure her nerves were on edge. Though you couldn't tell it from the relaxed expression on her friend's face. Lisa looked as chill as ever. She was braiding her hair and talking about wearing her "lucky underwear."

"What exactly is lucky underwear?" Amber asked, taking a seat on her bed.

Lisa turned to face her. "The underwear you have on when great things happen to you." She pulled out a pair of black lacy panties and twirled them around her finger. "I met Blake wearing these. I won the World games wearing these and qualified for the international games wearing these."

Amber tilted her head, then cracked a smile. "Ah, I see. Clearly they're your lucky underwear."

"Right?" Lisa slipped them on, then resumed getting dressed.

Yes, she was definitely in a good mood.

"Have you ever been in love, Lisa?"

She straightened and looked at Amber. "If you had asked me that a few months ago, I would have said no. Today the answer is yes."

Amber felt a warmth spread all over her body at Lisa's answer. "You're in love with Blake."

"Yes."

"Tell me how you know it's love."

Lisa sat on the bed next to Amber. "I was someone who loved playing around. I liked dating different men. The thought of settling for just one was inconceivable to me. Guys are fun, you know? They're like donuts."

Amber arched a brow. "Donuts?"

"Yeah. Some days you want chocolate crème. The next day you might crave rainbow sprinkles. The day after that you might be in the mood for a maple bar. Why settle for glazed every day of your life when there's so much variety out there in your donuts?"

"Oh. Gotcha."

"But now, the idea of being with another guy just turns me off. All I want is Blake. All I think about is Blake. I want to be with him all the time, and when I'm not with him, I miss him. And that's so unlike me. As soon as I realized that, I knew I was in love with him." Lisa shrugged. "He's my favorite donut and no other donut will do for me now."

Amber laughed. "I'm so happy for you."

"Thank you, honey. I'm happy about it, too."

"Is Blake in love with you?"

"He is." She sighed. "He told me, and it was sweet and romantic, and oh, God, Amber, I'm not the mushy romantic type. What the hell has happened to me?"

So this was what it was all about. "You've fallen in love."

"I guess so. The weird thing is, I used to make fun of people like me. You know, the gushy, 'Oh, look at me I'm so in love' type. The ones who couldn't stop talking about themselves and their perfect partner. And now I am that person. It's disgusting."

Amber squeezed Lisa's hand. "You are not disgusting. It's sweet. You've found someone to have feelings for. Feelings that go beyond one night of hot sex. Someone you click with on an emotional level. Who wouldn't want to celebrate that? You deserve it, Lisa. You're one of the nicest people I've ever met. You embraced me when I was closed off, not wanting to make friends. You dragged me into your circle and made me open up and enjoy the experience of the games. You didn't have to do that and I'm so grateful. I can't think of anyone who deserves love more than you."

Lisa's eyes filled with tears. "Dammit, Amber. I have to go be a tough bitch on the half-pipe soon. And now you're making me feel all soft on the inside. How could you do this to me?"

Amber moved over to Lisa's bed and put her arm around her. "Oh, somehow I think you've got it in you to kill that half-pipe, even if you are mushy and sweet and in love."

Lisa laughed. "You're right. I do. And I will."

"Plus, you have your lucky underwear on. How could you possibly lose?"

"You are so right." Lisa stood. "Now I'm pumped. And I need to get my ass out there."

After Lisa left, Amber texted Will.

Where are you?

She went into the bathroom to put on makeup and fix her hair. Her phone buzzed so she picked it up.

Game room with the guys. You?

She texted back. In my room. Heading to watch Lisa soon. You going?

He replied quickly with, Yeah. I'll meet you at your apt. What time?

They made plans to meet, she finished getting ready and left the apartment to head downstairs.

Will walked into the lobby a few minutes after she got there. Even though she'd seen him every day for the past couple of weeks, she still got that gut punch whenever he entered a room.

"Some of the guys are coming, too," he said after he drew her close for a kiss.

"Same with several of the skaters. We should have a good crowd."

"More fun that way."

They started out the door and toward the lift that would take them up the mountain. "How was your practice today?" she asked.

"Intense. Coach worked us hard. But we're ready for tomorrow night."

"I'm so excited to watch your game."

He took her hand. "And then you skate the following night."

She inhaled and let it out. "I can't believe it's already here, that it's almost over. These two weeks have flown by. Well, almost three weeks since we both got here early."

"Yeah. Feels like I've known you forever."

It did feel like that. Maybe because they'd spent so much time together since that first night. She felt like she knew so much about Will. That probably had to do with their situation, of being together here at the games.

She wondered if it would be different if they had met under different circumstances, like at a party or through Lisa or something. And if they'd liked each other—which they would have, of course—and started dating.

But how would that even have worked with her living in Long Island and him in St. Louis? He'd already tried the long distance thing once and it had failed.

And why was she even pondering this? She already knew what

she had going on with Will was just a temporary thing that would last only for the duration of the games. Once the games were over, so were they.

That thought left her feeling decidedly unsettled.

"You're sure quiet," Will said.

She lifted her gaze. "Thinking about skating."

He smiled as they entered the lift. "Yeah, it's hard to turn that off, isn't it?"

It was hard to turn off thinking about Will—thinking about the two of them and where they were going together. But she wasn't ready to broach that subject. Things were going well between them and she intended to take it day by day.

Because she was happy and content. So why worry about the future when the right now was perfect?

She laced her fingers with Will's and laid her head on his shoulder, enjoying the ride up the mountain. The sun was a shimmering gold disk over the mountain, making the snow sparkle. Amber took a deep breath of the crisp mountain air as they reached the top. It would be a perfect night for Lisa's event.

She spotted Blake as they got to the seats. He was already surrounded by some of the hockey players and several skier friends of Lisa's. Telisa and Robbie were there, along with Rory and Tia and Brandon and Sergei.

Lisa would have a large cheering section.

They watched as all the snowboarders warmed up. They would go through qualifying first, and then as the field narrowed, semifinals, until the final six ran two rounds. In Amber's opinion, they were all good. She could barely ride down a straight ski slope on a snowboard let alone fly through the air doing the kinds of loops these talented athletes managed. As far as she was concerned, they were all winners.

Of course, that's not how it worked. There was an intricate

scoring process, much like that in figure skating. Lisa had explained the scoring to her one night four years ago when the two of them had stayed up late talking and getting to know each other. They'd shared information about each other's sports.

In the end, neither of them had understood the others' scoring process. Which wasn't a surprise since judging was always complex. She understood the scoring in figure skating, but that was it. So she'd just watch the scoreboard and see how it went, with ever-high hopes that Lisa came out on top.

The three US competitors also had very good chances to medal as well. It was going to be an exciting competition.

Amber cheered on the US team, who performed exceptionally well. One had just finished, and her loops and rotations had impressed the crowd.

"Wow," Will said as Patty Jones's score came up. "That's impressive."

Patty currently sat in first place, with Chloe Masterson, the other US competitor, in second. An Australian athlete was currently in third by the time Lisa came up for her turn.

Amber leaned forward, grasping Will's hand.

"You nervous?" he asked.

"I'm always nervous when my friends compete."

"But not when you compete."

She smiled. "No."

"Anyone ever tell you that you're a little odd?"

"All the time."

Blake stood and yelled, "We got you, Lisa! Let's do this."

The excitement was palpable. Lisa dropped in and immediately swept up into her first rotation. She flew high, did a backside 540 mute that was perfectly executed and went right into her next movement.

Amber was mesmerized watching the flips Lisa did. She was

getting huge air, landing perfectly and sweeping into the next trick without hesitation. She looked amazing, without flaw. And when she finished with a huge lift into a double cork lien—hey, she remembered some of the names—Amber held her breath when Lisa landed.

She'd executed it flawlessly and the crowd showed their appreciation with screams and applause.

Amber, Will and Blake and everyone were on their feet, yelling and clapping for her.

Now they just had to wait for her score.

When the score came up, the crowd erupted with applause. Lisa was in first place.

"Oh, my God," Amber said. "I'm so excited for her."

"That's a high score," Will said. "She fucking shredded that half-pipe."

"She did."

She'd scored so high she'd automatically qualified for the finals, which was amazing. The lower scoring competitors had to run again to qualify for the top twelve.

It was a grueling wait for the finals. Amber couldn't even imagine what it was like for Lisa to wait it out.

Blake had been unable to sit. He'd finally gotten up and moved down to where the crowds stood at the scoreboard.

"He's nervous for her," Will said.

"Yes, he is. It's sweet. You can tell he really wants her to do well."

"If I could be on the ice with you when you compete, I would be."

She leaned into him, then wrapped her arm around his. "That is so sweet. It would also be terribly distracting."

"Yeah, you'd probably crash into me while you were doing a jump."

"Which might affect my score a little."

"Or a lot."

She laughed. "Okay, so you could just sit somewhere and cheer me on instead."

He sighed. "If you insist." Then he winked at her.

She watched the end of the Swedish snowboarder's run, then turned back to Will. "Hey, if I could be on the ice with you during a hockey game, I would be. It causes me severe anxiety watching you play."

One corner of his mouth lifted. "We could sneak you out there, hand you a stick. No one would notice."

"Ha. Yeah, no one would notice the chick in the skating skirt."

"I didn't say we'd let you play in your sexy skating outfit."

She trailed her fingernail over his hand. "Oh, you think my skating outfit is sexy."

"Babe. You could be out on the ice wearing a hot dog costume and you'd still look sexy."

"I'm trying to picture myself doing a triple axel in a wiener costume."

He slanted a half grin at her. "Now I've got that picture in my head. Maybe not as sexy as I first thought."

She shoved into him. "You can't take it back now that you said it. You have to accept me as a hot dog."

With a sigh, he said, "I never thought the day would come that I'd be in a relationship with a wiener, but you are kind of irresistible."

She laughed. "That's very progressive of you, Will."

Banter completed, they watched both Americans fly through the half-pipe on their second runs. Chloe stunned with an amazing run, but it wasn't high enough to beat Lisa's score.

Oh, shit.

Amber looked over at Will, who grinned back at her.

"Lisa just won gold," Amber said.

"Hell, yeah."

Chloe's score put her in silver position and Patty had earned a bronze medal.

All in all, a stellar day at the half-pipe.

They got up and followed the crowd out of the stadium. Amber was elated for her friend. She turned to Will. "I'm going to hang out for the medal ceremony, and see if I can get anywhere near Lisa."

"Okay. The guys and I were going to go outside the village to grab a bite to eat. Do you want me to ask them to wait for you so you can go with me?"

She loved that he considered her. She shook her head. "Thank you, but that's unnecessary. You all go on and have fun."

"Okay." He drew her against him and kissed her. "I'll catch up with you later."

Now she was even more euphoric. Instead of just blowing her off, Will had thought about her before going to hang out with his friends and teammates. Her chest was filled with joy. She was sure the majority of that was for Lisa, but she couldn't help but feel that a tiny corner of it had to do with the way she felt about Will—or how she perceived he felt about her.

Since she was utterly clueless about relationships, she had no basis for comparison. But somehow what was happening between them felt right.

With a satisfied sigh, she went in search of Lisa. She had to congratulate her friend.

And commend her on her lucky underwear.

It was obvious that Amber was going to have to get herself a pair of lucky underwear.

TWENTY-FIVE

WILL TOOK A LOOK AT HIS PHONE. IT WAS ELEVEN thirty. Kind of late. He and the guys had ended up hitting a couple of clubs outside the village, just to burn off some steam before tomorrow night's game. They'd shot some pool and sat around and talked strategy.

Obviously he wasn't the only one on the team who was pent up and nervous about tomorrow's game.

Regular season games? He was chill. Even postseason didn't affect him much. He'd feel a heightened sense of anticipation, but otherwise, he could handle it.

But here they were playing for gold. It was an entirely different hockey game. They all felt that tension. Getting out tonight and letting go a little had helped. They'd met some locals, talked hockey and had a great time. It had been low-key and fun, exactly what they all needed.

Now he needed to go to bed, but he still felt that adrenaline pumping through his bloodstream. He wasn't ready to settle in yet. He knew Amber had an early practice tomorrow. So did he. He shouldn't bug her. He'd texted her a couple of times while he was out. She said she was in her room, reading a book and relaxing.

He really wanted to see her, even if it was just to say good night.

He didn't know when she'd started to matter so much to him, and tonight wasn't the night to start dissecting his feelings. The only thing that mattered was he wanted to be with her, now.

He pulled out his phone and sent the text message.

You still awake?

Hopefully, if she was asleep, she wouldn't get the message until tomorrow morning.

She answered right away. Yes. What are you doing?

He typed back: Back at the village. Hanging around outside.

She replied with: Come see me.

Happy she'd replied, he texted and told her he'd come right over. Since he'd already been on the way to her apartment building, it didn't take him long to get there. She was already downstairs, wearing her pajama bottoms and her coat.

Whenever he saw her, he felt that jolt, low in his belly. She wore her hair up, pieces of it brushing her cheek. He wanted to take that clip off and slide his hand into her hair, to feel the softness of it, to kiss her until she moaned against him.

His cock twitched as he walked through the door she'd opened for him.

Damn, he needed her. He hadn't realized how much until just now. And maybe that was just pregame stress and she was his outlet for it. He didn't have explanations for how Amber made him feel. Only that whenever he was around her, he felt a lot. And what he was feeling for her felt more than just physical.

She put her arm around him as they walked to the elevator. "How was your night? Did you have a good time?"

"Yeah. We ate, played some pool and hung out with some lo-cals and talked hockey."

"That does sound fun."

When the elevator doors closed, he turned to her. "I missed you. I tend to miss you when I'm not with you."

She looked surprised. He'd been surprised as well. He hadn't intended to say that, but the words had just fallen out. He couldn't even blame alcohol since he hadn't had a drink tonight.

She tilted her head back and studied him, and there was a look in her eyes that told him her heart was there.

"Same," she said. "Like, really, Will. The same."

The elevator doors opened and they made the short walk to her room.

"Is Lisa here?" he asked as she entered her key card.

Amber shook her head and opened the door, turning to face him. She walked backward into the room. "She's out celebrating. She and Blake went down to Vancouver to spend the night."

He shut and locked the door. "So we're alone."

She pulled off her coat, then dropped her pajama bottoms, leav-ing her in a skimpy tank top and her panties.

His dick took notice, coming to life in an instant.

"Yes, we're alone."

He dropped his coat and came toward her. "I had really in-tended to come say good night. Give you a kiss. Then leave."

She nodded, then sat on the sofa, propping her feet on the table and spreading her legs.

His cock went fully hard.

"That's probably a good idea. You have a big game tomorrow. You need your sleep."

He pulled off his shirt, toed out of his boots, then unzipped his pants and let them fall to the floor. "Yeah. I should go. After I get my kiss."

She slid her hand into her panties, and his balls quivered.

"I could use a kiss."

He stepped over the coffee table, then got down on his knees between her legs, watching as she rubbed her pussy.

"Does it feel good?" he asked.

She gave him a wicked smile. "It would feel better if you were doing this."

"Oh, I can do more than just touch you."

He peeled her underwear over her hips and down her legs, discarding them. Then he spread her legs, teasing his fingers along her inner thighs, listening to the sound of her breathing, watching the way she watched him so intently.

"I told you I came here for a kiss."

He leaned in and pressed his mouth to her sex, breathing in the musky scent of her as he licked around her satiny skin. She lifted her hips and he cupped his hands under her buttocks, lapping around her clit, easing into pleasuring her. He wanted to take her there slow and easy, with no rush, so she could enjoy every second of what he was doing to her. Because he sure as fuck enjoyed tasting her.

As she started pressing against him, he increased the pressure, giving her more direct contact.

She moaned, writhing, moving her body into the position she liked.

"Oh," she said. "Right there, Will. Put your tongue right there and suck."

He had to give Amber credit. She was a fast learner, she wasn't shy about sex and she gave instruction well. And when he found the right spot, she could come with wild abandon. He loved to watch her let go, like now, when he felt her body jerking against him and knew she was right there.

"Ohhh, yes. That's it, I'm coming."

When she came, she bucked against him, shuddering as she pushed against his mouth. He fed off the pulses as she ground against his face. There was nothing sweeter than feeling a woman come and knowing he had given her that pleasure.

He held onto her butt and gently licked her to bring her down, taking in each quake as she rode the last of her orgasm, finally settling.

He rose, shed his boxer briefs and stepped away only long enough to grab a condom. Then he was back, tugging Amber against him. He pulled the clip out of her hair, watching as the blond waves tumbled down over her shoulders. He slid his hand in her hair.

Like silk. She was so beautiful, lying there looking at him, she took his goddamn breath away.

She reached for him, wrapping her arms and legs around him. He scooped his hand under her butt, then slid into her with an easy stroke.

She tightened around him in welcome, pulsing and squeezing his cock as he moved within her. He leaned forward to tease her nipples, watching her chest rise as she silently asked for more of his touch.

"Will. I like you touching me," she said, her voice a breathless whisper. "It feels amazing. My pussy comes alive when you tweak my nipples like that."

"And when you talk dirty to me like that it makes my balls quiver and all I can think about is driving my cock hard into you."

She reached up to rake her nails down his chest. "What's stopping you? I want to feel you, Will. I want to feel you hard inside of me."

He thrust, hard, then pulled partway out and pumped back in. She gasped.

"More. More of that. Deeper, Will."

She was driving him crazy, her eyes wild with the same powerful need he experienced. He couldn't get enough of her. He wanted to crawl inside of her and never let her go, never stop this connection he felt to her.

And when he felt her contracting around his cock, he knew she was going to go off. He took her mouth in a kiss and stayed that way all through her orgasm, all through his, too, feeling her breath, her body, everything as they rocketed together and held on to each other.

He moved his mouth from her lips to her jaw to her neck, breathing in her scent. She always smelled sweet, like summer mornings when the air was fresh and the day was new and anything was possible.

Fuck. He'd just thought poetic thoughts about a woman, and his gut was all tied up with emotion.

Ah, hell. He was falling in love with Amber. He raised his head and stared down at her. She smiled up at him, that innocence and freshness always present in her eyes.

It wasn't just about sex. It had never been just about sex with her. Even from the beginning, he'd been taken by her wit and intellect and zeal for life. He'd wanted to know more about her as a person, not as just someone to play with for a limited time. And as every day had gone by, he realized he wanted to spend more and more time getting to know her.

His dad had told him he'd realized he was in love with his mom after a week.

It had been nearly three weeks. Could he trust this? Was this real?

He didn't know. All he could go by was what he felt. He'd dated a lot of women. He'd loved one. He knew what love was.

This was love.

"Do you have a cramp?"

He frowned at Amber. "What?"

"You look pained."

"Oh. No. I'm good."

Her lips curved. "Yes, you are definitely good."

"No, you're good." He stood, picking her up with him and depositing her on her feet.

They went into the bathroom to clean up. She turned to him, resting her butt against the sink counter. She wound her arms around his neck.

"Thank you for coming over."

He kissed her. Her lips were warm and inviting, making him want to sink inside of her all over again.

"You're kicking me out, aren't you?"

She nodded. "Much as I'd love for you to stay over, so we could wrap ourselves around each other for the rest of the night, it's already late and you have an important game tomorrow."

"Yeah, I know."

She pressed her lips against his. "And you need sleep."

He grabbed her hips and rubbed against her. "I need you."

"I need you, too. But if you stay here, we'll be up all night making love."

He breathed in deeply, then let it out. "That sounds really good to me."

"It does. But not good for resting. So out with you."

He was about to move toward her, but she skirted around him and the counter and headed into the bedroom.

Damn. The logical side of him knew she was right. So he stayed in the bathroom for a minute to get his wayward cock under control. When he came out, she was in the kitchen sipping from a glass of water. She'd also poured one for him.

"Drink this before you leave. You need to stay hydrated and you were sweating a lot."

She'd given him a glass of water. She was kicking him out of her apartment because she cared about him getting rest before his game. No wonder he felt all these goddamn feelings about her.

He took the glass from her and downed it in several swallows before setting the glass in the sink. "It's your fault. You make me work."

Her lips curved. "Think of it as a pregame workout. Or a pre-bedtime relaxation."

He went to get his coat, then came over to her, pulling her into his arms. "I'll definitely sleep well. Not as well as I would if you were next to me."

"Ditto."

He kissed her, lingering in the kiss a little longer than he probably should have given that his dick got hard again. But Amber stepped away, then smiled at him.

"Out."

"Fine," he said, smiling at her as she opened the door. "Talk to you tomorrow."

"Yes, you will. Good night, Will."

"'Night, Amber."

He realized as he made his way down the hall that he'd wanted to say something else to her before he'd left.

But it was too soon. And the timing wasn't right.

So those important words would have to wait until some other time.

TWENTY-SIX

"AND HOW IS IT OVER THERE?" HIS MOM ASKED. "ARE you getting enough to eat?"

That was always Will's mother's biggest concern. "The dining hall here is double the size of our street, Mom, and it's open twenty-four hours a day. There's no way I could ever go hungry."

"I'm so glad to hear that. But are you eating regularly?"

"Let it go, Lorie," his father said on speakerphone. "You know the boy. He's eating."

"Well I have to check."

"Why? You gonna send him a baloney sandwich if he isn't?"

Will grinned. If there was one thing that had been a constant in his childhood, it had been the bickering between Vic and Lorie Madigan. If his parents didn't snipe at each other at least once a day, Will would think they didn't love each other anymore.

"I'm eating. I'm getting rest. I'm having a great time. I wish you could both be here."

"We wish we could be, too, Will, but the bar has been packed every day since the games started," his dad said. "You know who stopped in the other night during your game?"

"Who?"

"Lucky Harrison."

"Really? I haven't seen Lucky since grade school."

His dad laughed. "That's what he said. He lives in Cleveland now. He's a warehouse manager. He was in Chicago for a conference and came by to see us, and stayed to watch the game. Caught up with some of the guys, too. He said to tell you good luck. I got his number, so you can call him when you get back."

"That's great. I'll be sure to give him a call."

"So you're meeting nice people there?" his mother asked. "You're not lonely?"

"I'm not lonely, Mom. There's always something to do and there's a game room. I've watched several events with my friends. And don't forget some of my teammates are here, too."

"That's right. You know I worry about you. I shouldn't, of course. You make friends everywhere you go."

He smiled at that. "Thanks."

"We miss ya, kid," his dad said. "Kick some ass tonight."

"I'll do that."

"Love you, Will," his mom said.

"I love you both. Talk to you after the game."

He hung up and shoved his phone in his pocket, grabbed his bag and put on his coat, then headed toward the arena. It was a huge night and Will felt equal parts nervousness and excitement. This was the big game—the last game.

They'd had a long practice this morning and again this afternoon, allowing Canada their time on the ice as well. The entire team had eaten an early dinner together and had talked strategy for dealing with a very talented Canadian team. It wasn't like it was a given they were going to win.

He breathed in the crisp air. It smelled like impending snow. Clouds had gathered earlier, that ominous look that spelled a storm was coming. Will hoped it wouldn't be too bad. Just enough snow to bring a fresh pack to the mountain for the events.

It was getting colder, too. He pulled the hood of his parka over his head to ward off the cutting wind. By the time he made it to the arena, snow had started to fall in big, thick flakes, coming faster every minute.

He made his way to the locker room, shaking the snow off his coat and hat and tucking his gloves into his pocket. He felt chilled clear through to his bones. He needed a nice hard skate to warm him up.

"My man," Drew said, coming up to shove his things into the locker next to him. "You up?"

"I'm up."

"Gold looks really good on me," Eddie said, his golden blond hair spiked straight up. He slid alongside them on the bench. "So don't fuck this up."

Will cracked a grin. "I don't plan to, Eddie. I'd hate to ruin your golden moment with the press, especially since you're having such a good hair day."

Drew snickered.

Eddie shot Drew a glare. "Hey, don't diss the 'do. This takes work."

"You do realize you're about to stick a helmet on your 'do,' right?"

"Not a problem. It'll bounce back in time for me to have my moment with the cameras."

Will rolled his eyes and got his gear on. He was more than eager to get out there on the ice.

Coach Stein gave them an incredible motivational speech about doing this for their country, who were all behind them. Will felt that love of country deep in his bones. He was ready.

So when they were in uniform and stood at the entrance, listening to the clamor of the crowd, he felt that first rush of adrenaline drilling right into his marrow. That noise, those cheers, got him excited and eager to play.

They skated out to earsplitting noise, American flags waving throughout the crowd. He'd never felt happier to be representing his country than he did at this moment. He could only hope to do his country proud.

He saw Tim McCaffery skate by, wearing his team Canada gear. Tim skated backward, grinned and waved. Will smiled.

It was still so weird to be playing against a teammate. He knew Tim would do everything he could to win for Canada, just like Will would give it all he had for the US.

And when it was over, they'd go back to being teammates on the Ice.

Each team did their warm-ups and got ready for the game to begin. Will used all that nervous energy and centered it into his gut, preparing to go for the puck. He knew Canada had a loaded team with a ton of talent and this game wasn't going to be an easy skate for them. It was going to be three periods of digging in and working their asses off, with no guarantee of a win.

Which meant it was time to focus.

At the puck drop, Canada got the advantage, skating to the US net. Hance, their goalie, captured the shot from McCaffery and punched it out to their defenders. Will ended up with the puck and dropped it off for Oster, who took a shot.

Denied. Their goalie was sharp.

Dammit.

It was a back-and-forth battle, the puck making its way to both ends on a frequent basis, which meant they were all skating their asses off.

When Canada slid the puck into the net at the end of the first period, Will felt that sinking disappointment all the way to his feet. He ignored the erupting crowd noise.

He had to shake it off. Still plenty of time, and the game was close. They could do this.

They all fought hard for a score, but the only team that scored in the second period was Canada. Again.

Shit.

They could not lose this game. They went into the locker room and he'd never seen his team so down. He remembered every game they had played here. And it looked like they had already given up.

He stood. "Hey, guys."

They all glanced up.

"Take a look around this room. You know most of us play against one another all season. You know the talent in this room. You know how good everyone is. There is no way we can lose this game."

"Yeah, I'm sure the other guys in the other locker room are saying the same thing," Miles said.

Will laughed. "Probably. But you know what? We're just as good. No, we're better. That second period shot was lucky as hell and we all know it. And scoring two goals in a period? How many of us have done that in a game? Or more than that?"

"Plenty," Drew said. "So what's stopping us from scoring three?"

That's what Will needed to hear. "Exactly. This is it. This is for gold. This is what we came here for and we're not leaving without it."

They all stood in unison, sticks in the air, and shouted, "Yeah!"

They came out in the third period with a renewed sense of determination. They could come back from this and win it all. They *would* come back from this and win it all.

And when Drew sank one into the net within the first thirty seconds, that bright light of hope beckoned to Will. He felt the spark that jazzed him up like nothing else. This was that last game and they wouldn't give up.

They scored the second goal on a shot from Oster to Will, who slid the puck in between the goalie's legs. He had no idea how the goalie missed that block. What's more, he didn't care. They were tied and the arena was going crazy. Just the way Will wanted it to. Because they were tied and there were still five minutes left in the game.

Defense was going hard at Canada, and Hance was blocking every shot.

They were firing on all cylinders now and Will could feel it in every one of his bones. They had the crowd behind them, and the team was a fucking machine. They had this game.

But after four blocked shots, and the clock dwindling down, he wasn't sure they had this game in regulation. None of them wanted to do this in overtime, but if they had to, they would.

They were on the US side now, and Will was waiting for defense to do their job.

When the shot came his way, he and Drew hustled their way down the ice. He passed to Oster, who lined it up while Drew and Will fought their way to the goal. Canada's defenders were all over him as he skated his way to the interior. But he wrestled the puck and dropped it off to Drew, who took the shot.

Holy shit, it went in. It went in. They'd scored.

The crowd erupted and all Will could see was the lamp light up. He practically flew over to Drew.

"You fucking did it." He wrapped his hand around Drew's helmet and pounded him on the head.

"With a hell of a pass from you, buddy."

Will grinned. "Now let's close this out."

Will's heart was beating so fast he could barely catch his breath. He glanced up at the clock. A minute and a half left. It seemed like an eternity, because Canada could still score.

But defense was relentless, and Hance seemed to make himself even larger at the goal, blocking everything that came his way.

The buzzer signaling the end of the game was the sweetest sound Will had ever heard.

They'd won. They'd won gold. It wasn't like four years ago when Canada had beaten them by one goal. This time it was their turn.

Will had never experienced this kind of elation before. As he skated to center ice to celebrate with his teammates, he felt as if he were floating on his skates. They all smacked one another on the head, hugged and skated around in circles.

It was total euphoria, all played out to the backdrop of screaming fans.

He knew his parents and his brother were watching, knew they'd be as excited as he was. He hoped the bar was packed and everyone had been buying drinks all night, that the bar's take tonight would be awesome.

Because he felt awesome.

He looked up at the crowd, knowing that Amber was somewhere up there.

They did their handshakes with the Canadians. Damn, he felt awful about Canada losing. A lot of these guys were his friends. He'd been on that side four years ago, so close to gold you could taste it.

But a silver medal wasn't too damn bad to come home with, either.

Once they finished shaking hands, they skated around the ice, waving to the crowd, some of whom threw the flag to them. They skated with the flags, proud of being Americans. The Canadians did the same.

It all felt damn good.

The medal ceremony later felt even better. He fought back tears when the national anthem was played, and in the end, just let the tears fall, knowing his teammates were crying, too.

It was an emotional moment to play for your country, to know you'd given everything you had out there, and had come out victorious.

It was a moment he'd never forget.

AMBER HAD CRIED WATCHING WILL AND HIS TEAMmates receive their gold medals. She'd been so moved, watching those guys tear up, letting their emotions out.

She knew she wouldn't see Will tonight. He and his teammates would have so many interviews with the media, and they deserved to celebrate their win. She sent him a text message letting him know how proud she was of him, how amazing he'd played and she'd see him in the morning. She had her own big day tomorrow, so she needed to get some rest.

She and all her friends had been there to watch him. She was hoarse from all the screaming she'd done. It had been the most incredible game she'd ever watched.

Lisa had told her she was going to hang out with Blake at his place, so after saying good night to them, she made her way back to her apartment alone.

Her phone buzzed. It was her mother. She punched the button. "Hi, Mom."

"Hello, Amber. What are you doing?"

"I went to the hockey game tonight. Now I'm heading back to my apartment to get ready for bed."

"I see."

Her mother did not see. "Did you watch the game?"

"I did not. Your father flew in tonight."

Amber felt that twinge of excitement she always did when her dad was mentioned. "He did? So he's going to be there for my performance tomorrow night?"

"Of course he is. We thought perhaps you might like to have breakfast with us tomorrow morning."

"I'd love to. I have practice at nine a.m. Is seven thirty too early?"

"No, that'll be fine. Where would you like to meet?"

Amber named a restaurant just outside the village.

"We'll be there. So you're going to sleep now?"

"As soon as I get back to the apartment, yes." Though she was so hyped up from the game, she doubted she'd fall asleep for a while.

"That's good. You need your rest. Tomorrow is a big day."

"Yes, it is. I'm very excited about it."

"We'll talk about it tomorrow, Amber."

"Sure, Mom. I'll see you then."

She hung up and tucked her phone back in her pocket.

Will had such an amazing night. She was so thrilled for him.

Hopefully she'd have an equally great night tomorrow. She was so excited about her skate tomorrow, she wished she could will away the next several hours. She was ready now.

Seeing them place that medal around Will's neck, watching that smile on his face, motivated her like nothing ever had.

She wanted that gold medal. And she intended to get it.

Tomorrow.

TWENTY-SEVEN

"HOW'S WORK, DAD?"

Her father looked up from his phone, then smiled at her. "Oh. Busy, like always. Just picked up a new client in Manhattan. Prestigious one, too. They have branches all up and down the eastern seaboard, so it'll require some travel, but worth it."

He resumed scrolling through his e-mails.

"Great."

Amber waited, but he hadn't once asked about her or how she was doing, or comment on her short program. Had he even watched it? Surely he had. She hoped he had.

She started to ask, then stopped herself, tapping her fingernails on the table of the restaurant where she was having breakfast with her parents.

"You sure you feel prepared enough? That you've practiced enough?"

Amber tried not to be offended by her mother's questions. "Yes,

Mom. I'm totally ready for this. If I could have skated last night, I would have. I'm very excited."

"That's good. You know how nervous I get before you skate."

Her mom was always way more nervous about her skating performances than Amber was. "It'll be fine. I intend to be amazing."

"You're always amazing," her dad said without looking up from his phone.

"Thanks, Dad." At least she knew he'd been listening. Or at least partially listening, which was more likely.

"And how are your . . . friends?"

Her mother had used the word "friends" like one would ask "And how is your rotting garbage?" She'd even grimaced. Then again, Mom had never been one to mask her displeasure.

"My friends are awesome, Mom. We hang out together all the time."

"And this Will person that you seem to focus on. Is he what you might call a . . . boyfriend?"

And "boyfriend" was referred to along the lines of some kind of growth that her mother would like removed from her daughter immediately. Amber would have laughed if it wasn't so freaking irritating.

"I don't know. We haven't defined our relationship yet."

Her dad lifted his head from his phone. "Wait. What? You're in a relationship with a boy?"

"He's hardly a boy, Dad. You do realize I'm twenty-four."

Her father slid his glasses down his nose. "You are? When did that happen?"

She laughed. "I don't know. The past twenty-four years?"

He took his glasses off and laid them on the table on top of his phone, then looked her over. "So it did. And you might be dating a guy. Did you hear that, Denise? Our baby girl has a boyfriend."

Her mother wrinkled her nose. "She did not say 'boyfriend.' Either way, it's not a good idea for Amber to be seeing anyone."

"Why not? It's good for her to get out and meet new people, date some guys, have some fun."

Mom looked at Dad. "Oh, really, Alan. Right before the biggest performance of her career, you think she should be carousing with some guy, out 'til all hours, doing God knows what?"

Her dad shot her an open-mouthed shocked look meant to make fun of her mother.

"Oh, my God, Amber," he said. "Are you carousing?"

Amber bit down on her lip to keep from laughing. "I'm not carousing. Promise."

"Go ahead and laugh at me," her mother said. "But when you lose focus and fall on the ice tonight, don't blame me. Blame the guy you've given all your attention to. And your friends."

"Denise," her dad said. "That's uncalled for."

Her mother threw up her hands. "What am I supposed to say? That we've spent the majority of Amber's life preparing her for this moment, and it's okay that she throws it all away because suddenly she wants to go have some fun?"

Her dad gave her mother a look, then turned his focus to Amber. "Have you been practicing?"

"Every day."

"How do you feel about your program?"

"Solid."

"And your chances of winning gold?"

She smiled at her dad. "I feel really good about it, Dad."

He turned back to Amber's mother. "Relax, Denise. Let our daughter enjoy herself a little. She's been working her entire life for this. She's also an adult now. Give her the chance to prove she knows what she's doing."

Her father had been the busiest man she'd ever known. He'd

often missed some of her critical performances. Sometimes he was off in his own world, focused on his work.

But when he was on and with her, he was really with her.

"Thanks, Dad."

Her mother, on the other hand, had been with her every step of the way.

And it was still hard as hell to get her mom to believe in her.

And it broke her heart.

TWENTY-EIGHT

AMBER HAD TWO HOURS TO KILL BEFORE SHE HAD TO report to the ice arena. Lisa and Blake had gone down the mountain today, but Lisa told her they'd be back in time to see her performance.

Will had some media interviews this afternoon, but they'd talked on the phone this morning. He'd told her he'd see her before she went on tonight. She just didn't know when or if he'd even make it on time. Often interviews went longer than expected. Which would be fine. She didn't have to see him.

So when there was a knock on her door, she had no idea who it was. She went to the door and looked out the peephole, her heart squeezing when she saw Will standing outside. She quickly opened the door and threw herself into his arms.

"I didn't expect to see you," she said.

He put his arms around her and hugged her tight.

"Hey, I told you I'd see you."

They walked into the apartment and she shut the door. "But I know how interviews go and they often run longer than expected."

He took off his coat and laid it on the hook by the door. "Yeah, these were about to do that, but I asked our rep to get them wrapped up. I had a very important appointment."

"Oh, you did?"

"Yeah." He led her over to her sofa and sat, then pulled her onto his lap. "My lady has a big night. I needed to see her before she goes on and wows the crowd with her skating."

She inhaled a deep breath. She kissed him, a long, slow kiss meant to convey how she felt about him. When she pulled back, she smiled. "Congratulations on last night. It was epic."

"It kind of was, wasn't it? I can't even put into words how it felt. It was a hard game."

"Yes, it was. It was so tense, and when Canada went up by two goals, I realized it was going to be a rough comeback for your team."

He rubbed his hand over her hip, causing skitters of delightful goose bumps to break out all over.

"You didn't say you thought we'd lose."

She cocked her head to the side. "What?"

"You didn't say when we went down two goals you thought we might lose."

She searched his face, surprised he'd even think that. "I never thought you were going to lose, Will. I knew you had it in you to win that game, no matter the score."

"I love you, Amber."

Her breath caught. "What?"

"I love you. Do you want to know why?"

Her heart was beating so fast she could feel her blood pumping. "Yes, please."

"You're the sweetest woman I've ever met. You always think of other people. You're thoughtful, insightful and smart. And smart women are sexy as fuck. You're also the sexiest woman I've ever known."

That comment surprised her and her brows went up. "I am?"

"Hell, yes. You throw yourself into your sexuality wholeheartedly and without restraint. Do you have any idea how hot that is?"

"No."

"It is. No matter how many times I've been with you, Amber, you always leave me wanting more of you. And last, but not least, you believe in me, and that touches my heart in ways I never expected. I told you I believe in love." He raised his hand to show her the tattoo. "I've seen it firsthand. I know what love is. And I feel it when I'm with you."

She felt like she was going to hyperventilate she was breathing so fast. "I didn't expect this. I don't know what to say."

He smoothed his hand down her arm. "You don't have to say anything."

"Yes, I do. Because I've had all these feelings—all these emotions having to do with you—that I didn't know what to do with. But I don't know if what I'm feeling is love, Will, because I've never been in love. I do know I have very strong feelings for you. How could I not? You're honorable and kind and funny and smart and athletic and sexy and hot and everything I could ever want in a man."

He smiled at her. "But I'm also the first—and only—guy you've ever been with."

She shrugged. "That doesn't scare me. I know my own mind. I know what I want and what I need out of life. It's not like I need to go out and have sex with five more guys before I decide you're the one I want to be with. I'm not that kind of person."

"I'm actually glad you didn't blurt out 'I love you, too.'"

"You are?"

"Yes. Because if you say it back it has to be because you feel it. Because you mean it."

Relief washed over her. "Thank you. That means so much to me."

He slid her off his lap and took her hand. "I didn't intend to tell you that when I came over today. You have enough pressure going on with your performance."

She half turned and draped her leg over his. "You do realize that you telling me how you feel about me doesn't put any pressure on me, right?"

"I'm glad to hear that. Because I don't want anything to change between us. We can continue to hang out and have fun. I just believe in being honest. Honesty is important to me."

She nodded. "To me, too."

"Good. So let's just hang out together until it's time for you to go."

They ended up watching some of the day's events on television. She laughed when he told her they'd done tequila shots last night at the bar they'd ended up at, and that one of their players had thrown up in the trash can outside the bar.

"Oh, hopefully no media was around," she said.

"No, they weren't, but we all got it on our phones and we showed it to him this morning. He was so hungover it made him sick all over again."

She let out a sympathetic laugh. "Oh, that was mean."

"Yeah, it was. After interviews he said he was going back to his apartment and back to bed."

"He must feel miserable."

"He's twenty-one. He needs to learn his liquor limits."

She laid her head on his shoulder. "It was a big night. You can't really blame him for wanting to celebrate with all of you."

"I guess not."

When it was time to go, she stood and walked Will to the door. She lifted up on her toes to kiss him. "Thank you for being here with me today. And for your declaration. I don't even have words for how much it means to me."

He cupped her neck and brought her closer, then kissed her in a way that made her toes curl right into the wool of her socks. If she didn't have to be at the arena, she'd keep him right there with her to explore that kiss, to get him naked and spend the entire rest of the day playing with him.

But not tonight. Rarely would there be anything of a higher priority than her spending time with Will. Except now, when she had to skate for her life.

It was Will who finally broke the kiss. "Now my dick's hard and I'm going to have to calculate stats in my head on the way to the elevator."

"Stats, huh?"

"Yeah. My official stats. Boring as fuck. Guaranteed to deflate my erection."

She grinned. "Sorry about that."

"It's okay. You can make it up to me later."

"Consider it done."

He grabbed his coat. "Go kill 'em out there on the ice, babe."

"I intend to."

He walked out and she shut the door, then turned and went into the bedroom to get herself ready for tonight's performance.

TWENTY-NINE

HAVING A GUY TELL YOU THAT HE LOVES YOU WAS A strong motivating factor when preparing for your last performance in the games.

Amber had always connected to her music, to her movements, but this time she felt an emotional link that had never been there before.

First, though, she had to wait. Since she was in second place after the short program, she'd skate second to last.

She had warmed up and now she was in her tracksuit, staying limber, doing squats and wall stretches and hanging out with Tia, who seemed nervous as hell. So she decided to distract her.

"What's the first thing you're going to do when you get back home?" she asked.

Tia dragged her gaze away from the French skater. "What?"

"The first thing you're going to do when you get home?"

"Oh." Tia thought about it for a few seconds, then answered

with a wide smile. "I'm having a large sausage and pepperoni pizza with extra cheese."

"Oh, God, Tia. That sounds so good."

"Doesn't it? Then I'll go back to training, but I have to have a pizza or I might die. Oh, and loaded nachos. And a huge cheese-burger with grilled onions."

Amber's lips curved. "Clearly you've been thinking a lot about food."

"My mother's a nutritionist. So she makes sure I eat well, but she knows I have a thing for pizza. And nachos."

"And cheeseburgers?"

"Yes. With bacon cheese fries."

"You are killing me here."

Tia laughed. "It's good to skate hungry. It makes you perform better."

"Who told you that?"

"My trainer."

"Ha. She lied."

"I know. But it got me through a few more salads with grilled chicken."

Amber wrinkled her nose. "I don't want to see another salad with grilled chicken for a while. I think I'll take at least a week off from the healthy diet as well."

Tia bent forward at the waist and grabbed her ankles to stretch her hamstrings, then turned her head to look at Amber. "What's your indulgence?"

"Chocolate marshmallow milkshakes."

"Oh, that does sound good."

"And pie."

Tia stood and stretched her back. "What kind of pie?"

"I don't even care. Any kind. Apple, cherry or peach. With ice cream on top."

"Mmm."

"Oh, and a huge steak, with a loaded baked potato. And, of course, a cheeseburger. Who can resist a cheeseburger?"

Tia's eyes widened. "Yum. We should go out to eat tonight after the performance. Something really disgusting."

"We do have the gala Saturday. So we'll still have to fit into our skating outfits."

"I didn't say eat twenty pounds of food. We'll eat tonight, then run in the morning."

"You've got a deal."

When it was time for Tia to skate, Amber hugged her. "Leave it all out there, and most importantly, have fun with it."

Tia nodded and smiled. "I will."

Tia skated a clean program, which Amber had hoped for her. She looked beautiful out there, too, and the crowd was behind her. And while she lacked the power and technicality that some other skaters had, her performance had been lovely and without flaws. Amber applauded loudly for her when she came off the ice.

Tia sat with her coach and trainer and waited for her scores.

When they came up, Amber cheered. They were higher than her short program scores.

She came off the ice and hugged Amber.

"You did so well," Amber said. "I'm incredibly proud of you."

"Thank you. I'm proud of myself."

They watched as Hua Ping and Olena Brutka skated. There was something off about Ping's performance, and it was glaringly obvious. Amber thought she might be nursing an injury, because her jumps weren't as high, and she stumbled on one. That just wasn't like her, since Ping was always technically proficient. Plus, she had no luster.

It showed in her scores, too. She dropped quite a bit, down to sixth, which helped Tia's positioning.

Brutka skated well and ended up getting decent scores. But Amber knew she could do better.

Amber changed into her skating outfit. She stared into the full-length mirror, making sure her hair was perfectly done. She wore the front part of her hair braided, the back falling straight. All the beading on her outfit had been set to perfection. Her outfit was lavender and blue, the beading made to look like a starry sky.

She was skating tonight to rock music, and she intended to rock the entire arena.

She inhaled a deep breath, let it out, then repeated the action.

She had waited a lifetime for this moment. This was her last chance.

And now it was time to find out if the past four years of preparation, if her new program, was worth all that effort she'd put into it.

Yegor braced his hands on her shoulders.

"You have prepared four years for this," he said. "No one is more talented than you, more confident than you. I believe in you. Now go and show the world your magic."

She nodded and made her way onto the ice, taking in the cheers of the crowd. She set her toe pick into the ice, waited for the queue of the music. When it started up, so did she.

Normally she didn't think at all during a performance. She just went through the motions, prepared for one jump, went into the other, making sure she had it all in line.

Tonight was different.

She was loved, and she was going to let that love flow through her, to show the audience what it felt like.

She'd always held herself in check. Tonight she let her emotions free, showing the beauty, the angst, the uncertainty of love.

She felt it from her skates all the way to the tips of her fingertips—the power of it as she flew into a triple axel and followed it up with a triple flip. She sailed out of that and swirled over the ice, letting her heart take over, showing the audience and the judges the freedom of love as she spun out of control.

Only she had the control, and when she came out, she went on, hoping she showed the audience how beautiful love was, how it could change someone. How Will had changed her, how he'd opened her up.

She'd never felt this free, had never skated so openly before. Each jump felt so easy, each connection an extension of her skates.

When she finished, she glided onto one knee on the ice, raised her hands and her face toward the rafters, and expressed the joy on her face.

She knew love. She was loved. She was happy.

The music stopped and the crowd noise was incredible. She rose to her feet and smiled, waved and knew she had given it her very best.

Win or lose, she was satisfied. She waved to the crowd and skated off.

Yegor and Valeria were there to hug her and accompany her to the waiting area.

"That was the best I have ever seen you skate," Yegor said.

She smiled. "Thank you. I felt really good about it."

Valeria kissed both of her cheeks. "You were magnificent."

She squeezed Valeria's hand. "Thank you."

They sat and the waiting began. Her heart pounded and her pulse raced. She had all the control when she skated. But the judges had all the control now.

"You will receive very high scores," Yegor whispered in her ear.

She hoped she wasn't setting herself up for disappointment. But she knew she'd done the best she could, the best she'd ever skated. It had to be enough.

When the scores came up, her eyes widened, her entire body and mind in shock.

She'd never scored that high before. The marks for both technical and program elements were higher than she'd ever received. Her hands flew to her cheeks and she looked over at Yegor, who nodded at her.

"I told you. High marks."

"I cannot believe this. Did it just happen?"

Valeria rubbed her back. "Believe it. Believe in yourself. You were wonderful."

"And now you are in first place."

She could hardly breathe. Now only one thing stood between her and the gold medal she'd worked all these years for.

Sasha Petrova.

And she had no control over that, either.

Amber knew that for Sasha to beat her, she'd have to skate a flawless program. She'd let Yegor figure out the math on what it would take, because Amber wanted to take these last few minutes and float on that cloud of bliss. Her entire program had been an out-of-body experience.

She had Will to thank for that.

Okay, that wasn't entirely true. Will had given her additional motivation, but she'd skated the program of her life. She had to give herself the credit. It had been her on those skates, feeling those feelings and translating them into what she felt was a beautiful performance.

She was proud of herself.

But now it was time to watch Sasha.

Amber tried to watch Sasha skate from a dispassionate angle. There was no doubt she was technically proficient, and her jumps were very good. But Amber just couldn't be objective where Sasha was concerned. She mentally picked out every perceived flaw—probably even where there weren't any—hoping to ascertain where the judges might take off some points.

She wanted to walk away, not watch, but Sasha's performances were always mesmerizing. She drew you in with her magical movements, then made you gasp with the height and perfection of her jumps.

Amber felt the gold slipping away with every minute of Sasha's performance. There was no way she could match that level of precision.

But she thought back to her own performance. She'd skated better than she ever had. She'd been flawless, too, and she knew her program had a level of magic that had captured the audience.

She closed her eyes and clasped her hands together.

Believe in yourself, Amber.

She was just as good as Sasha Petrova. No, tonight she had been better. She had to believe that.

As was typical, Sasha received loud applause and cheers from the audience. She had skated a great program. Was it flawless? Amber didn't know since it wasn't possible for her to be objective. Not tonight, anyway.

All she could do was wait until Sasha's scores came up.

No matter what, Amber would receive a medal. Considering the talented figure skaters here, that was amazing. She was thrilled.

Yegor came up behind her and laid his hands on her shoulders, both of them watching and waiting for Sasha's scores to come up. It seemingly took forever. Amber knew Sasha was nervous as well.

When the scores went up, Amber just stared.

Oh, God.

She felt the squeeze of Yegor's fingers on her shoulders, but she was numb. She heard the roar of the crowd, but it seemed as if they were far, far away, that she wasn't even in the ice arena any longer.

She'd just won a gold medal.

Her lifelong dream had finally come true.

Yegor turned her around and picked her up in his arms. She was already crying. Valeria was crying. Yegor hugged her, and when he put her down, there were tears in his eyes.

"You were magnificent tonight," Yegor said. "You fought for it and earned the gold medal."

Valeria hugged her next. "I'm so proud of you, *moya myla divchyna*."

Valeria had often called her "my sweet girl" in Ukrainian when she was little, but now it made the tears prick her eyes again. She squeezed Valeria around the waist. "Thank you. Thank you both. I couldn't have done this without you."

"Go out and wave to the people. They want to see you."

She nodded, swiped at the tears, then walked out to wave at the crowd, who burst into applause and cheers.

It was an incredible moment and she soaked it in, because it was one she'd never forget.

After, she did several quick media interviews, then went over to congratulate Sasha, who had won the silver medal, and Olena, who'd won the bronze.

"You were amazing," Sasha said, giving her a hug. "I have never seen you skate so well. You deserve the gold tonight."

"Thank you," she said. "You are very hard to beat."

Sasha smiled. "That is a very nice compliment."

Since Sasha was only twenty, Amber knew she'd be back in four years. Amber wouldn't.

This was the end-of-game competition for her. But she'd gotten what she wanted.

Tia came up to her and hugged her. "Oh, I'm so happy for you."

Even Tia was crying. "Thank you. And congratulations on fourth place. That's amazing."

Tia smiled. "Thank you. My coach said for my first time it's very good."

"It is very good. In four years when you come back, you'll be on the medal stand."

Tia squeezed her hand. "Thank you for that."

When she stood on the medal stand and that gold medal was draped around her neck, she fought back tears again. She'd waited a lifetime for this, and when the national anthem played, she put her hand over her heart and let the tears fall freely. She was so proud to represent her country, and she hoped she'd made the US proud.

She did several interviews with networks and journalists after the medal ceremony. It was nearly midnight by the time she finished. When she grabbed her phone, she saw several text messages from her mother and father. Her mother had also left her a voice mail. She had several text messages from Will.

She texted Will: You still up?

He replied right away with: Hell, yeah. Been waiting for you. Where are you?

She sent him a reply letting him know she was leaving the arena. He told her he was on his way to meet her. She smiled at that. Then she sent a text message to her mother letting her know she was just now getting out of the arena after interviews, that she was exhausted, and she'd call her first thing in the morning, so they could meet for breakfast.

She was actually looking forward to celebrating with her parents.

She only made it a short walk outside the arena before she met up with Will, who swept her up in his arms and swung her around in a circle.

"You kicked ass tonight."

She laughed when he put her down. "Thank you."

He took her bag and slung it over his shoulder, then grabbed her hand. "You looked like a princess out there, babe. Actually, that's not right. You looked like a warrior princess. You were fierce and bloodthirsty, but also elegant and beautiful." He stopped and turned to look at her. "Does that even make sense?"

She sighed, lifted up on her toes and grasped his chin to kiss him. "You couldn't have given me a better compliment."

His lips curved. "Good. So where's the medal?"

"Around my neck, under my clothes. I might sleep with it on tonight."

He dropped her bag and tugged her close. "Just so you know, I've never made love to a woman wearing only her gold medal."

"Really. Well, you might get a first tonight."

"I'll bet it looks really sexy nestled between your beautiful breasts."

A swell of heat fluttered through her. She could already envision the two of them naked, with Will inside of her. She already knew how good it felt. It would cap off this incredible night perfectly.

"Your place or mine?" she asked.

"Elias has already left. His brother is getting married, so he had to go back to Sweden."

"Your place it is."

"You don't want to go somewhere and celebrate?"

She leaned into him. "We are going somewhere to celebrate."

"I like the way you think."

She noticed when they resumed walking that Will had accelerated his pace. That made her smile. She had to admit she was in a hurry to be alone with him, too.

When they got to his apartment, he shut and locked the door, then set her bag down on the kitchen counter. Amber unzipped her coat and hung it on the peg by the door.

"Let's see it," he said.

"See what?"

He walked over to her, cupped her jaw, then trailed his finger along the column of her throat, then along her collarbone and down her sternum. "You know what."

Her lips curved. "Oh. That. I don't know why you're so interested. You have one, too."

"Yeah but mine isn't resting between your breasts."

"So true." She moved to the sofa, slipped off her boots and pulled off her socks, then stood and peeled off her leggings and panties. Her long V-neck shirt fell to her thighs, which made Will cock his head to the side.

"That seems unfair. I can't see the goods."

"Soon enough. Start stripping."

He reached for the hem of his shirt and pulled it over his head. "You're very bossy when you win a gold medal."

She laughed at that, then got serious about pulling her shirt over her head, followed by unclasping her bra, letting the straps slide down her arms before tossing it to the floor.

"And you're messy, too," he said.

"Oh, shut up."

He dropped his pants and shrugged out of his boxer briefs, then moved toward her, his erection bobbing up and down as he walked. She took in a deep breath.

"Got a condom?"

He lifted his hand and waved the pack back and forth. "Always ready for you."

"I'm so glad to hear that."

He picked up the medal and rubbed his thumb over it, then lifted his gaze to hers. "Gold is your color."

"Thank you." She rose up and wrapped her hand around the nape of his neck to draw his head down for a kiss. His lips were warm and his tongue wrapped around hers, making her quake with desire.

Whenever he kissed her, she felt that kiss everywhere. Not just on her lips, but tingling pulses through every nerve ending. She felt warm and quivery. Every time he kissed her felt like the first time, giving her that take-your-breath-away feeling that never failed to make her weak in the knees.

She moved backward, directing him toward the bedroom.

He pulled his lips from hers. "Got something in mind?"

"Definitely." She turned him around and pushed him onto the bed, on his back. Then straddled him.

"I like where this is going," he said, running his hands up and down her thighs. "And I like you on top of me."

"Me, too. I like the way your cock feels when I'm on top. You fill me up, and when I rock against you, it sparks all this delicious sensation in my clit."

"Well let's make that magic happen for you. Bring that pretty pussy over here and slide down on my cock."

After he applied the condom, she lifted up and took her time easing down over his shaft. Their gazes collided and held and she grasped his hands as she slid all the way down onto his cock.

She gasped, her body acclimating to his thickness by quavering and tightening around him.

"Fuck, yeah," he said. "Do you know what that does to me, feeling all those tremors your pussy makes when I'm inside of you?"

She shook her head. "No. Tell me."

He lifted his hips, moving slow and easy. "It makes me want to drive hard inside of you until I come. It also makes me want to prolong this so we can do it for hours, because it feels so fucking good."

"Mmm, I know the feeling. The way you rub up against me feels incredible. It's like this magical sensation I don't have words for."

He lifted the medal from her chest and wrapped his hand around it, his knuckles brushing the inside of her breasts. "It's warm from resting against your skin."

She should feel silly for wearing the medal, but at the same time the medal was the last thing on her mind when Will was inside of her. She shifted forward, then back, and the only thought in her head was how his cock felt, how her clit was sparking with all these sensations, and how close she was to coming.

And when he brushed the palm of his hand over her nipples, then brought her forward so he could take a nipple into his mouth and suck it, she cried out, her orgasm taking her by surprise.

She ground against him, trying to get as much out of her climax as she could while simultaneously attempting to drag him into an orgasm with her.

She succeeded because he groaned, gripped her hips and lifted into her, shuddering against her as he came. It was the sweetest sensation feeling her own orgasm and his as well, to see his features go hard with tension as he released.

When he finally went lax, she lay forward to rest against his chest, listening to his heartbeat. He rubbed her back and she drew circles around his shoulder with her fingertips. It was nice to just lie here and do nothing as they both came down from that incredible high.

She finally lifted and climbed off him and he went into the bathroom to discard the condom. He returned to the bed and pulled her against him. She wrapped one leg over his hip.

It was late. She knew she should go back to her room, but she just didn't want to move. She finally lifted her head.

"I should go."

He arched a brow. "Why?"

"I don't know. I told my parents I'd have breakfast with them in the morning. I know they're excited and they want to see me."

He brushed her hair away from her face. "I'll wake you."

She wanted to stay with him, to wrap herself around him and sleep with him tonight.

"Okay."

"You're easy."

She laughed. "You sure know how to flatter a girl."

He kissed the top of her head. "I might wake you in an hour and make love to you again."

"Okay."

She closed her eyes.

"See? Easy."

She shoved into his chest.

He laughed and she climbed on top of him.

"Just for that I'm going to keep you up all night long."

He smoothed his hand over her back, his fingers making a slow trek toward her butt.

"Ooh, punishment."

Somehow it didn't seem a fitting punishment, but as he rolled her onto her back, she figured they'd both benefit, so . . . whatever.

THIRTY

AMBER COULDN'T BELIEVE IT WAS ALREADY THE CLOS-
ing ceremony. The past three weeks had gone by so fast.

The gala had been incredibly fun. It always was. Skating without
being judged was always stress free. It wasn't practice, it wasn't to
hone your skills, it was just for the crowd, a final showcase with no
pressure, and the audience always enjoyed it. And because the audience had always been there for her, she loved performing for them.

She'd had a great breakfast with her parents on Saturday morning. Her mother had told her she was proud of her. Her father had
hugged her and said he'd always known she could get that gold
medal.

Then her mom had announced that she'd gotten her a gig on
that dancing show where several former figure skaters had gone—
and many had won. She was set to report in the late fall.

Amber was stunned, but it was a great opportunity. Especially
since she hadn't been the only skater to win a medal. Brandon had

won gold, Rory had won a bronze and Telisa and Robbie had won a silver medal. And their friends Darren and Christina had won a silver medal.

These games had been good for the US figure skaters.

And Sergei had won silver. He didn't seem to mind since he and Brandon were now solidly a couple. She had no idea how that was going to work once Sergei made his way back to Russia, but she hoped he and Brandon could find a way.

Now she was going to have to figure out the whole after-competition thing. She'd never had an agent, but she supposed it was time to get one. She'd never thought too hard about life after skating, other than maybe teaching skating to kids. She was going to have to think about what she really wanted to do now.

For now, though, she stood beside Will and all her friends and watched the end of the games. The showcase was beautiful, but it always made her a little sad.

This time, especially. Her entire life had changed at these games. She'd made so many new friends, and as she looked over at Tia and Rory and Telisa and Robbie and Lisa and Blake and Brandon and Sergei, she realized these people would be friends forever.

And then she looked over to her left at Will, who was watching the ceremony with several of his friends, some of whom were also her friends now, too.

That sense of warmth settled over her again, as it always did whenever she looked at Will.

He turned to her and gave her a grin.

"Isn't it great?"

She nodded, then turned to watch the ceremony with him.

When it was over, they all decided to leave the village and head to a party Lisa had told them about. Tia wasn't going, so Rory was staying to hang out with her.

The party was at this beautiful home owned by a friend of

Lisa's. It was a two story set high on a hill, with amazing views of the mountains.

The inside was incredibly spacious with tall windows everywhere you turned. The place was filled with skiers and snowboarders and bobsledders and skaters and just about every athlete imaginable.

"Come on," Will said, following Lisa and Blake to the expansive kitchen, where a bar had been set up. "What would you like to drink?"

She really wanted a drink. "Vodka with soda."

Someone was bartending, so he got her drink and a whiskey for himself. They made their way around the house, finding a bench seat near a set of windows. For a while they watched the goings-on. Loud music, people dancing and just cutting loose.

"I think everyone feels the same as I do," Amber said to Will.

"What? That it's finally over and we can all relax?"

She laughed. "Yes."

He nodded. "There's so much pressure all through the games. It's nice to just cut loose and let it go. Win or lose, it's over now."

"Exactly. Last time I stayed until the end, but I was happy to rest in my room and relax. There was no more pressure."

"Yeah but you stayed in your room. Isn't this better?"

She leaned into him and wrapped her hand around his arm. "Much."

"When do you leave?" he asked.

"Tomorrow afternoon. You?"

"I have a six a.m. flight."

"Wow, that's early."

"I know. I have to get back to work with my team."

"Oh, right."

She thought about that, about what it meant for the two of them. She half turned to face him.

"So now what happens?" she asked.

"You mean for us?"

She nodded.

"You know how I feel, Amber. That hasn't changed. I go back to my regular schedule, which means half the season of home games, the other half on the road. What about you?"

"The whole ice skating team will go on tour. There will be interviews after the games are finished. I'll be busy for several months, no doubt. And then there's that dancing thing my mother set up for me."

"Which is very cool."

"Thank you. I'm not sure how I feel about it."

"So you haven't accepted it yet?"

She shook her head. "On the one hand, it's a great opportunity. On the other . . ."

He studied her for a few seconds. "You're not sure it's the next step for you?"

She nodded.

"Only you can decide that for yourself. But if you want to talk about it, you know I'm always up for that."

Of course he would be. "Thank you."

"And no matter what, we'll carve out time to see each other. Plus, there's a New York hockey team that we play against."

"Drew's team."

"Right. So whenever I'm in New York I can see you. And if you're going on tour, that means we can work out a schedule for when we're either nearby or in the same cities."

As he talked about it, she realized it was a disaster in the making, and a lot like what Will had gone through with his last girlfriend.

She knew how that one had ended. She also knew he had a schedule that couldn't be altered. And she had no idea what hers was going to look like, but she'd gone on tour after the last international games, and it was months and months on the road with no break.

How would they ever have a relationship when they never saw each other?

She refused to be another woman who broke his heart, because she couldn't give him what he needed.

She knew now she was in love with him. She hadn't told him, because she hadn't been sure she knew what love was.

Now she did know. Love meant letting someone go before you hurt them.

She wasn't going to hurt him, wasn't going to drag out this relationship for months, only to have it end with both of them hating each other, or blaming the other for the lack of time together. She loved him too much for that.

Which meant she had to break it off now. Just the thought of it made her chest ache.

But every minute she thought about what life would be like for them—what their relationship would be like—reminded her of his last relationship. She knew how much that had hurt him.

She couldn't do that to him again.

She looked down at her hands. "So I've been thinking."

"About?"

This was so hard. She wasn't good at lying. But she had to, for Will.

She finally lifted her gaze to his. "About us."

He smiled at her, and it was like a punch to her stomach. "Yeah? What about us?"

"You know I've had a wonderful time with you these past few weeks. It's been the most incredible experience of my life, Will."

"Why do I sense a 'but' coming?"

She inhaled, let it out. "But my life and your life don't mesh. We don't live in the same city, your life is going in one direction and mine is going in another. And while we had fun together, I just don't see a future with you."

Oh, God that was so hard to say. Because it wasn't true. The one thing she wanted most was a future with Will. But it could never happen. And she wouldn't pretend that it could. She wouldn't hurt his heart later, when it would be so much more painful.

Because it was painful enough now.

And when she saw the smile on his face disappear, replaced by hurt and pain, it crushed her.

"Oh. Okay."

That was it? "I'm sorry, Will."

"Hey, don't be. If you don't feel it, you don't feel it."

She wanted to cry. She wanted to crawl into his lap and tell him she loved him, that she was lying, and beg him to forgive her. But she had to stay strong.

"I feel really bad about this."

He stood, and pulled her up with him. "I'm gonna make sure Lisa and Blake get you back to your apartment safely, and I'm gonna take off, okay?"

She reached out for him, but he took a step back.

"Will—"

"I think you're amazing, Amber, and I hope you find everything you're searching for. I want you to be happy."

He picked up her hand and kissed the back of it, then turned and walked away.

She couldn't breathe. She fell back onto the seat and tried to find a way to get through this devastating sense of loss.

That's where Lisa found her. She didn't know how long she had been sitting there. It felt like hours. Days. Because Will was gone and she already missed him.

"There you are." Lisa sat next to her. "Will said he was leaving. What's going on?"

She lifted her gaze to her friend. "I broke up with Will."

Lisa frowned and pulled Amber against her. "Oh, honey, no. Why?"

She explained why to Lisa, and then she burst into tears.

"Oh, Amber."

Lisa told her to stay there. It wasn't like she had a coherent brain cell to move at the moment anyway.

She'd thought this would be easy. She'd been so wrong. When you loved someone, breaking their heart was the worst thing ever. What had she been thinking?

Lisa came back. "Come on, honey."

Lisa helped her stand. They got their coats and headed back to the apartment.

They were halfway there when Amber realized it was just the two of them. "Where's Blake?"

"I told him to stay and hang out with his friends."

Amber stopped. "Lisa, I'm so sorry. Go, have fun. I can make it back on my own."

"Don't be ridiculous. You need a friend right now and that's me. We're going to sit in the apartment, and you'll cry and tell me why you made this dumbass decision."

Amber laughed, then burst into tears.

But Lisa was right. She needed to talk it out with someone. Not that she'd change her mind, because she knew she'd made the right decision.

But why did it have to hurt so much?

She just needed to get out of Vancouver. Get back home and back to her life. Stay busy, and move on.

Then everything would be all right.

THIRTY-ONE

BEING IN NEW YORK SURE AS HELL WASN'T HELPING Will's mood.

It had been two weeks since he last saw Amber. He'd been back at work, had even played against Chicago so he'd seen his parents and his brother.

At least that part had been fun. He'd gone to the bar, had downed a beer with the regulars, showed off the gold medal and shared a meal with Mom and Dad and his brother, Ethan.

He hadn't even mentioned Amber, though his mother had known something was up with him. What was it with moms and their freaky intuition anyway? He told her he was tired from the games and he'd be fine once he got back on schedule.

She didn't believe him. Imagine that.

But now he had a game in New York tomorrow night. They'd just flown in this morning and checked into the hotel. He'd made contact with Drew Hogan, hoping that connecting with Drew might help keep his mind off Amber.

Will had invited Drew out for drinks, but Drew told Will he could just come to his place and they could have lunch. Carolina was out of town on a buying trip and Drew said he'd order takeout for them.

It sounded like a great idea, so Will had a car take him to the nice-looking apartment Drew and Carolina owned on the Upper West Side of Manhattan. It was modern and well furnished and, considering the location, very spacious.

Drew opened beers for both of them and they sat on the white leather sofa.

"Guess you can't toss your shit around in this place," Will said.

"I've learned to live a little neater, but I have a game room in here that Carolina lets me slob around in."

"Then why the hell are we sitting in here?"

"Because food's coming soon. I don't know about you, but I'm hungry."

Drew ordered Thai food for them, which sounded great because Will was hungry, too. They ate and drank a couple of beers and talked shit to each other about tomorrow night's game.

"Too bad your goalie's hurt and your team is playing a backup," Will said. "I don't know why you're even bothering to show up."

Drew finished his plate and wiped his hands on his napkin. "Because even with our backup goalie we're going to drag your asses all over the ice?"

Will laughed.

"So are you glad to be back to regular business?" Will asked.

"Hell, yeah. I mean the games were fun, but holy shit that was some pressure. I've got enough pressure going on here."

"Here being the high castle? It is fancy."

Drew leaned back against the sofa. "Yeah, well fancy's going on the market. Carolina's pregnant."

"No shit? Congratulations, man." Will leaned forward to shake Drew's hand. "When's the baby due?"

Drew sprouted a wide smile. It was obvious he was really happy.

"Thanks. Baby's due in August. We're both pretty damned excited about it. But this place"—Drew looked around—"isn't suitable for a baby. So we're moving out of Manhattan."

"Yeah? How's that gonna work with Carolina's fashion career?"

"She has a talented staff of people working under her that can deal with the day-to-day. She intends to take the first year with the baby, and she'll handle a lot of the minutiae from home."

"I'm really happy for you, Drew."

"Thanks. Hey, you and Amber seemed to hit it off. Maybe it won't be long before you're headed in this direction."

"Yeah, that didn't work out."

Drew frowned. "It didn't? Why not?"

He shrugged. "I don't know. I told her how I felt. She just . . . didn't feel the same way."

"I find that hard to believe. She was really into you."

"That's what I thought, but sometimes it doesn't go the way you want it to."

"Huh. I'm sorry, Will."

"Me, too."

The last thing Will wanted to talk about, think about or dwell on was Amber. "But hey, you've got great news and some exciting things to think about. So let's talk about that."

"Oh, yeah. Like putting this place up for sale, buying a house, moving, dealing with a hormonal wife, finishing up this hockey season, trying to figure out the million different baby things to buy and worrying about what kind of dad I'm going to be. Or even if I know what the hell I'm doing."

"See? Like I said. Exciting things to think about." Will shot Drew a grin and a nod.

Drew laughed. "Asshole."

"That's what I'm here for, buddy."

And as long as they could talk about something—anything—other than his wrecked love life—Will would be happy.

Though he wasn't sure he'd ever be happy again.

THIRTY-TWO

AMBER HAD A PERFORMANCE TONIGHT AT MADISON Square Garden. She loved doing a touring performance there, and the crowds were always fantastic.

Normally being in Manhattan would perk her up, since going into the city was always one of her favorite things. Instead, she sat in her hotel room, looking down at the bustle of the city, the traffic, the people, and felt as far removed from it all as she could.

She didn't want to be here.

"You seem down."

Amber lifted her gaze to her mother. "It's nothing."

"It's not nothing. Tell me what's bothering you. Is it one of your fellow skaters?"

Her mother would think that. "No."

"Then what is it?"

She might as well tell her. "I broke up with Will before we left Vancouver."

Mom stared at her for the longest time, then finally nodded. "Well, that's good."

Amber blinked. "Good? How can you say that?"

Her mother came over to her and sat in the chair across from her, taking her hands. "Honey, it frees you. Now you don't have the bonds of that relationship to tie you down. You can concentrate on your skating, on your career, on your future."

Amber jerked her hands away. "That's all you ever think about? My career?"

She stood and paced the room, her heart aching.

"Sweetie, you'll feel differently when you have some time—and some distance. You have so much to look forward to. Don't look back."

Amber pivoted and glared at her mother. "He told me he loved me. And I never told him I loved him, Mom. Which I do. I love him."

Her mother waved her hand back and forth. "You hardly know him. You'll get over it."

She stared at her mother, unable to fathom her lack of empathy. "I'll get over it? How can you say that like my feelings mean nothing?"

Her mother leaned back in the chair. "What do you know about love, anyway, Amber? You've never even dated. You were in a bubble at the games. It was a fling."

Amber sighed. "It was more than a fling. I love him, Mom. He loved me. And I hurt him."

"Give it some time. You'll move on. You have your career to think about. Now's not the time to get involved with someone. There are big things on the horizon for you. That's what you should be focusing on right now."

She sat across from her mother, wishing she understood. "Just once I'd like you to consider my feelings."

"What do you want me to say? What do you want from me, Amber?"

"You know what I'd like? Just once, I'd like you to act like my mother instead of my manager or my coach or my trainer. I'd like you to be sympathetic to my feelings, instead of thinking of me as a figure skater. I'm hurting here, Mom, and all you can think about is how awesome it is that I broke up with the man I love because now my relationship won't get in the way of my career.

"You know what I expected of my mother? A little empathy. Maybe a hug. That maybe you would actually care that my heart is broken. Instead, all you care about is how it affects my career. That's not what a mother does. That's what a manager does. I don't need a manager. I need a mother. I've always needed a mother and you've never been one to me. And that breaks my heart."

She was crying by the time she finished. She'd never been so outspoken with her mother, but it had felt like a catharsis. She'd held all that emotion inside for years and it needed to come out. And now that it had, she wouldn't take it back.

Her mother stared at her, giving her that same judgmental look she'd given her her entire life. "I've always done what was best for you."

"I know you did. And I'm so appreciative to you and Dad for everything you've given me. I've had a wonderful career. Now I need you to step up and be my mother."

She waited for the lecture. And waited for her mother to blow up at her.

"I'm . . . I'm sorry, Amber. I had no idea."

Amber was shocked.

"I've been so hyperfocused on your career, that maybe I have overlooked the emotional side. As you know, I'm not very emotional myself. But I can see you get your emotional side from your father. It's a part of you I'll probably never be able to understand. But I can learn to appreciate it."

"So you do love Dad?"

Her mother frowned. "Of course, I love your father. We've been married for twenty-seven years."

"You can be married and not love the person you're married to."

"Well, what would be the point of staying married to someone you don't love? I love your father, Amber. I always have. I always will."

"But you're not . . . affectionate with each other."

"In front of you, no. In public, no. That's just not how your father and I operate. We prefer to keep our . . . passion for each other private."

She could tell how uncomfortable this conversation was for her mother. "I appreciate your honesty. And I'm sorry if it makes you uncomfortable."

"Profoundly uncomfortable. But it's important for you to understand that just because we don't show emotion doesn't mean we don't feel it. Your father and I love you very much, Amber. We always have."

Amber felt a swell of emotion. "Thank you. I love you, too, Mom. But I need you to know that skating isn't my entire life. I love it. But I don't know that I want to become a professional skater. And I'm not sure about the dance thing. And I think I have to fire you as my manager."

Her mother blinked. "Oh . . . okay. Why?"

"Because it's high time you and I have a mother-daughter relationship. I think I've reached a point in my life where I really need a mom."

Her mother's eyes welled with tears. "Very well, then. I can accept that and I will switch my focus in the future to giving motherly advice only."

Amber smiled. "Thank you."

"So tell me what happened between you and Will."

Now they were getting somewhere. For the first time, Amber had hope. Not that she thought her mother would give her good advice, but they were talking, and it wasn't all about skating, so they had a start.

They talked for a couple of hours, and then her mother left. They'd even hugged, and it was a genuine hug.

But she still had no answers for her misery about Will.

Maybe getting outside would help. It was cold, but it wasn't raining or snowing, so some fresh air might clear her head. She put on her coat and hat and grabbed her gloves and her purse, then took the elevator downstairs and went outside, joining the hum of humanity.

She walked briskly, keeping up with the flow of people going to and from—wherever they were going. They all walked with a sense of purpose and confidence, something she was decidedly lacking in.

These past couple of weeks had been utterly miserable. She was utterly miserable.

Even with the gold medal, she didn't enjoy skating anymore.

And, worse, she missed Will.

She lacked that sense of purpose, and her heart hurt. She'd had several conversations with Lisa since she'd gotten home. Lisa had invited her back to Vancouver, had told Amber she could come to her house and just chill and chat.

She'd been tempted, but that would be hiding. She couldn't hide from what she'd done. She had to face it.

She walked for a while until she ended up in Times Square, a bustling activity center for tourists. She found a place out of the way of pedestrian traffic and looked up at the video screens.

Something immediately caught her eye and she turned back to look at the news and sports screen, waiting for it to repeat. It took several minutes, but when it did, her heart leaped.

The St. Louis Ice were in town to play the New York Travelers tonight. Which meant Will was here.

She pulled out her phone.

Don't do it. You already hurt him.

What would it accomplish to see him? To hurt him even more? Or could she repair the damage she'd done?

She walked for over an hour before sending the text message, knowing she had to do it. Because she'd made a huge mistake in Vancouver.

And she had to make it right.

THIRTY-THREE

WILL STARED AT THE TEXT MESSAGE, UNABLE TO BE-lieve he and Amber had found themselves in the same city at the same time.

She was performing at Madison Square Garden tonight. She asked if he'd be willing to see her. She wanted to talk.

What the hell did they have left to talk about? She'd made her feelings clear in Vancouver. She didn't feel it with him.

But, God, he missed her. You didn't fall out of love with someone you were in love with overnight. Those feelings were still there, and his heart jumped when her name came up on the message.

Meeting with her would be stupid. He could get over her faster if he just cut ties.

But maybe he needed to say good-bye. He'd been so shocked by what she said in Vancouver that all he could think to do was walk away.

He shouldn't do it. More good-byes would only hurt more.

Yeah, but he was an adult, and this wasn't his first breakup. The only way to get through saying good-bye to someone you loved was to actually *say* good-bye, to close that door for good.

He could handle it. And then he could move on.

He texted her back letting her know he'd be at Madison Square Garden tonight, and he'd meet with her after her performance.

He got in touch with the ticket center and reserved a ticket.

Then he sucked in a breath.

Okay, man. Time to say good-bye.

THIRTY-FOUR

WILL SAT IN THE CROWD AND WATCHED AS ALL THE skaters—some of them his friends—performed.

Telisa and Robbie made an incredible pair, on and off the ice. They were amazing and the love they had for each other showed in their skating.

Brandon put on a hell of a show, too. So did Rory and Tia, and hell, he liked all of these people. It was great to see them all again.

When Amber came out, he couldn't help but feel that squeeze of pain in his chest. But hell if she didn't look like the most beautiful thing he'd ever seen. Her hair was up tonight, and she looked like a mermaid in her multicolored skating outfit, all blue and green and purple. Like a siren, she called to the audience, mesmerizing everyone with the way she moved, her jumps so damn perfect he wondered how she did them.

But something was different tonight, something that wasn't

there the night she won the medal. She lacked that passion, that love and energy he'd felt when he'd watched her in Vancouver.

Obviously no one else noticed it because the audience cheered like crazy for her, which was good.

But there had definitely been something lacking.

After it was over, he went backstage and gave his name. Amber had texted him and told him she'd have a backstage pass for him. Security gave him the pass and he strung it around his neck, then followed the guard's instructions and made his way down the hall and to the right to Amber's dressing room.

He sucked in a breath and knocked on the door.

She opened the door, her face scrubbed clean from all the glitter and eyeliner and lipstick she wore when she performed. She wore a flowered robe that showcased her legs.

"Hi, Will."

He nodded. "Amber."

"Come on in."

He walked in and she closed the door.

"Thanks for coming."

He turned to face her. "You looked good tonight."

"Thanks."

This was so awkward, but he was here, so . . . "Your performance was off."

She cocked her head to the side. "It was? How so?"

"It lacked passion. It's like you didn't put all of yourself into it or something. It wasn't anything like your skate that night in Vancouver."

She sank onto the chair. "You're right. I don't feel it anymore. I haven't since the night you and I—"

He went over and sat next to her. "Why?"

"Why what? Why don't I feel it anymore?"

"I guess."

He heard her sigh. "I don't know, Will. I guess that night in Vancouver I was inspired. You'd told me you loved me. I skated with my heart filled with love. And now it's not there anymore."

He let out a short laugh. "You ended things with me, Amber."

"I know. And I need to be honest with you about that. It wasn't because I didn't have feelings for you. I did—I do. I still do. I was just afraid that we'd end up like your last relationship."

"What do you mean?"

"We were talking about doing the long distance thing. And that's what blew up your relationship before, because it didn't work out."

It finally dawned on him. "Oh. So you thought we'd end up the same way."

"Yes. I'm so sorry. I didn't want to hurt you. I thought if I ended things with you then, I could spare you being hurt again down the road."

"You know you and I aren't like my last relationship."

"I know that. But I was afraid and I thought you'd end up hurt. That we'd end up hurting each other, and I didn't want that." She shuddered out a sigh and he saw the tears in her eyes. "I made a mess of everything. I hurt you, I hurt myself. God, I've missed you so much. I love you, Will. I just don't know how we could have made this work."

He should be pissed. But how could he be when all she'd done was try to avoid hurting him. "Okay, a couple of things. First, don't ever lie to me about how you feel ever again."

"Okay."

"Second, the reason my last relationship ended was because neither of us was that heavily invested in making it work. That's what love is all about, Amber. When you find that person you want to be with, you'll move mountains to make it work."

"Oh."

"And third, you never gave us a chance to try."

He saw how hard she was fighting to hold the tears back.

"I'm so sorry. You're right. I totally screwed this up and all I ask is for you to forgive me. I don't expect you to want to be with me. I just want you to understand why I did it. It wasn't out of malice, and God, I did love you. I do love you."

He leaned in and kissed her, and as always, she fired him up, body, heart and soul, like no other woman ever could. When he pulled back, he took her hands in his. "Amber. Look at me."

She did.

"I'll move mountains to make it work with you."

Tears streamed down her face. "Now I understand. This is love. This is how it works."

"Yeah. This is how it works."

She kissed him back. "Love hurts sometimes, Will."

"Yeah, it does."

"Also, I don't want to dance on that show."

"You don't?"

"No. When my mother told me about it, I kept waiting to get excited, but I wasn't. And I'm not. And that's because it's not what I want to do."

"What do you want to do?"

"Remember when I told you I wanted to teach skating to kids who have the talent but can't afford it?"

"Yeah."

"I want to open a school, to teach skating to young kids, so they can find their passion early in life."

He nodded. "That's a great idea."

"But I still have this tour."

"And hockey is over by May if we make the playoffs."

"Which you will."

He loved that she always believed in him. "Thanks. So when that's done, where you go, I go. And after that, we'll figure it out."

She threw her arms around him, then climbed onto his lap. "I love you, Will."

"I love you, too, Amber." He put his arms around her. "We'll make this work."

"Of course we will."

He laughed. "Don't ever doubt it. Because as long as we love each other, nothing will stop us."

He kissed her, and lost himself in the feel of her body against his.

He pulled back. "Did you ever get your skating tattoo?"

She shook her head. "Not yet."

"We're taking care of that right away."

"Okay. I didn't want to do it without you, anyway. You being the expert on tattoos."

He laughed. "I'll hold your hand through the whole thing."

"Thank you. Oh, and one more question."

"Yeah?"

"Can you get me a ticket to your game tomorrow night?"

He grinned. "Well, I know a guy who plays for New York. So I think I can score a ticket or even a few in case you want to bring some of the skaters."

"Awesome. Now you'll have a New York cheering section."

"Right now I'd like to have some sex in your dressing room."

She slid her hand under his shirt. "I already locked the door."

His mouth met hers and he murmured against her lips. "See? We're meant for each other."

"Oh, and another thing. I have lucky panties."

He arched a brow. "Lucky panties?"

"Yes."

He cupped her butt. "Would you happen to be wearing them?"

"Of course. I wear them for every performance now. They bring me luck. I own several pairs."

He lifted her robe to reveal hot pink satin and lace underwear. "I like these."

"The other pair is black."

"So you can wear those tomorrow night to bring me luck when I play."

She skimmed her fingertips over his shoulders. "Of course."

"We're a hell of a team, Amber."

She leaned in to kiss him, her lips soft and warm. "Yes, Mad Dog. We certainly are."

TURN THE PAGE TO READ A SPECIAL EXCERPT
FROM THE NEW HOPE NOVEL BY JACI BURTON

One
Perfect Kiss

AVAILABLE SEPTEMBER 2018
FROM HEADLINE ETERNAL

ZACH POWERS READ OVER THE LIST OF GRADES, THEN scrolled down to his two football players who been placed on academic probation. His gaze narrowed when he saw which teacher had been the one to put them there.

Josie Barnes.

"Dammit, Josie." He clenched the paper in his fist and left his classroom in search of the woman who was trying to ruin Hope High School's football season.

He found her in her classroom, looking content and calm and gorgeous in her long skirt and white short-sleeve button-down shirt, so unlike the outfits she wore outside the classroom. Here she was buttoned up and professional, always nodding and smiling at him in the halls, but never giving away anything other than polite teacher-to-teacher glances.

When they were out with their friends, though, she flirted with him. Nothing had happened between them yet, but Zach knew she liked him.

He liked her, too. Or he had, until now.

He knocked on her door. She looked over, then waved him in. She always wore her hair cut short, which did nothing to detract from her stunning face. In fact, it brought out the amazing sea blue of her eyes and her generous mouth, which today was painted a pale, shimmering pink.

If she'd been his teacher, he would have never been able to concentrate. Like right now, when he was supposed to be pissed off about those grades.

He opened the door, then closed it, coming over to hover over her desk.

"What's this all about?" he asked, shaking the paper at her.

She looked at his hand. "What's what all about?"

"You put Paul Fine and Chase Satterfield on probation."

She leaned back in her chair and gave him a confused look. "I have no idea what you're talking about."

He dropped the paper on her desk. She opened it up, read it, then lifted her gaze to his. "Oh. Football."

She said the word "football" like she had no idea what it meant.

"Yeah, football. You know, that thing that's my life here."

"Huh. I thought teaching history was your life here." She finished her statement with an arched brow.

He narrowed his gaze at her. "Don't play games with me, Josie. Paul's my best wide receiver and Chase is my center."

"Uh-huh. Whatever. We're four weeks into the semester and Paul's missing four assignments. Chase is missing five. Which means neither of them is passing my class. I'm just doing what the school board requires by submitting progress reports."

Zach clenched his jaw. Bureaucracy always got in the way of his players doing what they did best—play football. Some of the other teachers understood this and were more . . . lenient with grades for his players, giving them a sliding scale to work with. But those were typically players that were on the cusp.

Five assignments? Jeez.

He took another glance at Paul's and Chase's grades in the class. They were both F's.

It wasn't like you could "sliding scale" your way up to a passing grade when you were already on your ass.

"How bad is it?" he asked.

"Take a look."

She took out her grade book and showed him. "Chase has only turned in one assignment. Paul two. And the two Paul turned in—" She looked up at him. "I tried to give him the benefit of the doubt, Zach, but honestly? They were bad. I couldn't even say he was phoning it in. He hadn't even picked up the phone."

This was where he needed to remind himself these were high school students. High school students who had potential college careers ahead of them, which meant they also had to do the academic work.

He unclenched his jaw. "Fine. Tell me what they need to get done and I'll make sure it's turned in before the end of the week report comes in."

"Sure." She got out a piece of paper, opened her laptop and jotted down the list of assignments. When she handed it to Zach, she looked up at him. "And Zach, make sure they're the ones doing the assignments, okay?"

"What the hell does that mean?"

"It means not bullying any of my stellar students to do the work for them. Or, even worse, buying the work online. Because I'll know it if they do."

"Christ, Josie. What kind of guy do you think I am? What kinds of guys do you think my athletes are?"

She sighed. "Let's just say I've seen students like this before. They get in a jam, and they're desperate and more than willing to do anything—and I mean anything—to turn in passing work."

He laid his hands on her desk and leaned in. "My guys aren't like that. And if they are like that, they won't play for me for long."

She didn't flinch away. She held his gaze. "I guess you should make sure you know your players well, then."

"I intend to, because these two will be sitting with me every day after school this week doing these assignments while their team-mates are on the practice field. So I can guarantee you, Ms. Barnes, that when this work is turned in, it'll be work that both Paul and Chase have done themselves."

Her lips lifted. "I'm glad to hear that. And I'm sorry about all that classwork you'll have to do this week. If you need any research assistance, feel free to give me a call."

"I think I can handle it. After all, I've been to school myself, ya know."

She laughed. "Yes, I'm sure. But that was a long time ago. And I require a lot of my students."

"How hard can it be?" He looked at the assignments and bit back a curse.

"Poetry? A journal of thoughts and feelings? Aww, hell, Josie."

She smiled. "You did say you were going to help them, right?"

He pushed off the desk and pivoted, already halfway to the door. "Yeah, yeah."

Once out the door, he stopped and read the assignments again. Poetry. Journals. Ugh.

A small part of him understood Paul and Chase blowing off the homework. He'd hated poetry in English class. All that evaluation of shit that had never made sense to him. But he'd sucked it up and done it. And had maybe learned a few things in the process. He might have not enjoyed it, but he'd done the work.

Not doing the work was lazy, and he wouldn't accept that from any of his players.

He headed toward the field.

Time to kick a couple of asses from here to next week.

JOSIE PONDERED HER CONVERSATION WITH ZACH ALL the way home, then ended up deviating toward the library, where hopefully Jillian Reynolds would be working this afternoon.

She'd made friends with so many wonderful women in the time she'd been here in Hope. But she and Jillian had grown closer in the past few months, likely because, out of their group of women friends, they were the two single ones. Everyone else was either coupled up or married, and several of their friends even had kids or were expecting them. So Josie and Jillian had started hanging out more and more lately.

Plus, it didn't hurt that they shared a lot of things in common. Jillian was the head librarian, and she loved all forms of literature. As a language arts teacher, Josie had loved books and reading from the time she was a kid. She had started hanging out in her local library as a means of escape from family drama, but it had turned into a love of reading that had developed into a voracious appetite.

She could still remember Elda, the librarian at her small town library, who'd introduced her to countless books when she was a kid. She'd fallen in love with classic literature and poetry and mysteries and romances and science fiction and fantasy. She'd returned day after day to turn one book in and check out another. She'd also spent hours at the back of the library reading and soaking in the quiet.

After all, no one was drunk or on drugs or screaming at her there. It was peaceful and she could lose herself in a story of magic or fantastical worlds, or escape into romantic escapades.

Reading had been her life, and the library had been her salvation.

And meeting Jillian had evoked warm memories of those early years, because Jillian ran her library the same way Elda had all those years ago. She was fierce and protective and fostered a love of books in every child she met.

Josie spotted Jillian in her office at the back of the library, so she went over there. She was working on her computer and she didn't want to bother her if she was busy, but Jillian happened to look up and smiled, then motioned for her to come in.

Josie opened the door, then closed it behind her. "You looked busy. I didn't want to bother you. I just stopped in to say hello."

"It's okay. I was ordering some books."

Josie sighed. "How fun."

"Yes, it is. How was your day?"

"Good, mostly. Until after school when Zach came into my room and told me I was ruining his football team."

Jillian leaned back in her chair. "Really. And how did you manage to ruin his team?"

"A couple of his players aren't passing my class so now they're on probation."

"Oh, Josie. How could you? Don't you know football is king here?"

"Uh-huh. Well, in my classroom, literature is king and I'd like my students to do their assignments. And actually pass the class."

"So did you two have words? Was it a hot and passionate argument?"

Jillian always turned any heated discussion into a hot and passionate argument. In her imagination, anyway.

"No. I gave him their assignments and he's going to work with them this week so probation doesn't turn into a suspension."

"How disappointing. I mean, not for the kids, of course. But I was hoping you two would end up making out on your desk."

Josie laughed. "I don't think the principal would appreciate that."

"Who cares what the principal appreciates? I would have appreciated it immensely."

"I think you need a hot guy to come make out with you on *your* desk."

"Don't I ever."

"He's out there for you somewhere."

Jillian waved her hand. "Not looking for him. I'm busy."

Josie sighed. "Aren't we both. Which doesn't mean I'd turn down some hot guy throwing me across anything and making out with me."

Jillian pointed a finger at her. "See? You wouldn't have turned down Zach throwing you across your desk."

Josie laughed. "That wasn't the topic of conversation at the time."

"But you like him."

"Yes, I like him. Most days, anyway. Just not this afternoon."

They fortunately got off the topic of Zach and onto other things, mainly Loretta and Deacon's deck party this weekend and what they were going to bring, food-wise. Then Josie left so Jillian could get back to work.

But she still stewed about Zach on the way home. He could be so sweet to her when they were all out with their friends. Then again, at school, they had to be all business. Teenagers had the uncanny ability to zero in on any type of flirting or attraction.

Working with someone you were attracted to had its disadvantages. And she didn't know how she was going to handle it. Because she and Zach had been dancing around each other for months now.

So far, nothing had happened between them other than friendly hanging out in groups with their mutual friends.

Maybe that's all it would ever be. But as she thought back, there'd been glances. And touches that felt like a lot more than just causal friendliness.

So maybe it wouldn't be just friendship between them.

It wasn't like she needed another relationship. The last one had ended badly—really badly—and she wasn't looking forward to wading in those waters again.

But still . . . Zach was hot. Very hot. Impossibly tall and muscular and incredibly good-looking with dark hair and those steely gray eyes that would catch and hold your attention like nothing Josie had ever experienced before. That man could make her melt like a stick of frozen butter in the hot summer sun.

So maybe she'd just dip a toe in and test the waters.

She just wouldn't go for a swim.

AND READ ON FOR A SNEAK PEEK AT
THE LATEST PLAY-BY-PLAY NOVEL

The Final Score

AVAILABLE NOW
FROM HEADLINE ETERNAL

ONE

"SO, HERE WE ARE, ONCE AGAIN LIVING IN THE SAME city." Mia Cassidy took a sip of her green tea and looked over at Nathan Riley. "How did that happen?"

Nathan, the epitome of tall, dark, well-muscled and absolutely hot, leaned back in his chair and grinned at her. "Easy. You're obsessed with me so you followed me."

She laughed. "I don't think so. You knew I was thinking of starting a business here so you decided you had to get drafted by the San Francisco Sabers."

Nathan took a swallow of his iced tea and set the glass down. Mia tracked the movement of his hands. He had really big hands. She remembered that night several years ago in college when he'd used his hands to touch her—all over. They'd only had that one night together, but it sure had been memorable.

Yeah, the guy had magnificent hands.

"I've been here a year already, Mia. You just got here. So like I said, you followed me."

Her lips quirked. "And aren't you happy to have me here?"

"Actually, I am. Although who would have thought this kind of major shit would go down for both of us? You were going to get your PhD, and instead, you've got a start-up sports management company. I thought I'd end up in Cleveland or maybe in L.A., but not here in San Francisco, taking over as the Sabers quarterback now that my dad has retired."

Mia clutched her glass, feeling the cloud of anxiety rain down over her. Which was why she'd asked Nathan to have lunch. His charm and humor had always been a distraction for her, and oh how she needed it today. "Big changes for both of us for sure. How is your dad? Is he okay with the decision he made to retire?"

"He seems fine with it. The Sabers won the championship last year, and he had the knee issue that plagued him at the tail end of the season. He's thirty-seven, so he felt like it was the right time for him to step away."

"And you don't think he did that for you, to give you a chance to play?"

"I asked him that—more than once. He said no. Knowing my dad, he'd never walk away from football if he wasn't ready. He loves the game too much."

Mia nodded. "Since I have three brothers who play football, I believe that. You should believe him, too."

She knew Nathan had been worried when his dad announced his retirement at the end of last season. She also knew it added some pressure for Nathan, because he'd take over as starting quarterback this season for the Sabers. He'd had all last season to learn from him, but succeeding someone as high profile as Mick Riley wasn't going to be easy. Plus, Mick was his dad.

Now she was doubly happy she'd made the decision to launch

her company here in San Francisco. Besides being a prime location for her, she and Nathan had always been close in college. Despite their one night together—which had definitely been a mistake—they'd remained friends. It was a bonus that now they would be in the same city.

"How's your company coming along?" Nathan asked.

"Just getting things rolling. I told you Monique Parker came on board as my executive manager, didn't I?"

He grinned. "Yeah. She'll make sure nothing falls through the cracks."

"I know. She's incredibly organized, even more than me."

"If that's possible. I've never known anyone as anal as you."

"Hey, I'm good at everything I do."

He waggled his brows at her. "Don't I know it."

She laughed. "We promised we wouldn't bring up that mistaken, drunken night ever again."

"No, *you* made *me* promise it wouldn't happen again. I thought it was amazing."

Her body heated at his words. "It was amazing. But we're friends, Nathan."

"And friends can't have sex?"

"I don't know. Do you have sex with your friends?"

He cocked his head to the side. "You know what I mean, Mia."

"I do. But we agreed after that night it wouldn't happen again."

"You made me agree. I wanted to keep you in bed with me the next day."

She laughed. "We were drunk. It was a mistake. And I'd much rather have you as a friend than a lover."

"Oh, so now you're implying the sex wasn't good enough?" He leaned over and grasped her hand, the contact instantly electrifying. "Because if that's the case, I'm calling you out for faulty drunken memory loss. If I recall, you came three times that night."

At least he whispered that last part. And if he kept talking that way she was going to have an orgasm right there in her chair. So much for pushing those memories aside. She snatched her hand away. "That is not what I meant and you know it."

"Fine. We're friends."

"You need me as your friend, Nathan. Who will get you past all your training camp anxiety?"

He frowned. "Who says I have training camp anxiety?"

She twirled the stirrer around in her tea glass. "Don't you?"

He leaned back in his chair again. "Maybe. Don't you have a little anxiety, too, miss big-shot business owner?"

"Yes, I have anxiety. Like you would not believe. Which is why I'm glad we're friends. I need you, Nathan. As my friend."

He glared at her. "Shit. Fine. You know I'm always going to be here for you."

He had no idea how much his friendship and counsel meant to her. "Good. Now let's order lunch because I have to get back to work."

"You're a tough woman, Mia Cassidy."

"But I'm also your best friend, Nathan Riley. And don't ever forget it."

These next few months were going to be critical—for both of them. They were going to need each other more than ever.

As friends. And nothing else.